Echoes of Silence

Also by Marjorie Eccles:

ECHOES OF SILENCE

Marjorie Eccles

Thomas Dunne Books
St. Martin's Minotaur ⧉ New York

THOMAS DUNNE BOOKS.
An imprint of St. Martin's Press.

www.minotaurbooks.com

ISBN 0-312-30880-9

First published in Great Britain by Constable,
An imprint of Constable & Robinson Ltd

First U.S. Edition: September 2003

10 9 8 7 6 5 4 3 2 1

Echoes of Silence

1

It had always been a favourite walk of theirs. Approaching the top of the world must be something like this, Richmond used to feel, not being accustomed to hills as Isobel was, who'd been born and bred here.

The view from the top was more than worth the hard pull, especially on clear, sunny days, and exhilarating, with the wind that always blew across Clough Edge, though it was bitter today, enough to cut your face in two. He left his Volvo by the side of the reservoir and steadily began to climb the stony track between the coarse moorland grass, hunching his shoulders into his jacket, bracing himself to walk into the wind. Early, transient snow powdered the higher hills, unexpected for the last days of October. Premature even here, where winter came early.

His long strides took him to the top in minutes and, directly below him, there it was: Low Rigg. The old Hall and its cluster of cottages.

And below that, where the moors ended, was Steynton, situated at the beginning of the urban sprawl of what he still liked to think of as the West Riding: a small, grey industrial town with roads climbing from the valley bottom at forty-five degree angles, a town built of weathered northern gritstone. Its life-blood had once been wool and its accompanying trades – washing, combing, dyeing, spinning and weaving – until its *raison d'être* had declined with the advent of man-made textiles and cheap imports. Now, other enterprises and initiatives had brought it back to life. The once-predominant smell of greasy wool had been blown away, soot-spreading mill chimneys had been felled, and the many-storeyed mills which had created a dark tunnel of the main road were slowly being demolished, revealing views of the Pennine slopes not seen for a century and a half.

He'd hoped and intended never to return. This town had always made too many demands on him.

Yet he'd always felt it to be a basically good place, a compact, workaday town with a sense of permanence and solidity. Stone viaducts spanning the deep valleys, foursquare mills, old stone houses set with their backs to the hillsides, growing from them like a natural outcropping, part of the landscape – unlike the new estate of red-brick bungalows, visible for miles, like a rash on the far side of the valley. Even Rumsden was better than that, the suburb where rigid rows of Victorian back-to-backs were overshadowed by the bulk of Brackenroyd's Carpets, still the town's biggest employer.

Rumsden. That small area cut off from the rest of the town, not by distance but intangibly by tradition and perhaps by super-stition as well, and physically by a park of serpentine shape, its form ordained by the beck tumbling through it. Less of a park than a mere recreation ground, really, it was called East Park and its name just about summed it up – nondescript, with scrubby grass and melancholy shrubberies, the odd municipal flowerbed that was planted up in summer serving only to underly its inherent dreariness. The respectable residents on its western side avoided it, even choosing to exercise their dogs elsewhere. It was known as a place where Rumsden youth hung around, away from questions about their activities. Or as somewhere to get rid of the kids for a few hours by shunting them off to amuse themselves on the slide and the swings. An empty space for amateur soccer teams to kick a football around. There wasn't anything else to recommend it.

Against himself, Richmond's gaze was drawn to seek the old bandstand, unused for its original purpose in decades, but he saw with relief that it had gone, vandalised or dropped to pieces; it scarcely mattered which, now. A raised octagonal wooden structure it had been, decorated with curlicued Victorian wrought iron and with a space underneath to store deck chairs for hire on hot summer days by those without gardens, when even a park like this seemed appealing.

Deck chairs . . . and once, something infinitely more sinister.

He went on looking for several more expressionless moments, then turned abruptly away from bitter memories of an investiga-tion that had never been brought to a satisfactory conclusion, one that he'd lived with ever since. The murder of a child – any child – was something in which every police officer dreaded being involved, the ultimate in evil, in this case made worse by failure to find the perpetrator. He'd been glad enough to leave the town after it, for that and other reasons.

The day was rapidly closing in and lights were springing up in the valley as he drove circumspectly down into Steynton, along the road that wrapped a protective elbow around the hill. Built on an ancient track trodden out centuries ago by plodding packhorses carrying wool between outlying farms and weavers' cottages, it was steep and dangerous in bad weather. There was an escape road to the left and a nasty hairpin bend at the bottom, but it was less used now that the M62 strode the landscape a few miles away. He drove right past the turning to Low Rigg, straight down to the town's main hotel, where he'd booked in. Tomorrow he'd get himself back down to Bristol and make his arrangements for leaving. It wouldn't take him long. He'd learned to travel light, and there was nothing, and nobody, that he'd regret leaving behind. The mess he'd once made of his life had redounded on to other people; since then, he'd steered clear of involvement.

The final interview that afternoon had gone well, better than he'd anticipated. In some perverse way, he almost wished it hadn't, so that the decision would be out of his hands. In another it was encouraging that they were prepared to have him back, even pleased. He'd always felt they regarded him as a cold bastard, a stuck-up foreigner from down south. The warm handshakes today had been a surprise. Money, he thought with wry amusement, wasn't the only thing Yorkshiremen didn't give away easily. They kept their feelings pretty close, too.

'She can't be serious!'

'How can you say that? Your mother's never anything but, when it concerns her,' Sonia retorted with unusual acidity, but with such self-evident truth that Ginny didn't bother to refute it. She went on rustling through the wrappers in the box on the table beside her while she thought about the news her sister-in-law had just imparted, looking doubtfully at the chocolate that emerged between her manicured fingertips before popping it into her mouth and then grimacing. Another cracknel! She never learned, they were always the ones that were left.

'How much is this woman going to charge?'

7

'Money wasn't mentioned.'

Ginny raised an eyebrow. 'No, I don't suppose it would be.'

Freya had always been close about money matters, even in the days when there wasn't much to be close about – or when her children had thought there wasn't. They'd grown up used to believing themselves poor. If you were told often enough there was nothing to spare for pocket money, sweets or outings, you came to believe it. Became resigned to hand-me-down clothes, and food that was invariably of the mince and stodge variety, though as they grew older they realised this last was not solely for reasons of economy but because Freya's early preoccupation with keeping her figure had resulted in a long-term lack of interest in food and she really didn't care what they were given to eat. As children, it had never occurred to them that 'poor' was a relative term. That the unpolished, neglected furniture with which Low Rigg, the chaotic old house on the edge of the moors, overflowed, might be antique, and valuable. Or that money must come from somewhere to run the primitive, wickedly expensive heating system that made the draughty old place marginally bearable to live in – not to mention the possession of the vener-able Daimler and Nagle who drove it. At least not until the girls began to want records and make-up and new clothes like their friends, until Peter needed drawing materials and art books. Only then had they begun to take exception to their mother's regular visits to the hairdresser, her exquisite clothes – so unsuit-able for life as a Yorkshire schoolmaster's wife – her theatre and shopping binges in London, when she stayed heedlessly at the best hotels. All these had to be paid for – sometimes by having to send Nagle over to Leeds to pawn or sell some of her remain-ing jewellery.

If anyone ever dared question her, they would be given the Look, that famous, limpid stare from her beautiful eyes that meant: *What? Am I to be accountable for my every action?* before she swept from the room. But nobody took any notice of this. In her younger days Freya had been a model, who showed off beautiful clothes to rich women or was photographed for top magazines – a fashion model, not an artists', although just as outlandish in many Steynton eyes. She had come to accept that this entitled her to do as she pleased – which was to drift about in a vague and indecisive manner, until she unexpectedly dug in her heels over something she considered important. None of her children resembled her much: Ginny, a pretty, plump child with sleepy eyes who nevertheless missed nothing, and Peter, dark and secretive and clever, like his father. And Polly.

Of the three, only Polly had ever openly rebelled against Freya's subtle but inflexible dominance. She had a sturdy determination that matched her mother's velvet-clothed iron will and, needless to say, they often clashed. Sonia wondered what she'd have to say about this latest development. But Polly wasn't here, yet. One part of Sonia wished that she was, another was glad enough to shrug off the moment when she would arrive and start dealing with the situation.

Like a large and very elegant blonde cat, a lioness perhaps, good-natured Ginny, in her caramel sweater and soft wool trousers, lay supine along the sofa cushions, guzzling chocolates, stretching out a languid hand to pick through them, disregarding the inevitable day of reckoning. If there was nothing else in her of her mother, she had, inbuilt, Freya's love of luxury. She, the eldest of the three children, nursed a long-term remembrance of the lack of amenities in her childhood and had married Leon Katz partly because lack of anything could never be associated with him.

Solidity was a word that came to mind when one thought about Leon, especially here in Garth House, this large, roomy house which his father had had built just before the war. Square and confident, without fripperies, it stood alone on a corner, high above the junction of two roads: built of dark dressed stone, with a sloping garden and a central flight of steps to the front door. Inside, despite two super-active children, this room of Ginny's was filled with well-kept luxury: silk and velvet; cushions and thick Chinese rugs; gleams of gold and the sparkle of cut glass. The stifling heat brought out the scent of patchouli from the bowls of pot-pourri scattered around, adding it to the heavy perfume of hothouse white lilac in the huge black jasper vase on the marble-topped table. Sonia fought back the urge to scratch the patch of psoriasis on her neck and felt rather sick, especially when she remembered the charmless vicarage she must go back to.

'Well, honestly, an advert! Or that's what it amounts to,' Ginny said at last, in the tone of voice that probably meant she wouldn't rouse herself to do anything about it – though you could never be quite sure with Ginny. She was amiable, easy-going and languid, but not lazy; self-indulgent, but not selfish. Though her marriage to Leon meant she had no need to lift a finger had she been so inclined, she nevertheless ran a small, efficient business, with premises in a converted woollen mill which had been gutted and made into four storeys of well-designed flats, its ground floor given over to shops where hand-made jewellery, hand-blown glass, speciality breads and wine proliferated. Ginny sold made-to-measure knitwear and employed a couple of women to design the garments and an army of outworkers to knit them up. She sold reasonably and people came from miles around to buy. She was never less than beautifully dressed, never seen without make-up. Thick, creamy skin which Sonia, sallow and mousy, envied passionately. Well, anyway, I'm slimmer than she is, she comforted herself, breast-less as a boy.

'Anyone who has to tout for business to get a book published can't be much good,' the object of her envy added.

'Oh, Ginny, you're missing the point!' (Or deliberately mis-understanding, which Ginny was extremely good at.) 'She's not the one whose name will be on the book – and after all, I don't suppose we need worry. It won't be for public consumption.'

'You know what I mean, though.'

Sonia did, in a way. But the woman to whom Ginny was referring hadn't been advertising her own wares – only her expertise. She had, it appeared, written to Freya out of the blue. It was a standard letter, personalised, offering her skills as an experienced writer to anyone who wished to see their memoirs, or their family history, in print, but didn't feel capable of under-taking the task of writing it themselves. She buttered up the recipient by saying she had learned what an interesting and varied life they had led, what a well-known and respected family they were part of, and what a pity it would be not to record this for posterity. If her offer was taken up, the book would be privately published and quality-printed in as many handsome, leather-bound volumes as required, all for an extremely modest outlay. *How* modest Freya hadn't been pre-pared to divulge. She had pounced on the opportunity with delight and promptly engaged the woman.

10

'Interesting and varied,' Ginny repeated. 'You could say that. Once upon a time.'

'Oh, but she *was* famous, Ginny, for quite a long time, you can't deny that.'

'Now she must be stark raving bonkers – sticking her neck out like that! She can't have given a thought to anyone else – all that muck's bound to be raked over again.'

Sonia snuffled into her handkerchief. The hot, dry air in this house always gave her trouble with her sinuses. 'It needn't be. Peter says we must all make a stand about that – though I think it's probably too late. She's been at it for weeks, without telling anyone. I wouldn't have known anything about it if it hadn't been for Dot Nagle.'

Ginny shut her mind off, as she always did at 'Peter says'. With his dog-collar, her brother had assumed the right to tell them all how they should run their lives. She hadn't yet forgotten the stewardship campaign in the parish a couple of years ago, when he'd presumed to dictate that everyone should pay a tithe of their income to the Church. A tithe of *Leon's* income? Peter had never forgiven Leon for laughing so uproariously. Nor had Sonia, quite, Ginny thought, though she could always forgive Leon more easily than the rest of them, simply because he wasn't a Denshaw.

'I wonder why Philip hasn't tried to stop her?' she mused.

'Oh, you know Philip!'

'Yes,' Ginny came back, rather sharply. 'And he's no fool, Sonia. But perhaps he has tried. Freya only takes notice of him up to a point.'

It had always been Freya's way to listen vaguely, appear to agree, but then to go her own way, and Sonia acknowledged that Philip Denshaw, despite appearances, was smart enough to see through this. He was Ginny's uncle, her father's brother, a mild and self-effacing man who, after his wife died, had accepted the widowed Freya's invitation to live at Low Rigg Hall. It was a convenient arrangement all round – company and (since Philip had married a Brackenroyd, thereby setting himself up for life) a way of gaining a contribution to the upkeep of the house for Freya.

Ginny scrabbled hopefully in the chocolate box again and was triumphantly rewarded with a coffee cream. She bit into it with her strong white teeth and said through the mouthful, 'More to the point – what are we going to do about Elf? How will she react?'

There was a silence, full of resonances. The gas-coal fire roared wastefully up the chimney, the porcelain clock on the mantelpiece chimed a silvery five. Sounds of uproar issued from upstairs, where Harriet, Polly's eight-year-old daughter, was being entertained by her cousins. Sonia, hopefully assuming the question about Elf to be rhetorical – there wasn't, after all, a great deal one *could* do about her – shrugged her shoulders and said awkwardly, 'Well, I suppose I'd better get Harriet back up to Low Rigg.' Always an interminable leave taker, she looked round vaguely for her bag, but made no other move to go. 'Did Polly say what time she expects to be back? She didn't tell Freya – or if she did, Freya's forgotten.'

'Oh, sometime this evening,' Ginny answered carelessly. 'It's a long way from Norwich, in that little car, and there's no telling what the traffic'll be like. Depends on what time she got away anyway, I suppose. Polly never did have any sense of time.'

'Peter isn't sure she's doing the right thing, coming back to live here, with Freya.'

'Nobody's sure, love, least of all Polly! Anyway, I can't see them living together for long – it's only until she finds somewhere of her own.' Ginny swung her long elegant legs off the grey velvet sofa and stood up so that Sonia was forced to do likewise. 'If she finds dear Mama too much, she knows she can always come here.'

Upstairs, a record player emitted noises indicative of someone having killed the cat. 'They seem to be having a high old time,' Sonia said nervously, but Ginny didn't turn a hair.

'They're all right. It's time Harriet had someone of her own age to let go with.'

She guided Sonia out into the hall, where she shouted at the top of her not inconsiderable voice, 'Come on, you lot, time for Harriet to go!'

Two pairs of feet presently pounded down the stairs, the ten-year-old twins jostling for first place and Sam winning, cannoning down two at a time and putting the brakes on by swinging round the newel post at the bottom, only just missing knocking over the large Chinese jar that stood there.

'Don't *do* that,' Ginny, unfazed, said automatically, without any obvious expectation of being obeyed.

'Sorree,' Sam answered, without any obvious appearance of being so.

Ginny ruffled the hair of her identical sons with a carelessly affectionate hand and Joey began an amiable wrestling match with his brother, an attempt to get even with him for coming first down the stairs. Sonia occasionally thought she might like to have children, but shrank at the thought of rough boys like these. It was someone like Harriet she wanted: Harriet, whose face was now flushed with unaccustomed excitement, but who had come sedately down the stairs after her cousins and was already into her coat, saying thank you for having me, in the nice, polite way she'd been taught and never forgot.

She was a sensible, composed child, normally pale-skinned and clear-eyed, with a fringe of silky dark hair. She wasn't like either of her parents: neither her charming and disgraceful father, Tony, now separated from wife and child for good, nor Polly (christened Paulette, but she'd soon disposed of *that*) with her whirlwind energy and her sometimes disastrous enthusiasms, of whom the departed and unlamented Tony Winslow was a prime example.

'Has Mummy got back yet?' Harriet asked with carefully controlled anxiety.

Polly had done her best to teach her independence but, though she wasn't a clinging child, she was only eight years old, after all, and had already lost one parent and couldn't really bear to be away from Polly for too long. Her mother was the centre of her life, always late, always on the rush, too much to do. Lighting up a room when she entered it, energising it, even inanimate objects seeming to take on a life of their own. Talkative, quick-tempered sometimes, bright clothes reflecting warm colours into her face. A magic smile – Harriet's smile as she nodded now, appearing satisfied when Sonia said, 'She hasn't rung, love, but I expect by the time we've driven up to Low Rigg she'll either be there already, or she won't be long.'

2

The light had gone by the time Sonia had left the town behind, had negotiated her car round the hairpin bend at the bottom of the hill, and was crawling up towards the moors and Low Rigg. The houses grew progressively fewer, the hills loomed either side and the headlights reflected sharp sparkles of frost from the road surface. Sonia, who was a timid driver at any time, and especially in the dark, decided she wouldn't stay for supper, even if Freya should ask her, which was by no means certain. She didn't mind the thought of leaving Harriet with her mother-in-law. The child and the old woman got on together, which was just as well. If Freya didn't take a shine to anyone, she could be very unkind, as Sonia knew to her cost.

Harriet, strapped into the front seat, had fallen asleep within minutes of getting into the car, as she invariably did, lulled by the motion, and tired out tonight by the exuberance of her cousins. Sonia would have liked to have listened to what was left of *PM* but didn't want to waken her. In the silence, her thoughts rambled inconclusively, undirected.

She wondered if Peter would remember that she'd left the remains of last night's stew for him to heat up in the microwave. Probably not, or if he did, he wouldn't bother with it. He professed to hate anything that came within nodding distance of the new technology, even pecking away at his sermons and other parish matters on an ancient portable Olympia and refusing to think of a dishwasher. Not that they could have afforded one, anyway. He'd frowned on the microwave as an unnecessary luxury, but it had been a present from Sonia's parents, who didn't approve of her marriage to Peter and ecclesiastical poverty. Sonia would never have bought the microwave herself, but she blessed it for its usefulness.

She didn't care about luxury, as such. As servants of the Church, you weren't supposed to, anyway, but she truly didn't. Never having been deprived in her childhood, having *chosen* her vocation of being married to Peter, rejection of material things was easier for her than for him. She didn't have to prove it so much, as it were.

Sometimes, she wanted to tell him to relax, but as a second wife, and one of only a few years' standing, she still had to tread carefully. He was a difficult man, and there were areas of his life which were still uncharted seas to her. She didn't, for instance, have a clue why he'd married her. She was pushing forty and not attractive, had no skills as a parson's wife (though she worked harder in the parish than he did, and with more joy), he wasn't interested in the prospect of what she'd inherit from her parents, and as for sex . . . That was something she preferred not to think about.

You had to watch your step with Peter. She felt it must surely pain him to realise he wasn't much of a success as a parish priest and she tried to make allowances, telling herself it was that which made him so touchy, and very often angry. She wished the bishop would offer him another living, send him where he might be appreciated, to some High Anglican city parish where the parishioners called him 'Father'. In this chapel-orientated society where they lived, he was just tolerated by the dwindling minority of the faithful at St Wilfrid's C of E, and regarded with scepticism by the rest.

He'd always intended to take up some sort of career in the world of art but then, while still at art school, had apparently experienced a sudden conversion to Anglo-Catholicism. Saul on the road to Damascus could not have been a more fervent convert, Sonia thought. He burned with – was it missionary zeal, religious fervour? We-ell, perhaps. He preached love and forgiveness, turned the other cheek, he embraced sacrifice – and yet . . .

And yet, there was an unforgivingness about him she found hard to understand. Moreover, although he accepted living without luxury, she didn't miss the way his eyes lingered lovingly and rather wistfully on various *objets d'art* when they visited Freya at Low Rigg – at least, those objects you could see under the layers of dust.

Her thoughts skittered away with some relief from her marital dissatisfactions as she approached the narrow turn-off that led up through the hamlet which had given Low Rigg Hall its name. Rounding a bend of the hill, she steered the car between the last

15

habitations before the moors proper began: nothing more than a cluster of old dwellings and the ancient inn that was called the Moorcock, then the rambling bulk of the big house glimpsed in the headlights after the last exceedingly steep few hundred yards.

The house had been built in the seventeenth century as a farmhouse-cum-manor for the thriving little weaving community of Low Rigg, to stand overlording its domain. Low-built, of solid stone that had been quarried from the heart of the hills two miles away, and weathered to darkness by time and industrial pollution; mullioned windows, low, sweeping, stone-slated roofs. Crouched with its back to the side of the hill, seeking shelter from the scouring winds, it was surrounded by what had at one period been a garden, which was, in turn, encircled by a dry-stone wall. The moor rose up behind, with nothing beyond but bare stretches of heather and bilberry and cotton grass.

The garden was bare now, save for gaunt, stunted elms bent by the prevailing winds, in which crows and jackdaws nested. Nothing much had been done to it for years so that most of the time it looked a mess. The only time Sonia thought it approached anything like attractiveness was when the daffodils, unchecked for decades, covered the garden with sheets of gold in spring, blowing and dancing in the wind. Or when the great, blowsy, sugar-pink rambling rose of unknown origin was in bloom: a vulgar, heavily scented beauty with wicked thorns, festooning the back wall of the house in summer. One day, vowed Polly, one day I'll get at that garden . . . But she was never there long enough.

Inside, it was never really quite clean, despite Dot Nagle's half-hearted attempts, except when Polly visited and saw to it that at least some of it had a brisk going over, which annoyed both Dot and Freya. And even so, in the lesser used parts, dust gathered in corners and spiders swung from the ceiling, mice scampered behind the wainscotting. Freya, so fastidious about her person, either didn't see it or didn't mind – or probably, as Polly maintained, enjoyed the drama of it. Her working life had been spent in the glare of the cameras and it wasn't inconceivable that she saw it as an *outré* background for one of her outdated fashion pictures, like the one where for some reason she was shown draping a mink stole across a windswept mudflat, her back-combed hair and side flick-ups still immaculate. But Polly was right about one thing – nothing, dust, cobwebs or anything else, could make any real difference. The house resisted change, it would never be anything but its implacable self, Sonia thought with a shiver, as she drew up on the flagged frontage.

'There's Mummy's car!' cried Harriet, waking up as the engine died.

And there was Polly at the open door, light spilling on to the flags, arms wide for Harriet to rush into.

Only one vacant space was left in the car-park of the Woolpack when Tom Richmond arrived. He slid into it, surprised at the number of cars there, mid-week. He'd chosen the Woolpack for the simple pub he remembered, a free house, unpretentious, situated in the centre of Steynton. It didn't take him long now to realise that one of the breweries had got hold of it and given it a face-lift: conference rooms had been added, and the old, leisurely, shabby comfort had gone. It was now a clone of every other hotel, all co-ordinated fabrics, wallpapers and curtains, background Vivaldi, and a so-called French chef.

'Dinner will be served in the breakfast room tonight, sir,' he was informed by the receptionist, a pretty girl with a warm, bright smile and broad northern vowels, Caro by her name tag. 'We've a function on in the main dining-room. Actually,' she added confidentially, 'you'll be on your own, if that's not a problem for you? We're full up, but all the other residents will be at the dinner dance.'

'Dinner dance? Not above the music, my bedroom, is it?'

She smiled, understanding his alarm. 'No problem, sir, you're at the front. You won't hear a thing.'

Richmond, who had been contemplating a light snack alone in his room, glanced into the breakfast room, saw a roaring fire and changed his mind, and was glad he had when he'd located and surveyed the accommodation allotted to him. A northerly aspect, though warm and comfortable enough, if a bit cramped, as single rooms in hotels invariably were. A hard-stuffed, upright armchair and a huge television set dominating the small space. The steep streets of Steynton dipped and rose and swung away at crazy angles from the market square and somehow the window of this first-floor room was level with an aerial on the roof of a tall building below. A row of melancholy rooks sat on it and stared in at him as he unpacked. A decent meal, and afterwards a glass of scotch in a comfortable chair in the lounge with a book was a tempting thought. But after dinner he had business to conduct.

'I'd like to eat at half-past seven, if that's all right?' he'd asked at the desk. 'A Mrs Austwick will be coming in to see me at eight fifteen, so I want to be finished by then.'

'No problem, sir.'

'Anywhere my guest and I can be private?'

'The dinner's a reunion for Brackenroyd's retirees, so they won't be bothering with the residents' lounge. You'll be quiet there.'

Richmond had already noticed more than the usual quota of elderly couples wandering around. *Retirees.* Well. 'All right, I'll wait for coffee until Mrs Austwick comes and we'll have it in the lounge.'

'I'll have them bring it to you there,' returned Caro with a bright, professional smile, adding, yet again, 'No problem, sir.' She handed him his key. 'Number 14, there you go.' She turned to answer the telephone, leaving Richmond wondering whether a training in American-speak had been a mandatory require-ment, as part of the hotel refurbishment.

3

Sonia had stayed to supper after all, since Polly was there.

Polly, energetic and smiling, wearing the glossy brown waves of her long hair drawn back either side and fastened behind with one of her big slides. An art nouveau one tonight, oval, with an asymmetrical design, picked up from a market stall, she said. The layers of dark patterned velvet and other rich materials that Sonia could scarcely have described and would certainly never have dared to wear probably came from the same place. The leaping firelight caught the glow of the velvet, the crimson waistcoat and the curve of the silver slide whenever she turned her head, the huge silver and amber ear-rings swung; Sonia watched, half-jealous, fascinated, as Polly sat with her arm around her daughter and talked so airily of how she had disposed of most of the tangible evidence of the last unhappy years of her life – along, presumably, with her memories of Tony Winslow. She had, she said, put her few remaining things into storage. 'All done and dusted, but let's hope it won't be for long.' She smiled down at Harriet, as if the upheaval had all meant nothing, but perhaps the show of cheerfulness was for the child's sake. 'Now we must look for somewhere to live, Hattie. There's that house I saw last time I was here. Maybe it's still on the market.'

'You can't mean that one in Ingham's Fold?' Freya protested. 'That's ridiculous! It's only a little old terraced house!'

'It's a very nice one, for all that. The best of those I can afford. I can just about scrape the deposit together.'

'You could surely get something less . . .' Freya paused. 'Something with more character.'

'Not at the price.'

Freya had been on the verge of saying something like 'less working class', Polly had no doubt, was surprised she hadn't come right out with it, but sometimes even Freya remembered such remarks might prompt reminders of her own origins, and that was something she never cared to discuss.

'I don't see what's wrong with staying here,' she insisted. 'We're not exactly short of room. But I suppose you'll do as you please.' She'd withdrawn, as usual opting out, putting up a barrier between herself and anything unpleasant. She'd always been able to act as if on another planet, but only when it suited her. She could be as practical as Polly if she chose.

Polly, in fact, was ambivalent about staying here at Low Rigg, she and her mother living in such close proximity . . . there was no surer recipe for disaster. She would get irritated by Freya's vagueness and the way the house was being – well, allowed to take over. Or that was what it felt like. But if she said what she thought, it would create an atmosphere. It would be wiser, if only for Harriet's sake, to move out as soon as possible.

The small house she'd inspected on her last visit wasn't Low Rigg by any means, but it was solid, square and decent, and moreover had a back door *and* a front one – not in a back-to-back street as it might have been for the price, but in a little cobbled cul-de-sac and with its rear windows overlooking an unobscured view of the town. There was no front garden, but the flagged back yard had been made into an attractive sitting-out place by the present owners, and it had an apple tree in the corner. It wasn't what she would have chosen, but it was a hundred per cent improvement on the various rented accommodations they'd suffered in the last few years.

'Why don't we find a flat, like Elf's?' Harriet remarked into the grown-ups' silence, polishing off her portion of the delicatessen treacle tart Polly had brought as a coming-home treat for Harriet, knowing she loved it and correctly surmising that there would be no pudding provided by Freya.

'Elf is different,' Freya answered shortly, looking displeased, but silenced.

Elf had once lived in one of the old weavers' cottages down in the village, the last to belong to the Denshaws. It crouched at the end of a row, and had tiny windows and draughts, but after Low Rigg Hall, with its low roofs and cold corners and stone-flagged floors strewn with a varied assortment of rugs, liable to trap the unwary, Elf had declared it held no terrors for her. For a time, she'd had the fanciful notion of using it for its intended purpose. She'd had a loom installed in the original loom-chamber upstairs, where she wove pieces of cloth and Rya-type rugs, by which she tried to make a living, selling them in craft shops and fairs. It was an ill-conceived idea, not at all suited to her temperament. She'd tried other things, finally ending up managing a small art gallery, which she'd recently bought from the owner. She had a flat in the same mill-conversion where Ginny had her shop, smart and self-contained, like Elf herself. When she moved out of the little house, the Nagles had moved in, after Freya had been persuaded into some modernisation.

Perhaps thinking of the draughty cottage, Freya shivered and said now, 'Throw another log on the fire, Polly, please.' The fire didn't need it but Polly obliged. Like Ginny, Freya complained if her surroundings were not always at Turkish bath temperatures. Yet most of the house remained chilly, even in summer, except for this room. She called it the morning room, if you please, a grand name for a good-sized parlour at the back of the house which the Denshaws had always used as a family living-room, since it was on a south-west-facing corner of the house with windows to either side and consequently received the sun for much of the day. So much sun was a mixed blessing – it had faded and rotted the yellow silk curtains and cracked the white paint on the window sills and panelling, which should never have been painted at all, since they were of oak. But Freya had liked the idea of a yellow and white room, an antidote to so much dark panelling elsewhere, and so, yellow and white it was.

'Anyway, good news,' Polly said. 'I've got myself fixed up with a temporary job, starting after Christmas – at your school, Hattie. A teacher's had to leave unexpectedly. How's that for a bit of luck?'

'Oh, wicked,' said Harriet.

'It's not a permanent solution, but it'll do until I start at Dean House.'

Working as she did, teaching children with special needs, she'd counted herself lucky in being promised a permanent position at the one school in Steynton dedicated to such. The position wasn't available to her for six months, so this temporary job was welcome, enabling her to keep Harriet at the school she was already attending, the twins' school, one with an excellent reputation.

Teaching ran in the family: their father, whose whole life it had been; his brother Philip who, while practising as a doctor for forty years, had also taught music in his spare time to generations of Steynton schoolchildren. Polly herself had chosen the profession almost in default, not knowing what else she wanted to do, though now, specialising as she did, she couldn't imagine any other kind of work she'd like better.

'Well, I shall be too busy to help you settle in, whatever house you decide on.' Freya smiled beatifically, as if that had ever been a possibility. Apparently, she'd decided to go along with Polly, for the moment. 'Due to these memoirs of mine, you know,' she added, and paused. 'Which I really wanted to keep a lovely secret, but alas! Dot's been very naughty, telling you. She never could keep anything to herself,' she added roguishly, an attitude so at variance with her usual one it was not to be taken seriously.

Sonia glanced at Polly, saw that this announcement was no news to her. Well, of course, Dot Nagle, once having let the cat out of the bag to Sonia, would have had enough sense to lose no time in telling Polly as well. Sonia shifted uneasily, waiting for the outburst as Freya's limpid gaze turned from one to the other, but Polly, having been prepared, wasn't rising to the bait.

'Not a bad idea, really,' she said mildly, with a swift warning glance at Sonia. 'It's a pity not to leave a record of the family to posterity.'

Freya's rare smile appeared. Catlike, satisfied. 'Absolutely right, Polly! And when I say *my* memoirs – well, I really mean the book will be about the Denshaws – but I am part of them, after all! There'll only be a teensy little chapter on me.'

'Edited, I assume,' Polly said.

There was the slightest of pauses. Then, 'Of course!' Freya declared, but it was accompanied by the Look. The one that had once made her famous on two continents, the haughty smoulder that had started a whole new generation of look-alike models. A new creation, a new face, right for the time, it had launched her on a meteoric career. Now she allowed it to remain only for a moment, then determinedly cleared her expression. 'I shall need your help when we get to the family bit, Polly. Yours and Philip's. You two have always been so keen on that sort of thing – you know so much more about it than I do.'

By which Polly assumed that, although Freya had apparently

been working with this writer woman for nearly two months, they hadn't yet got beyond the 'teensy little chapter' on Freya herself.

'I'd be delighted.' The intrinsic interest of it apart, it would mean that she and Philip could keep an eye on what was said – if that wasn't already too late. Freya could be discreet, stubbornly so when it suited her, but if she wanted to say anything, nothing would deter her.

Tall and willow-slim still, she was seventy, and could have passed for younger had it not been for the arthritis which had crippled her of latter years. She hated having to walk with the aid of a stick, she who had once pranced so elegantly down catwalks in many of the world's capital cities; she loathed the heavy, orthopaedic shoes she was forced to endure, drawing attention away from them as much as possible by wearing trousers or long skirts, though this was hardly a penance, since they further served to accentuate her grace and slenderness. Tonight she was immaculate as usual, in beautifully tailored dove grey slacks and a heavy silk shirt the colour of aubergines, with a lilac cashmere button-through jersey thrown casually around her shoulders; big pearl ear studs gleamed beneath the immaculately cut curve of dark silver hair. She was one of those women whose skin, through luck – or constant pampering – had stayed soft and elastic, and tonight, in the glowing lamplight, it looked radiant.

Polly was never quite sure whether love or admiration predominated in her wary relationship with Freya. She'd always stood her corner, challenged the hidden steel in her mother's personality, but inevitably she'd been drawn back by Freya's – charm, was it? Charisma?

Call it what you would, combined with her striking looks, it was a quality which had knocked out their father, already middle-aged, the successful and respected headmaster of the local grammar school, when he first set eyes on her. They'd met at a dinner party given by old friends of his, at a time when Freya had come north to model clothes at a prestigious charity fashion show in one of Yorkshire's stately homes, and Laurence's hosts had regarded their guest as something of a catch. What had possessed him, a supposedly confirmed bachelor, to ask her to marry him? To assume she'd be prepared to throw up her glamorous modelling career to become the wife of a mere school-master – one with a big house, local status and a small private income, to be sure, but none of them anything to write home about? Maybe he hadn't really expected her to say yes, but she had. Their marriage had apparently been the subject of bitching and speculation in all the newspaper gossip columns and those reputed to be in the know gave it three months, yet it had endured for the next twelve years, until Laurence had suddenly died of a heart attack at the age of fifty-four.

It was a bit daunting, growing up knowing that your mother had been the most talked of fashion icon of her day, the Naomi Campbell, the Kate Moss, the Evangelista of her time. Polly had embarked on a school project on women's magazines in her senior year, and had come across her mother's striking face on so many old covers of *Vogue* and other magazines that she'd shrunk with embarrassment and been tempted to give up the project in favour of something else. She'd been heavily into feminism at the time, and ashamed of a mother who'd been, for heaven's sake, a *model*! A lovely face and nothing between her ears.

Well, those were just feminist clichés, the sort of excess baggage that Polly had long since thrown overboard, and had they ever been true of Freya? Something of a lightweight she might be, but her shrewdness was never in doubt. That, presumably, was why she'd married Laurence, calculating that time was not on her side, that her fame and glory couldn't last for much longer. Cameras showed no mercy and she was knocking thirty. She was untrained for anything else and she'd always lived extravagantly. Perhaps she'd felt it better to withdraw while she was still at the height of her success and grasp whatever security was offered to her.

Marriage. Whoever, outside it, could tell whether it was successful or not? Polly had no means of judging that of her parents, since Freya gave no indication and Laurence had died when she was only three. But Freya had never showed signs of regretting what she'd done – though she talked and gossiped endlessly, wistfully, with Dot Nagle about those glamorous years, dropping the names of couturiers and fashion photographers still famous. Encouraged by Dot, her erstwhile success grew in her mind, exaggerated beyond what it had been. Yet she seemed to have accepted without grumbles the vastly different life she'd found, playing the headmaster's wife when strictly necessary with charm and grace – providing she could make her own rules and have her little expeditions up to town now and again. Though still, as she'd always been, Ruth among the alien corn.

As a widow, her life hadn't altered appreciably. Never known to lift a duster, content to leave the care of house and children to Dot, she read endlessly – romantic fiction, family sagas – tried painting, until darling Peter's talent exposed the lack of it in herself. Then she taught herself to embroider. Tapestries, cushions, bedspreads. At first clumsily, then more competently and afterwards exquisitely, with tiny, beautiful stitches until what she accomplished were works of art in themselves.

All the same, there was a streak of wildness in her that ran through her stoic acceptance. Manifest in the wilful business of these memoirs. She'd made up her mind about that and nothing would stop her. Polly had a feeling of impending disaster. Why couldn't Freya let sleeping dogs lie?

'Well, I'd better be on my way . . .'

Sonia, Polly realised, was embarking on the routine of her usual protracted departure. 'Goodness, look at the time!' had been said some time since. Next, she'd be sorry to break up the evening, but . . . Just say good-night and go! Polly apostrophised silently.

She began to round up Harriet for bed. Maybe Sonia would take the hint, the equivalent of putting the cat out, she was thinking, when sounds were heard in the hall and Philip came in, interrupting the business of ritual protests and reluctant obedience on Harriet's part.

Philip had given up teaching the piano, but his life still revolved around music. He was deeply involved in helping to keep up the town's musical traditions. Music appreciation night classes every Monday. Tonight, choir practice at St Wilfrid's, where he was organist and choirmaster. Tomorrow rehearsing the Steynton Choral Society for their Christmas production, this year *Judas Maccabeus* . . . Handel was always a favourite.

'You're up late, Princess,' he remarked, smiling at Harriet, and to Sonia he said, 'Nasty out there, freezing like the clappers. Watch how you go.' He poured himself a whisky before settling his plump form into a chair and stretching out his legs to the fire,

25

smoothing his sparse white hair across his pate. 'Could be snow again before tomorrow.'

'Wicked,' Harriet said, above Sonia's cries of dismay as she thought of driving down the moorland roads, but at least the announcement had had the effect of propelling her a little nearer the front door. 'Mummy, if it does snow, can I build a snowman?'

The small, electrified silence was broken by Freya and Polly speaking at once.

'It won't stay, this time of year,' said Freya.

And Polly said, 'Hattie, I won't tell you again. Pick your things up and off to bed. I'll come up with you.'

Harriet lifted a token book from the sofa, still trying to spin it out, unaware of the tension her innocent remark had caused. 'We've saved some treacle tart for you, Uncle Philip.'

Philip rose to the occasion. Feigning horror, lightening the atmosphere with a joke. 'Didn't you know sugar's bad for me at my age? D'you want my teeth to fall out? Why don't we save it for you, for tomorrow?'

Polly could see Harriet was on the verge of asking interesting questions about why his teeth hadn't already fallen out and been replaced by false ones, like her Granny Winslow's . . .

'Harriet!'

'Your mum's getting cross, Princess. On your way, and I'll see you tomorrow.' His white, well-kept hand strayed to stroke the soft, dark hair for a moment.

A reserved and gentle man, not renowned for his verbal communication with adults, or his sense of humour, Philip was good with children. He should have had a family of his own, grandchildren by now, but he and his wife had either been unable to have them, or she hadn't wanted them. Poor Philip. Polly knew that innocent remark of Harriet's about the snowman had hit him right where it hurt.

Wyn Austwick was younger than Richmond had expected from her letter, but older than she wanted to pretend. Around forty, he judged, too short and chunky for the jersey pants suit and too old for that cropped, unforgiving haircut, too sallow-complexioned for that vivid lipstick. But she looked as though she knew what she was about. Matter-of-fact, and with a sharp gleam in her eye.

'I've never met a ghost writer before,' he remarked, after the waiter had brought coffee and the brandy that had been offered and accepted, setting the tray on a low table in front of them and leaving them to roast in front of yet another blazing fire.

She'd said she didn't smoke, but her voice was gravelly as if she might have done, once, and her laugh was grating. He couldn't quite place her slight accent, which wasn't local. 'I suppose you could call me that, but that's not how I refer to myself. They wouldn't like it, my clients. I have to be discreet, because they usually want the book accredited to themselves. Don't even want their families to know they haven't written it, sometimes – know what I mean? In any case, they usually prefer to call it a private memoir, or even an autobiography.'

'Do you get many clients?' She had a sort of sly, know-it-all manner which he found off-putting but perhaps not everyone did.

'Enough to make a better living than I did trying to get my own books published! I used to write romantic novels but all they want nowadays is sex, and I know my own limitations. Readers can spot it a mile off if you're only writing from theory.' Her face was deadpan, not wanting him to believe that, and he didn't. He thought Wyn Austwick, in the right circumstances, might be a very sparky lady. 'Anyway, this suits me better. You'd be surprised how many people are prepared to pay good money to see their name on the cover of a book. A lot of it's vanity, but on the other hand, some people have a genuine desire not to let their family history die out. Or else they're convinced their life's been exciting enough for other people to want to read.' She raised a mocking eyebrow. 'Which it hardly ever is, believe you me, but never mind that.'

Richmond drained his coffee. Never one for small talk, he now deemed it time to finish with this. 'You said when you wrote that you'd come across something of enough interest to warrant our meeting.'

'I knew that would bring you here.'

He wasn't going to let that pass. 'It's lucky I had business up here,' he said austerely. 'I wouldn't otherwise have driven all this way without knowing why.'

27

He detected a look on her face that suggested she knew better. 'It's not something I could write about easily in a letter.'

'You'd better explain, then.'

'I'm coming to it, but you'll have to be patient. To begin with, I've been working on a book for the last couple of months with Mrs Freya Denshaw.' She paused expectantly, but he said nothing, waiting for what was coming. 'Mrs Denshaw of Low Rigg Hall, the one who used to be –'

'I know who you mean.'

So it was what he'd suspected it had to be, even from the vague hints she'd given in her guarded letter. A coincidence, he'd asked himself, this woman writing to him, just at the moment when he'd decided to return here? He didn't believe in coincidences. Isobel would have said it was fate, in his stars, but Richmond found even coincidence preferable to believing that his life was subject to the movement of the planets, out of his control.

'So – you're helping her with her memoirs?' he prompted.

She took a sip of her brandy, looking at him over the rim of her glass. Her eyes were a curious light amber, the kind, it occurred to him, often seen in untrustworthy dogs, the sort of dog who'd let you walk past and then snap at your heels. 'Theoretically, it's supposed to be a family history but we haven't got very far with that. The truth is, she has a big ego, plus she's seventy, and wants to get her own version of her glamorous life down in case she doesn't make it before the book's finished. Can't blame her. Freya Cass was once quite a name. It surprises me she's never thought of writing her memoirs before, they're all at it, anybody that's been in the public eye for five minutes. But she'd never make a writer. She's the sort who extracts every drop of drama from a situation, but she over-eggs the pudding, she's not always strictly truthful, goes right over the top and makes it not credible.'

'All very interesting, but where do I come in?'

She savoured a mouthful of brandy before answering. 'I always have to have access to family papers, diaries and such. I make this clear from the start and people don't usually object.'

'But Mrs Denshaw did?'

28

'Just the opposite. Threw everything at me, she did, old diaries, letters, everything.'

He began to see where this was heading. Who would let this woman into their private lives? Not me, thought Richmond, but maybe that was just because he was a policeman, and in any case naturally suspicious, even beyond the call of duty.

'They needn't show me anything they don't want me to see,' she bridled, as if sensing his criticism. He was right about the smoking, he thought, hearing the slight wheeze. Either that or maybe she was just very tense, though he didn't think that was so. Rather the opposite, if anything. She seemed to be enjoying keeping him in suspense, and plunged her hand into the huge leather bag beside her chair, extracting a sheet of rough paper, holding it out tantalisingly towards him so that he could just see it was a flyer advertising a concert in the New Hall of the Girls' High School. Still keeping it between her fingers, she turned it over to show the back of it covered in pencilled scribbles, much of it crossed out.

'Freya's getting forgetful, though she'd never admit it. This was stuck in with a lot of other junk, among a pile of old fan letters. "Throw everything else but the letters away," she told me.'

'What's this, then, if not a letter? Looks very much like one to me, a rough draft, anyway.' He held his hand out for closer inspection of the paper but she ignored it.

'You noticed the date on the front?'

'I did, but I'm afraid I don't see what it has to do with me.' It was a lie which they both recognised as such. She watched him quizzically.

'Let's not beat about the bush. We both know we're talking about the murder of that child, nearly ten years ago.'

He kept silent, the hard, intimidating silence that could have suspects and witnesses alike pleading to be heard, giving Wyn Austwick look for look. She didn't flinch.

'I know you were only a DC then, and weren't on the case for obvious reasons, but you can't have forgotten it. However, just so's we're both singing from the same hymn sheet . . . the little girl disappeared and the mother then took her own life, leaving a note admitting she was the one who'd killed her daughter, right?' He made a sudden gesture, almost knocking the coffee pot over, then sat back, his hand covering his mouth and chin. She went on, 'The child was found four months later, with evidence to confirm that it was indeed the mother who'd killed her.'

The incandescent heart of the fire collapsed in a spurt of blue-green flame and a small ember of wood rolled to the hearth. Music to dance to sounded from down the corridor. 'Tie A Yellow Ribbon' had finished, and now the gentle sounds of 'Moon River' drifted along: the oldies' trip down Memory Lane, getting off to a good start.

'You know a lot about it.' His voice croaked, felt like razor blades being swallowed.

'Only what I remember, plus what I've read up again in the old news reports. I take my work seriously,' she added, unperturbed by his unspoken censure, by what he thought of the lengths to which she'd gone. 'I do a good deal of research, even if all of it doesn't appear in the finished narrative. Like an iceberg, you know, most of it's below the surface. And Mrs Denshaw's attitude made me frankly curious. We've mapped out a rough outline for the book, gone through her version of her early life, and listed every member of the Denshaw family she knows about, but she's never mentioned this child at all, or what happened. The mother, being her son Peter's first wife, yes, she was briefly mentioned, but not a single word about this child, Beth. However, she absolutely dotes on Peter, so I assumed the reason was she thought he might find it just too upsetting to read about when the book's finished. He was, after all, a suspect for a while, until the mother's confession. But then . . .'

She paused to pour herself more coffee, holding up the pot inquiringly. He shook his head. 'Then what, Mrs Austwick?' he forced himself to ask.

She waved the piece of paper. 'Then I came across this. Which I think you'll find very interesting. As far as I can tell, it suggests there might have been other people involved in the child's murder.'

He wouldn't ask to see it again, anticipating the refusal. 'Scribbles like that, even a rough draft, if that's what it is – a letter or whatever that might never have been sent out, that's useless. If that's all you have, I'm sorry –'

'I think the case should be reopened.'

A waiter appeared to replenish the fire and the coffee. Richmond waved him away on both counts.

'On what grounds?' he managed eventually. She tapped the so-called letter, and he shook his head. 'I've told you, it's useless. Unless you have anything further.'

She watched him assessingly. 'I might have.'

'You realise, if that's so, you could be charged with withholding evidence?'

'Not unless the case is reopened. And if it is, then I shan't withhold it.'

He disliked the woman excessively by now and wouldn't trust her an inch. The very fact that she'd breached her client's confidentiality was enough to raise his hackles. But it went deeper than that.

'Tell me,' he asked softly, 'what's in it for you? Why are you so concerned? Why are you, personally, so keen to have this case reinvestigated?'

'Why? Why do you think? I want to see justice done.'

He didn't believe that for a moment. There was something here he didn't understand, a hint of spite that suggested other reasons than altruism for her intervention in this.

'What do you think I can do about it, at this stage?' he countered, almost roughly. It was becoming increasingly difficult to hide his feelings.

'I don't know – but you will do something, won't you? After all, it was your daughter who was murdered, wasn't it?'

Time stopped. Lurched. Started again.

Your daughter. Your little Beth. Eight years old.

His application for the job here hadn't been made without a good deal of heart-searching. He'd known what he was letting himself in for – pain, reminders of the past that he'd rather not face. But years of trying to convince himself that it was over and done with, part of his life that he must put behind him, had made no difference. He'd been driven on, a relentless inner voice had never ceased telling him that it wasn't finished, that somewhere the truth was hidden, that some day it must come to light. But not like this. This wasn't how it should be. No way could he jeopardise his plans and begin his new job by initiating the reopening of an old case in which he had a strong personal interest – even had there been sufficient grounds.

'I'm sorry, Mrs Austwick. It's out of the question.'

'Don't dismiss it so easily. Think about what I've said. Just think about it.' She stuffed the flyer into the depths of the big leather bag and stood up. 'I'm tied up for the next few weeks, but after that, from the beginning of December, you know where to find me.'

4

Polly took Harriet upstairs, still protesting she wasn't tired, that she wouldn't *ever* go to sleep, leaving Sonia at last saying final farewells and promising to drive cautiously.

It was a not inconsiderable journey up to the bedroom, once Polly's, where Harriet now slept. Spooky, whispered Harriet, listening to the moaning of the wind in the chimneys, pleasurably frightened by the possibility of encountering one of the ghosts the twins had sworn they'd seen. She didn't believe them, but she held tightly on to Polly's hand all the same.

After dark, Polly thought, you were always more aware of how old the house was, of its sighs, creaks and groans, as if settling itself down for the night, like an old dog in its basket. More jumpy, at the echoes of its silence and the shadows in the corners. Silly, really, when every nook and cranny was as familiar as your own face – though when she was away, it was strange how she sometimes couldn't remember it properly. Coming back to Low Rigg was always a journey of rediscovery to her, wandering through the house and reacquainting herself with it, coming to terms with how she felt about it. She'd been born here and felt a passion for it which she was never sure was love, or hate. She did know that it frightened her sometimes, the power it held, its strangeness and remoteness from the life of Steynton.

She was almost as grateful as Harriet was for their warm hand contact, as they moved from one part to another, swinging arms and singing a nonsense rhyme, giggling the way she and Ginny, and Elf, too, had done. She ran her fingers along the honey-coloured walnut of a small table, caressed threadbare tapestry curtains, pausing only for a moment to glance at the portrait of old Josiah Denshaw. Too late for the ritual of a Josiah story for Harriet tonight, however short and amusing.

A third-generation woollen manufacturer he'd been, a character, a stout Victorian about whom tales were legion, looking down at them out of an important frame with full knowledge of a settled and rosy present, and confident expectations of even better things to come. It was as well he hadn't been able to see into the future: a succession of male heirs killed in two world wars, leaving only two great-great-grandsons, Laurence and Philip, neither of whom was interested in carrying on his hard-won woollen empire. Gathering up the remnants of the fortune Josiah had made, these last two had sold their shares for much less than they should have done and got out of the industry. Laurence had taken up schoolmastering and Philip, medicine.

Low Rigg had been in the possession of the Denshaws ever since Josiah had moved from the valley and acquired the old manor-house when his aspirations began to stretch to being more than the biggest wool-comber, dyer and spinner in the area and included hopes of being looked on as some sort of squire. He had bought Low Rigg Hall from the last descendant of its original owners, along with most of its sparse contents, and to his wife's chagrin had filled the empty corners, being too tight-fisted to buy new, with the sort of second-hand furniture at that time poorly regarded: old-fashioned Regency tables, Hepplewhite chairs and the like. Over the years they, plus the Elizabethan oak of the original pieces and later, Victorian and Edwardian additions, had grown into something to make an antique dealer's mouth water. Josiah's wife would never have credited what they were worth now.

As Polly reached out for the knob on Harriet's door she found grit under her hand, from where she'd trailed it along the walnut table. She rubbed her fingers together irritably. She wasn't finicky about housekeeping, but the neglected state of the house could always be guaranteed to reduce her to annoyance.

She ought to confront Dot Nagle with it, but knew she wouldn't. There were some things Freya would tolerate, but criticism of either of the Nagles was not one of them. She and Dot formed an unholy alliance, cronies from that former, distant, shiningly remembered world they had both once inhabited. Freya had few other friends, she was almost as much a stranger here now as she had been forty years ago, when she came here as a bride. Dot had been summoned as a mother's help when Elf had been brought into the family as a baby, Polly had known her practically all her life, but she was still wary of tangling with her unnecessarily.

She'd been a dresser at some couture house or other when she and Freya had met – nobody could ever do up eighteen back-buttons on a model gown like Dot, with her quick, deft fingers, declared Freya. Small and skinny, a Cockney sparrow to her fingertips, salty-spoken and with a trenchant sense of humour and a sharp temper, she was undeterred by the change in her lifestyle, by having to look after four children, simply dealing with them in the same rough and ready fashion as she'd been brought up herself. A clip round the ear when they disobeyed; solid food at mealtimes and if they didn't like it they could do without. 'You just thank your lucky stars you don't have to eat what I had to,' she told them. 'Fish and chips if we were lucky. Pie, mash and liquor. Jellied eels. And a good hiding if we didn't finish every crumb.'

Jellied eels! Ugh, yuk! they'd repeated, making sick noises.

Otherwise she'd left them largely to their own devices while she and Freya gossiped and reminisced. She wasn't so bad nowadays, Polly thought, as long as you were careful to keep on the right side of her.

Nagle had come on the scene later, just when, Polly couldn't now quite remember, ostensibly to drive the now long-gone Daimler. Eddie Nagle, retired marine, who hung about all day, except for the times he spent at various dog-tracks around the country, and working at his part-time job as an attendant at the fitness club in Steynton, otherwise looking macho and not doing much else that Polly could see. She'd been afraid of him as a child but now, the picture of him that came to mind – stocky and muscular, with that extraordinary pink, shiny bald head, square, almost completely cuboid, the rubbery lips – gave her only the usual shiver of distaste. She used to tell herself it was only that he *looked* frightening. Yet she unconsciously rubbed a hand down the side of her skirt, as if she'd accidentally brushed against him.

'Mummy?'

Harriet was snuggling beneath the duvet, eyes almost closing. 'Eddie says he'll get me a puppy, if you'll let me. Can I have one, please, can I?'

Polly didn't correct either her grammar or the way she called Nagle 'Eddie', though this was at his request. He was, she reluctantly had to admit, good with the children. 'Isn't one dog enough? There's Lady, isn't there?'

'She's not mine, she's Eddie's,' Harriet pointed out. 'And sometimes he won't let me play with her. Joey and Sam have one *each!*'

The two enormous, unruly mongrels that the twins had been allowed to choose from the animal shelter weren't much of a recommendation. 'If you're thinking of one like Sheba – sorry, Hattie!'

'She has a lovely disposition,' Harriet offered. 'Aunt Ginny says.' Polly smiled, half-way to giving in. One like Lady, a shivering, gentle, sweet-tempered greyhound who used to race but had been pensioned off and saved from the knackers when she grew too old to win – a rare sign of weakness in Nagle – perhaps wouldn't be so bad.

'Besides, Lady wants a friend to play with, as well,' Harriet said, the unconscious pathos of the 'as well' smiting Polly.

She brushed the soft fringe of dark hair back from her daughter's forehead, kissed her and promised, 'We'll see,' as she turned out the light.

At midnight Richmond realised the receptionist's predictions had been made in the spirit of wanting to please rather than in the interests of absolute truth. He could hear all too clearly the distant but insistent thump of the music. The 'retirees', he reflected, punching his pillow, evidently had more stamina than he had. It wouldn't have been loud enough to keep him awake had he been tired enough, but as it was, the memory of the meeting with Mrs Austwick jumped around in his brain, along with the distant beat, tormenting him, repeating itself over and over but getting nowhere.

In the end he gave in, switched on the lamp and the electric blanket to keep the bed warm, got up and padded over to the tea-making facilities in the corner. He made tea and sat in the bolt upright, hard-stuffed armchair, huddled into his dressing-gown while he drank it, and at last allowed himself to think of Beth.

Silver-blonde hair, a retroussé nose, small for her age. A bouncy, laughing, happy child, full of pep. From the moment she'd first been put into his arms, he'd adored her. The divorce from Isobel had been acutely painful, but the seperation from his daughter had been like cutting out a piece of his heart. Still was, shot through with regret and remorse at being too late, desperately as he'd tried, to save his marriage.

It had come as a shock to Richmond when Isobel married again so quickly after the divorce, more so that she chose to marry the young vicar of St Wilfrid's, although she'd been attending his church for some time, with all the earnestness and zeal of the newly converted. She was not a person to cope with the sort of stress life had thrust upon her and, though he didn't know Peter Denshaw, Richmond had to admit that perhaps she'd found the support and stability which the Church, and presumably Peter Denshaw himself, had been able to give her and he, Richmond, had not. What was certain was that Isobel was constitutionally unsuited to being the wife of a detective with inordinate demands on his time and energies.

Detective Constable Tom Richmond he'd been then, having married Isobel when she was only eighteen. Keen and full of ambition to the point where he hardly saw his wife and child. The usual story, I'm doing it for you, so that you and Beth can have a better future. Refusing to see that he was killing his marriage. Tom Richmond, the white hope of the CID, who couldn't see that, and hadn't been able to do a damn thing about helping to find his own child's murderer.

Orders had been issued immediately his involvement in the case was revealed, as soon as the powers-that-be learned that the mother of the missing child was Isobel Denshaw, Richmond's ex-wife, and that he was the father. It was standard procedure that he should be called off, there was every good reason for it. He'd been given compassionate leave which he hadn't wanted and didn't know what to do with. He hadn't been allowed to put so much as a toe into the investigation, though he'd picked up what information he could. He had never been able to rid himself of the idea that the case had been botched.

He'd read somewhere, recently, of the relationship between cancer and stress, and could well believe it. The note Isobel left when she took an overdose said there was no point in waiting for the cancer, recently diagnosed, to kill her. She'd no more desire to fight it, nor did she deserve to go on living when Beth was dead, when she was to blame for her own child's death.

How could anyone ever have believed that?

Never in a million years would he, at any rate, believe that Isobel, however neurotic or disordered by her illness, would lift a finger to Beth, never mind bludgeon her to death, any more than he himself would have done. But evidence had been given that there had been a quarrel between them the morning Beth disappeared, overheard by one of Peter Denshaw's parishioners – a quarrel which Richmond reluctantly had to admit was possible. Beth had been an innocent casualty of the divorce. She didn't understand the terrible splitting apart of her life, and her fear and bewilderment had manifested itself in behavioural problems. Happy, biddable little Beth had at times become naughty, cheeky and disobedient, Isobel reported. Richmond might not have believed that, either, except that he'd witnessed both, himself, once or twice, on the occasions when it was his turn to have her for the weekend. The last time she'd stayed with him, she'd wet the bed.

The music downstairs had finally ceased. He got back under the sheets that the electric blanket had kept warm and eventually fell asleep to the continued repetition of Wyn Austwick's confident assertion: *'You will do something about it . . . she was your daughter, after all.'*

And as he slept, he dreamed of Low Rigg Hall as on the only time he'd seen it, dark stone surrounded by daffodils in their thousands, blowing in the March wind, the bleak moors beyond.

The Reverend Peter Denshaw pushed aside preparations for his monthly letter for the next parish magazine and stared morosely out of his study window. The view of the outside was marginally better than that of the interior and might be of greater help in suggesting an analogy to the coming Christmas more acceptable to his parishioners than the rather clever and erudite one which had just occurred to him. Hands in the pockets of his cassock, he stared across at the church, but no brilliant revelation came to him.

St Wilfrid's, a Victorian edifice unremarkable for anything,

38

stood in a churchyard which was a subject of controversy within the PCC, most of whom wanted the gravestones laid in the grass for easy passage of the verger's mower. He watched Mrs Lumb, champion of those whom Polly called the Levellers, and stalwart leader of the flower arrangers, as she emerged from the church and passed through the wicket gate which led into the garden of his old home. The Lumbs had bought it and tarted it up and called it the Old Vicarage when the PCC deemed the upkeep was costing the church too much. Its sale had brought in more than enough to build a new vicarage on church land between the churchyard and the C of E school, though the hoped-for saving on maintenance of the vicar's home hadn't amounted to much, mainly because they'd employed Sykes & Co. to build the new one. They were the cheapest of those builders who put in a bid for the work, and the new house was jerry-built and full of problems, as anybody who knew Harry Sykes could have told them it would be. It was called, dispiritingly, the New Vicarage.

As the parish assumed he would, Peter humbly bowed to the inevitable and accepted the transplantation without demur. It would hardly be the thing, after all, for the vicar to grumble that the rooms of the new house were small, square and character-less, and the thin walls offered no privacy whatsoever, when overall the house was warmer, so much easier to run and to furnish, and there was very little garden to distract him from his parochial duties. He even embraced these disadvantages, and the central heating boiler which threw tantrums worse than those of the old boiler at Low Rigg. He stoically put up with Miss Spriggs across the road, who spied on her new neighbours from behind her intimidatingly white lace curtains, she who still donkey-stoned her doorstep according to how she'd been taught by her mother. It was cramped quarters inside the New Vicarage, and the extensive view across the beautiful old garden and into the valley, which the old one had enjoyed, was obscured by the bus shelter outside. Boys rode their bikes and skateboards round the shelter and teenagers of either sex gathered there at all times of the day and night, littering the ground with their take-away trash and their fag ends. The noise from the Red Lion car-park further along the road at closing time was impossible to ignore. There was a fish and chip shop within smelling distance.

If the meanness and the shabbiness ate into Peter Denshaw's soul, he felt it was no more than he deserved. And if envy and hatred of the Lumbs, sitting there in the Old Vicarage, in what should have been his own home, were mortal sins, that was something between him and his God.

A car drew up on the opposite side of the road and from it stepped the smart little figure of Elf, wearing a tartan fitted jacket, a short green skirt, black tights and shiny shoes. Peter's heart made an uneasy descent into his stomach. But instead of coming up the path to the front door, as he feared, she disappeared in the opposite direction.

With surprising speed, Peter abandoned his newsletter and was on his way up the church path before Eva Spriggs, pegging out her Monday washing at the side of the house, had time to see more than his long black cloak billowing out behind him. 'Ey up, what's the big hurry?' she muttered. The question went unanswered, being addressed to her cat, but Eva went on speculating, having noticed the car and knowing to whom it belonged, although she'd only ever once seen it there before.

Elvira Graham had been destined from birth, by her small physique as much as by the name bestowed on her at her baptism, to be called Elf by her adoptive family, the Denshaws. She was tiny, and neat. She had glossy black hair which she wore short and sleek, a pale, sharp face and taut skin over high cheekbones. Slanting black eyes with a sometimes malicious quality that accentuated the elvish fancy. Peter had been afraid of her ever since she'd been dumped as a shawl-wrapped bundle on his ten-year-old lap with the stern injunction to look after her, she was coming to live with them, because her parents had been killed in a roof fall during an ill-fated pot-holing expedition in the Dales. He was terrified of dropping her. Later, he'd grown afraid of her for other reasons.

She rang the bell at the New Vicarage after depositing in her car the apples she'd bought from the corner greengrocer's. Receiving no answer to her ring, she tried the knob and the door came open. 'Anybody there?' she called, not knowing she was calling into an empty house, that Peter had left in such a hurry he'd forgotten to lock the door. When no one answered, she stepped in and, calling again and receiving no answer, looked into the study and found it empty, likewise the kitchen. She went upstairs to avail herself of the bathroom facilities, renewing her lipstick and peeping into the bedrooms before she descended the stairs, raising her eyebrows at what she saw in two of them.

The parish had fitted a serviceable carpet throughout the house, with a dotted pattern that made her eyes cross and offended her taste; the walls still bore the original paint, magnolia from top to bottom. Sonia might at least have asked for the walls to be painted a more interesting colour, she thought, but then, Sonia hadn't the least idea when it came to making a home. Someone, Elf thought, feeling a sudden exasperated benevolence towards Sonia, ought to take her in hand. She was willing, but the flair just wasn't there, and as for Peter, who might have been thought to have some artistic feeling . . . Well, Peter detached himself from everything, these days.

Elf went into the kitchen and made herself a cup of instant coffee, since there didn't appear to be any other kind – well, there wouldn't be, would there, in this house? – and took it into the study, where the electric fire was still burning. Wandering around with the mug in her hand, she took a look at what Peter had been writing, noting the last crossed-out phrase with amusement. Typical Peter. Writing down to his parishioners, as if none of them would be capable of understanding this scholarly reference. Perhaps they wouldn't. She didn't understand it herself. She drank the rest of her coffee standing in front of the window. Across the street, a curtain twitched. She looked at her watch and took her empty mug back into the kitchen. She didn't wash it up.

A minute later, the door bell rang. She barely hesitated before going to answer it. 'Excuse me,' said the woman with sharp features at such variance with her rotundity who stood on the step, 'excuse me, but if you're looking for the vicar or Mrs Vicar they're both out. She went out early on, but he's just gone up to the church, not ten minutes since. I just happened to be pegging out and I saw you arrive, so I thought I'd tell you.'

Elf surveyed her coolly. 'Thank you,' she said. 'I'd rather gathered they were out, but I'll let them know how kind you are, keeping such a keen eye on their property.'

The woman flushed and looked uncertain. 'That's all right. You never know, do you, these days?'

Elf watched her cross the street and disappear down the narrow ginnel between the two houses opposite. Nosy old bat! She'd give it ten minutes, and then try the church.

Peter was kneeling at the altar rail when she shut the church door quietly behind her. The scent of incense, wax candles and Brasso lingered on the air.

Under Mrs Lumb's direction, the flower arrangers had lately taken to using silk flowers in the winter months when florists' blooms were expensive. A huge arrangement, mixed with preserved leaves, stood by the pulpit, matching two smaller ones either side of the altar. Very professional, even if roses were unconvincing this time of year. Pink roses, huge cabbage roses, lighting up the dark church, so real one could almost believe an overpowering scent came from them. Their pinkness suddenly swam in front of her eyes and for a moment, at the same time as Peter rose and turned to see a flash of tartan in the dimness of the nave, Elf, who never repined the past and normally wasted no time on what was over and done with, was so shaken by memory she broke into a cold sweat. She dropped into a pew and bowed her head, not to pray but because she was afraid she might actually pass out.

The action steadied her but behind her closed lids the picture still remained of that summer day in the garden at the back of Low Rigg, no one else at home except her and Peter. The insistent perfume of the huge pink rose climbing the dark stone wall assailed her nostrils and beat in her head. She saw her adolescent self, and Peter, home from art college, his easel set up to capture the rose in paint. What had happened that afternoon had seemed quite natural – until they'd been interrupted. The day after, Peter had gone back to college, announcing some time later that he was abandoning art and was going to enter the Church. When he

42

came home for holidays he barely spoke to her and the temporary rapport that had existed between them during the last year or two ceased to exist.

She looked up now to see Peter sitting at the end of the pew across the aisle.

'What do you want, Elvira?' he asked coldly.

5

There was one thing to be said for travelling light: it hadn't taken Richmond long to put his small house on the market, say good-bye to colleagues and the few friends he'd made in Bristol. Apart from a sore head after a generous farewell booze-up organised by CID – which he'd gone along with and tried to enjoy, feeling he owed them that – he had no regrets.

He returned once more in November to a cold, rain-drenched Steynton; after the south-west, Steynton was like a neat shot of iced vodka.

He was staying temporarily at the Woolpack, with time to spare before he started his new duties, time to find himself somewhere to live, to renew old contacts. The first of these was Charlie Rawnsley, whom he rang the morning after he arrived and arranged to see later in the day. After he'd spoken to the old man, he left the Woolpack and made his way along one of the small, sett-paved streets off Towngate to cast a quick eye over the properties advertised in the window of Whiteley and Horsfall, House Agents. Standing with his coat collar pulled around his ears, he scanned the photographs with their accompanying, extravagant claims for a while, then dived inside, out of the rain.

'You'll want to see Mr Whiteley,' a bored young girl with damson-coloured, Cruella de Vil lips informed him in a strong local accent when he stated his business. 'He's busy with a client at the moment but he shouldn't be long if you care to wait.'

Richmond said he would and took a seat on one of the row of chairs at the back of the premises while she went back to pecking desultorily on a word processor. There were magazines on the low table in front of him, more details of some of the properties shown in the window, none of which had stimulated his interest. Perhaps because he didn't know what he wanted, was unsure whether he should buy at this stage. Something to rent, something furnished while he got his bearings, would probably be a better spec. He put the papers down and looked across the shop to where the only other representative of Whiteley and Horsfall – a youth, all of seventeen, pink-cheeked, barely out of the egg – was sitting talking, or rather, listening respectfully to a woman client. By his flustered look, she was running rings round him.

At that moment, she gathered her papers together and swept them into a big shoulder bag as she prepared to leave. 'Well, you can tell them that's my last offer.' She bestowed a smile upon the young lad that caused the blood to run up his neck. His hand flew to the spot of acne on his chin. 'Give me a ring and let me know what they say.'

'Certainly, Mrs Winslow.'

Richmond stood up, ready to take her place and, as she passed him, their glances met. A momentary pause, a puzzled look in a pair of amazing brown eyes, and then, in a flash of yellow raincoat, she was gone.

The youth dragged his eyes away from the door and back to business. 'What can I do for you, sir?' he asked, gathering the remnants of his dignity and introducing himself with a straight face as 'Mr Whiteley'. Apparently still bemused from dealing with his previous customer, it took him some time to get to grips with what Richmond wanted. When at last he realised that his prospective client didn't have property to sell and didn't want to buy – the idea seemed to have suddenly crystallised into a certainty in Richmond's mind – he began to lose interest. 'To *rent?*' He blew out his lips. 'Poo-oof – not much chance of that at the moment, sir.' Making Richmond feel as though he were a vagrant begging a room for the night. But the list he eventually produced was indeed unpromising: some properties too far out, one or two in Rumsden – no, definitely not! – a few flats above shops and the like, and a bungalow on the Clough Head Estate, that one which stuck out like a sore thumb against the hillside, an idea that would only appeal if he couldn't find anything else.

Richmond thanked him, collected the details together and said he'd be in touch. It was still raining and he dived into the snack bar next door, where he began to go through them again over a cappuccino and a croissant, hoping some jewel might yet turn up amongst the dross.

'Excuse me.'

A shadow had fallen across the table, and he glanced up to see the woman who'd passed him in the house agents' looking at him with the same puzzled expression as she'd worn then.

'Do you mind if I ask you something?' she said quickly, then rushed on without waiting for an answer. 'Haven't we met somewhere before?'

There was a wisecrack here, if only he could think of it. Except that Richmond wasn't the man for wisecracks and she didn't look that sort of woman, either. He pushed his chair back and stood up. 'I'm sorry, I don't think . . . I feel sure I'd have known if we had.'

He hardly ever forgot a face, he was observant by nature as well as by training, and she wasn't a woman you'd easily forget, once having met her. Those brown eyes – not a muddy chocolate or liquid spaniel's, but a warm golden brown with flickering shadows in their depths. Long, thick lashes with raindrops clinging to them. The curve of a soft, sweet, red mouth, too wide for beauty, but made to smile, as she was doing now, hesitantly . . .

And yes, there was, the more he looked, some fleeting recognition. He indicated the chair opposite. 'Won't you join me?'

'Oh, look, I didn't mean – I really shouldn't have said anything.' Her eyebrows rose comically. 'Will I ever learn to think before I speak?'

'I'm glad you did speak, I think maybe we *have* met. Why don't you sit down and let's try and work out where? But first, can I get you a coffee, something to eat?'

'Thanks, but I'd better let you finish your croissant in peace.' The hint of a smile lifted the corners of her mouth as she turned to go. 'Contrary to the evidence, I don't usually pick up strange men in coffee bars.'

'You can't go and leave me with my curiosity unsatisfied,' he protested. 'I'll never sleep tonight.'

She hesitated. 'We-ell, if you put it like that.' The smile came out in all its glory. 'Just coffee, then, please.'

He came back with another cappuccino and set the cup down. She'd pulled off the furry hat which had obscured her hair and it fell in glossy, chestnut-brown waves to her shoulders. 'My name's Richmond, Tom Richmond,' he said, holding out his hand, 'and I know yours is Winslow because I heard "Mr Whiteley" call you that.'

A ripple of amusement passed between them. 'He's the heir apparent, this is his father's firm.' Then, suddenly, she caught her breath. 'Richmond. Oh God, I remember now.' And all the light went from her face.

'You have the advantage over me. I still don't remember you.'

'You wouldn't. You only saw me once – but I heard your name, often. I'm Polly Denshaw, or I was before I was married.'

It all came back to him. His previous sighting of her had been brief and he'd been in no condition to register permanently the presence of any woman, attractive or otherwise, when the only woman he'd ever loved was being lowered into her grave. After it was done, he'd walked out of the churchyard, alone, not wanting to speak to any of the other mourners, wanting only to be shot of the whole thing.

'What can I say?' she managed to get out, the soft lips trembling now. 'We must be the last people you want to see, any of us. I'm sorry about the coffee but I can't possibly stay now, can I?'

Before he could make any further protest, she was gone.

There was the inevitable pot of tea on the go when he got to Charlie Rawnsley's in the late afternoon. He'd walked up the hill, despite the weather. It was still raining, turning to sleet, and the wind was whipping it about in nasty spiteful flurries, tearing off what leaves still remained on the trees. The cold afternoon was already dark, presaging the real winter.

'Bloody awful afternoon, Charlie,' he remarked, as the old man wrung his hand and took his raincoat to hang up before ushering him into the warm back room.

'Aye, well, soon be Christmas. Sit you down, lad, sit you down! Grand to see you.'

He turned the simulated coal fire up another notch and the coals glowed, amazingly real, the flames leaped. He saw Richmond seated in the comfortable leather chair opposite his own, poured tea. Richmond sipped cautiously at a well-remembered, fierce orange brew that could have stripped paint;

Charlie's own taste buds had long been anaesthetised by thirty-five years of police canteen tea.

The house was reassuringly the same. Not quite as tidy, some of the surfaces not as lovingly polished as they had been in Connie's day, but the lamplit room was comfortable and warm as ever. A savoury smell of cooking issued from the kitchen.

Richmond was grateful that the older man hadn't removed the photographs from the sideboard of Isobel, Beth and himself which had always stood there, along with one of Isobel's brother, an airline pilot, with his wife and children, and the one of Connie, their late mother. They were Charlie's family, alive or dead, and to remove them before Richmond's visit would have been an admission that he suspected Tom couldn't cope with seeing them. It showed a delicacy in tough old Charlie Rawnsley that you wouldn't have expected, unless you knew him as well as Richmond did.

'I never thought you'd come back, you know,' he remarked, after the usual formalities had been exchanged, Richmond had been congratulated on his promotions and had learned, not to his surprise, that Charlie was uneasy in his enforced retirement. Reaching the limit of his police service ten years ago, he'd found himself another job, in the stock control department at Brackenroyd's. Then, reaching sixty-five, compulsory retirement had once more caught up with him. Since then, he told Richmond, he'd spent his time building himself a conservatory on to the back of his house, tending the veritable jungle of plants in it, painting the outside of the house. He took himself off for long walks across the moors. And he had his books, packed into shelves set in the fireplace alcoves – he'd always been a great thriller reader. Despite all this, it was obvious time hung heavy.

'But I'm damned if I'll join that there Golden Links club,' he added forthrightly. 'I went, once. They were singing "Daisy, Daisy".'

Richmond laughed outright. 'What about travelling? You and Connie always enjoyed that.'

'You sound like our David's lot! They were trying to get me on a lonely hearts cruise t'other week.'

Richmond grinned again, thinking Charlie wouldn't be a bad catch for a woman, at that. He was still an active man, healthy and well set up, balding and a bit thicker round the waistline than he had been, but otherwise in better nick than many half his age.

'Besides,' Charlie added, 'it wouldn't be the same without Connie.'

The wind in the chimney gusted the flames of the fire as though they were real. Another spatter of rain rattled against the panes, and the window shook in its frame. 'Well, then, what's made you come back, Tom? You've done well enough down south. I never thought to see you up here again,' he repeated.

Too ambitious for that, was obviously what he was thinking. It had taken a lifetime's patient service for Charlie himself to achieve his final rank of Chief Inspector. But mention the name of Charlie Rawnsley to the lowliest rookie constable in the Steynton police force, even now, and he'd know who you meant. CI Rawnsley was a name that had gone down in history, a legend in his own lifetime. He'd ruled the local nick like a benevolent despot, blunt and broad-spoken. He'd been born and bred in Steynton and what he didn't know about it, and the folks who lived in it, wasn't worth knowing.

He held up the teapot inquiringly, cosied in a knitted, brown-striped beehive Richmond remembered seeing on Connie's needles, and pushed across the plate of ginger biscuits as he waited for Richmond's answer.

'No thanks, Charlie. To tell you the truth, I hardly know why I've come back here, myself. Must be the climate.'

But joking wasn't going to put Charlie off. Silence fell as he busied himself with pouring another liquid stream of pure caffeine into his own cup, sugaring it heavily.

'Not got any daft ideas about trying to follow up the case? Because I'll tell you summat for nowt. You won't get anywhere going down that road. Don't think I haven't thought of it, myself.' Briefly, his eyes rested on the school photograph of Beth, a wide smile and two front teeth missing, and on Isobel's: a thin, anxious face and a cloud of dark hair. 'Nearly ten years. Who-ever it was must be thinking he's got away with it. But I keep my eyes and ears open, and one day he might slip up. If he does, I hope I'll be there, and the bugger'll wish he'd never been born.' Unspoken between them, no need for words to affirm it, was the tacit assumption of Isobel's innocence. Then Charlie shook his head. 'Naa, that's wishful thinking, I'm too old for them sort of games. Me, I'd have nowt to lose, mind, but you keep out of it, lad. I wouldn't blame you, wanting to, but don't do it.'

'I wasn't thinking of it,' Richmond said and knew Charlie knew he was lying. He'd been thinking of little else since his meeting with Mrs Austwick. In the last few days, anger had come and fuelled the slow-burning fire of resentment at the mishandling of the case. It would take very little for it to burst into flames. He found himself recounting to Charlie his meeting with Wyn Austwick, and reporting what she'd said, and his impressions of her.

'Wyn Austwick? Never heard of her. Sounds a right piece of work. But we get all sorts of comers-in nowadays,' Charlie said. 'Only Austwicks I know of, one of 'em's dead and his son's doing a long time in Armley jail.'

'It's *Mrs* Austwick, Charlie.'

'Mebbe that'll be young Trevor's wife, then. I heard tell he got married to some foreigner.' Foreigner, Richmond knew, meant anyone from outside a five-mile radius of Steynton.

'*Young* Trevor? Wyn Austwick's all of forty.'

'So's Trevor.' Charlie said nothing more for a while. 'And she expects the case to be reopened on what she told you?' he said at last. 'Must be off her head.' But there was a flicker of excitement in his eyes at the prospect of another lead after all this time, however tenuous. 'Unless there's summat else?'

'She says there is.'

'You believe her?'

'I'm not sure. She's grinding her own axe, that's certain.'

Charlie looked at the clock and said suddenly, 'I've a meat-and-tatie pie in the oven. You used to like that.'

'Still do.'

'Going to stop and have some with me, then? There's plenty. We can have a bit of a natter and I can bring you up-to-date with what's been going on in Steynton since you left.'

Suddenly, the prospect of venturing forth into the vile evening, and dining alone in solitary splendour at the Woolpack, even with the choice of fancy French dishes, stood no chance against a few hours eating meat and potato pie, and chinwagging with Charlie Rawnsley. 'Thanks, Charlie, I'd be glad to.'

The old boy's delighted grin showed Richmond that it was no

mere chance there was plenty food to share. He stood up, reaching into his trouser pocket for his key ring as he crossed to his desk, unlocked the bottom drawer and lifted out a thick file in a pink cardboard folder, which he put on the table in front of Richmond. 'It's all here. Go on, have a read while I see to the pastry, and you'll see what I mean about getting nowhere.'

But Richmond couldn't bring himself to open the folder immediately. There wouldn't be anything new in it, nothing that wasn't engraved on his memory as if on tablets of stone, so what was the use? He sat there in the lamplit room, with the heat of the fire on his face and the photographs on the sideboard and the slow, deliberate tick of the old wall clock measuring out the seconds. But in the end, he opened it.

There was plenty. It had been a big crime in a small town and it was all there, patiently collected by Charlie: newspaper clippings, with comments added in his big, forceful handwriting, his own thoughts and ideas. Press photographs, with 'Have you seen Beth?' above them. Photographs of Isobel, of Peter Denshaw, of Low Rigg Hall. And, not surprisingly, photographs and background gossip of Freya Cass, the once-famous fashion model. Descriptions of Beth.

An eight-year-old girl, small for her age, blonde, shoulder-length hair, wearing dark blue trousers and a red anorak, and a blue and red striped scarf, red wellingtons. A happy, friendly child who talked easily with anyone . . . the subtext being, Richmond thought savagely, that she might have disregarded warnings not to talk to strangers.

She'd been taken up to Low Rigg Hall that snowy, early January day by her mother, who'd left her there for her weekly piano lesson with Mr Philip Denshaw. She'd had her lesson, and afterwards, as it was Twelfth Night, had helped to dismantle the Christmas tree. She'd stayed for lunch, as she normally did after her lesson. At about half-past one, she'd gone out to play in the snow while she waited for her mother to pick her up and take her home. In the event, her mother, who, the paper reported, suffered ill health, had taken a sudden bad turn that had left her in no condition to drive, so it was Beth's stepfather, the Rev. Peter Denshaw, who drove up to bring her home. When he arrived at approximately half-past two, Beth had already disappeared, an abandoned, half-made snowman and one small,

51

scarlet woolly glove the only evidence that she had ever been there.

A hue and cry was put out, teams of police and volunteers working round the clock searched the town and later the surrounding moors, a search that went on for days, despite atrocious weather conditions, until at last it had to be called off.

Meanwhile, damningly, evidence of a quarrel between Beth and her mother at the vicarage that morning had emerged.

Peter Denshaw, it seemed, was something of an amateur artist, and the morning she disappeared, Beth had been found messing around with his oil paints, something she'd been strictly forbidden to do – and indeed, when she was eventually found, her fingers were still stained with bright smears of viridian. Isobel Denshaw, her mother, knowing how angry her husband would be, had scolded the little girl, a scolding which was overheard by the church verger, Mr Dennis Roebuck, who'd been visiting the vicar to report that the central heating in the church wasn't working properly.

Events had taken a dramatic turn when, after the search had eventually been abandoned, Isobel had taken an overdose, leaving a suicide note addressed to her own father, Charlie Rawnsley, in which she wrote: 'I shall soon be dead, in any case, so there's no point in carrying on. I was responsible for Beth dying. It's all my fault, Dad. I pray God will forgive me, and hope you will, too.' She'd given no clue as to where the child was to be found, however, and Beth's body wasn't discovered until four months later by a park attendant, opening up the storage space beneath the bandstand in East Park for the spring. She had wounds on the temple which, in the opinion of the pathologist, had been the cause of death.

Afterwards, questions were to be asked. Why had the bandstand never been gone through in the original search? The answer was that it had been, but not thoroughly enough, by a PC who'd already been voluntarily on duty for sixteen hours, was bone weary and was also developing flu symptoms. Although it was understandable why his probing among the deck chairs stacked underneath the staging hadn't been as diligent as it might otherwise have been, he'd been hauled over the coals, but whether Beth's body had been there or not at the time, the question was academic. She must have been dead already by then.

In charge of the investigation had been Detective Superintendent Brearley. Dan Brearley, thought Richmond grimly. A once-intelligent detective, by then a fat, hard-drinking, heavily smoking slob of a man who'd wanted nothing more than an easy life in the last few months before his retirement. To be fair, he'd pulled out all the stops to find Beth when she'd first gone missing, nobody could have done more. But he'd been only too happy to accept Isobel's 'confession', when it came, had been smugly confirmed in his easy acceptance of it when the body had later been found behind the stack of deck chairs, wrapped carefully in a blanket and with her head resting on a pillow – surely a mother's touch? Much good his retirement had done him. Within six months of leaving the service, he was dead of a massive coronary.

The pie was as good as any Connie had ever made, the crust crisp and golden, the beef moist and succulent, plenty of onions in the gravy. A glass of Webster's went down well with it.

'You were wasted in the force, Charlie.'

'Aye, but I've always liked my food. Connie wouldn't have wanted to see me starve myself.'

Connie had been a lovely lady, a great cook with a figure to prove it. A sensible, down-to-earth woman whose sudden death had shocked and saddened everyone who'd known her. Richmond had often wondered if Isobel would ever have contemplated divorce if her mother had still been alive. He somehow didn't think so. Isobel was one of life's frail creatures, a gentle person, easily defeated and overcome by the business of life. Everyday problems tended to assume gigantic proportions. She'd always run back to Connie when things became too much for her and usually received what Connie had called 'a good talking-to', robust advice that cleared the air and lifted the clouds of depression, so that things didn't seem as bad to her afterwards.

'I never did like the idea of our Isobel marrying him, that Peter Denshaw, too young and no backbone, and I told her so,' Charlie said suddenly, picking up his thoughts. 'Mebbe I should've kept my tongue between my teeth, but you know me. "He's a good man, Dad," she said. I told her that didn't follow, just because he's a vicar, but she wouldn't hear owt against him. She should've stuck to the chapel, like her mam and dad. What did you think of that note she left?'

'Ambiguous, as I told you at the time.'

'It were that, all right.'

In view of the reported quarrel between her and Beth, the manner in which the child's body had been left, the note had seemed to be as neat a confession as could be that she herself had killed the child. After all, shocking as it was, it wasn't unheard of for mothers to kill their own children, and Isobel had been known to be neurotic. An accident, maybe, a slap that had gone too far? Children could provoke a saint – even the best of them, and Beth at that time had not always been easy or amenable.

The note seemed to be an admission of guilt. '*All my fault*', Isobel had written. But to anyone who knew Isobel it could also have been interpreted otherwise . . . *My fault that I messed up all our lives? My fault I married Peter Denshaw?*

Richmond knew that she'd genuinely believed their separation was giving Beth a better chance of a normal life, that marrying Denshaw would provide the child with a substitute father – one, moreover, who wasn't always absent. The agonies she must have gone through when she found it wasn't working out that way! Especially when she'd learned she was terminally ill. Richmond hadn't known about this until he was told of her note, even though the divorce had been a so-called civilised affair and there was still good communication between them. For Beth's sake, they'd made a pretence of smiles and even jokes when they met. With hindsight, it was possible to see that maybe this hadn't made it any easier for the child to understand why they couldn't all stay together, had created even more confusion in her mind, but at the time, it had seemed the best thing for her.

There'd been more than one person willing to testify that the trouble at the vicarage had centred around Beth's dislike of her stepfather. She'd made up her mind to hate him. He'd never been able to win her round, plenty thought he hadn't tried overmuch and, for a while, Peter Denshaw had been Dan Brearley's prime suspect.

Around lunch time that Saturday, the day Beth disappeared, he'd gone across to the church to meet the verger and the plumber who'd been summoned to attend to the faulty central heating, wanting assurances that the church would be warm enough for the services on the following day. The plumber had just finished the job, and after some discussion, he and the verger had left to share a pub lunch. That had been around one o'clock, leaving a big time lapse between then and his own arrival at Low Rigg to pick Beth up. His explanation was that he'd stayed behind in the church after the other two men had left and then, after he'd returned home at twenty to two and found his wife prostrate, further time had been spent in ringing for the doctor and waiting until he arrived. Why had he stayed in the church so long? he was asked. To sort out his thoughts, to meditate and pray was the answer. Gruff embarrassment all round, because you didn't want to cast doubts on a vicar when he said he was saying his prayers. Even from Dan Brearley, who wasn't the man to have finer sensibilities about anything. As an alibi, it was useless, but as Denshaw pointed out, he didn't need to provide an alibi, since he was innocent.

'I see red every time I think about him,' Charlie said. 'For if he didn't do it, who did?'

There'd been suggestions of a random snatch, but as a credible theory, it had swiftly been abandoned, the idea of some unknown person driving up to the back of beyond and plucking Beth up out of the garden. The road which wound up through the houses below Low Rigg was clearly signposted as not being a through road. Only those on legitimate business used it, the Low Rigg cottagers were accustomed to the family at the big house driving through the hamlet and barely registered their comings and goings, but any strange car was bound to have been noticed with interest. Peter Denshaw's familiar car had, as it happened, been seen on its way up to the Hall at half-past two, as he said, though there was no one prepared to swear that he hadn't also driven up and away before that, taking Beth with him.

There was no one to say that Isobel hadn't similarly driven up, either, before then and taken the child away, that the quarrel with her daughter hadn't been resumed . . . The doctor stated that Isobel's collapse was genuine, but it could have been brought on by the stress of having lost her temper with the child and of having fatally injured her. It had never seemed a likely scenario to anyone who'd known her.

'There were a lot of them up there at Low Rigg that day, you'll have noticed that,' Charlie said. 'Family. It's always been my belief that some of 'em must know a lot more than they let on about what happened. Stands to reason.'

Richmond flicked the papers over, and scanned the names of those who'd given statements: Mrs Freya Denshaw. Her brother-in-law, Philip. Elvira Graham, a girl who lived with the Denshaws as one of the family – and the last person to see Beth, helping her to build her snowman . . . Eddie Nagle had been there and his wife, Dot. Leon Katz, who'd had business there earlier in the day with Philip, but not his wife Ginny, who had been expecting the birth of twins at any time. Nor the still unmarried Polly Denshaw, he noted, remembering a pair of warm brown eyes and an enchanting smile.

'Katz says he left before lunch and I can't see him lying. Too good a lawyer for that, too careful – unless he had to.'

Richmond recalled Katz: a solicitor with a small firm of lawyers in Steynton. The only son of an immigrant tailor who'd ended up owning a chain of dresswear factories in Leeds, reputedly wealthy enough to have no need to work, he was nevertheless now a hard-working lawyer with a busy law firm in Bradford, so Charlie informed him. He was a well-liked man in the town, generous of his time and money to charities.

It was after midnight when Richmond got ready to leave, and still raining.

'Pity you've booked in at the Woolpack. You could've stopped here tonight if you'd wanted, there's enough room, God knows,' Charlie said, as Richmond at last regretfully stood up to go.

It lay between them, the old man's unspoken offer, and Richmond's fervent hope that he wouldn't put it into words. Much as he liked and respected Charlie, the very last thing he wanted, or needed, was temporary accommodation here, which might all too easily slide into permanency.

'Thanks, Charlie, but I'd better get back. They'll be reporting me missing, otherwise. I shall have to knock the night porter up as it is.'

'Night porter! They've gone up in the world. Aye, well.' After a moment, however, he added, 'You won't want to be stopping there long, mind. I'll keep my eyes and ears open. Mebbe I'll hear of summat to rent that'll suit you.'

'And I'll have another word with Wyn Austwick – when I can get in touch with her.'

Charlie looked at him over his spectacles. 'You're going on with it, then? All right, don't answer that! Well, if you must, you can count on me.'

'Charlie, I appreciate it, but I don't want you involved – if there's anything to get involved *in*, that is.'

'You allus were a one-man band, Tom, but you're too late. I am involved.'

'One-man band? I prefer to call it being unorthodox.'

'Call it what you want, you're still an independent bugger.'

Charlie was right, of course. He'd always steered a lone course. Not always a good team member, and that had gone against him, had damaged his career prospects once or twice in the early days, until he'd learned to bend to the wind over the years. His ambition, which had once cost him his wife and child, was still strong, but if it had to be sacrificed in the process of finding out who'd killed Beth, he discovered it didn't matter a damn.

It wasn't until he was half-way back to the Woolpack, striding out, head down against the icy, needle-sharp rain, invigorating as a cold shower, that it occurred to him to wonder why he hadn't mentioned his meeting with Polly Winslow to Charlie Rawnsley.

6

Old Mrs Wadsworth lived in a little low house near the cottage which used to be Elf's and was now lived in by the Nagles. She still made her own bread, and when she was in a good mood she made extra, selling it to those of her neighbours who had either no time or no inclination to follow her example. No doubt against some trading standard or other, but who was going to tell on her when it was so delicious?

Freya was making her breakfast coffee when Dot Nagle arrived with one of Mrs Wadsworth's teacakes, still warm from the oven. Freya poured another mug of coffee and they shared the bread, liberally spread with butter. Dot, lean as a skinned rabbit, had never had to worry about gaining weight and Freya had occasionally thought lately, astonishing herself, why worry? At my age? It didn't seem to make any difference to her figure. She still measured the same as she had forty years ago.

'I've come to a decision, Dot,' she announced, pouring herself more coffee.

Dot raised her eyebrows. 'Don't tell me – you're going to change your will.'

Freya smiled faintly, then looked dismal. 'As if what I have to leave would matter to anybody!'

'I wouldn't go around saying that, if I was you,' Dot said bluntly, lighting a cigarette and leaving Freya to wonder exactly how much more Dot knew than she'd been told.

Dot was nominally housekeeper here at Low Rigg, though her duties were unspecified and more often neglected than not, and their relationship was far more complex than that of mistress and employee, or even close friends. There was deep affection between them, though at times sparring partners might be a more applicable term. Although the Nagles didn't live in, Dot spent more time at the big house than she did in her own, and when Eddie wasn't dog racing or working at his part-time job at the health club, he was always around the kitchen or in the snug corner he'd made for himself in what had once been the stables, which had latterly accommodated the legendary Daimler and now gave house room to a sedate Rover.

Freya had to put up with Eddie for various reasons, one of them being Dot, though she detested him and couldn't for the life in her see what Dot saw in him. For one thing, his unfortunate appearance repulsed Freya, to whom physical beauty was paramount, and for another, she suspected he had pocketed a substantial sum from the sale of the Daimler several years ago – vintage models like that surely sold for far more than he said it had fetched? – but she had no means of proving it now. His attitude appalled her, and sometimes frightened her, too, but he was useful around the place when he felt like being so.

Having swallowed the last delicious morsel of bread and butter, she returned to her original remark. 'I've been having second thoughts. About the Austwick woman. I think maybe I ought to give up the idea. She's been getting too nosy.'

'I could have told you she would,' Dot responded tartly. Which in fact she had, several times, but Freya had chosen to brush aside the warnings. It cost her something now to admit that she'd been wrong: Dot had been antagonistic to Wyn Austwick from the start, more so to the very idea of the memoirs, but she herself had been impressed with the notion of seeing her achievements laid down in black and white, in an actual book with some of her best photographs included. She gave Dot a half-hearted version of the Look which, as always, was lost on Dot, who merely shrugged and said, 'Send her packing, then.'

'It's not quite as easy as that . . .'

'What do you mean? You haven't been saying anything you shouldn't, have you?'

For a moment, she looked quite as inimical as Eddie at his worst and Freya shrank. 'Of course I haven't *said* anything, but she's been poking around among my papers and I don't like that. I'm not sure I ought to trust her.'

'Let her poke around all she wants, there's nothing to find.' She paused. 'Is there?'

'No,' Freya said.

Dot continued the long, considering stare. 'She won't like getting the push. You've got yourself into this thing, so just you watch you don't let your tongue run away with you.' She blew a cloud of smoke across the table and Freya pointedly put the lid on the butter dish. She'd told Dot hundreds of times she didn't like her smoking in the kitchen, but it made no difference.

'It's not only me, you know,' she said, looking aggrieved.

'Nobody else is going to say anything, not now, why should they?'

Why, indeed? For years there'd been silence, nobody had said anything, not even to each other. Low Rigg Hall had become a house of secrets, a family together, but apart, each keeping their own counsel. None of them ever spoke of that time, but for Freya at least it was never absent from her thoughts. She had turned it over in her mind – the way things had happened and the way she wished things had happened – so often that everything had grown muddled and sometimes she wasn't clear as to what the truth actually was. Added to that, her arthritis was troubling her so much she could think of little else and there were times when she didn't need to pretend to be confused. And now – Wyn Austwick . . . She wished she'd never heard of the woman.

'When she gets back from Benidorm or wherever, she's going to talk to Elf.'

'Elf?' Dot asked sharply. 'What on earth does she want with her?'

'She says she can make a better-rounded book if she speaks to everyone connected with the family.'

Dot snorted. 'She won't get anything out of Elf, I'll guarantee that!'

Freya did not feel reassured. You never knew, with that young woman. Her daughters thought she judged Elf too harshly, but she was so wilful. From the moment she'd been introduced into the family, all their lives had begun to alter. A little, changeling thing, even as a baby but a few months old, she'd disrupted the household as none of the other children had ever been allowed to. Temper tantrums, sulks, screams, disobedience . . . there was no controlling her, there never had been, she did exactly as she pleased, except with Dot, who wouldn't tolerate such behaviour from anyone, despite having a soft corner for the girl. But Elf never showed much affection for anyone except Philip – and then, for a short time, Peter, though that hadn't lasted. It had always been Philip who had the patience to make the sun shine again for her . . . though alas, now even Philip was *persona non grata*. As the girl grew up, Freya came to think of her as an evil spirit, but she couldn't turn her out. And she'd grown out of all that nonsense now, of course, she was a controlled, self-possessed woman, who rarely lost her temper – but she never gave out her thoughts, either. And Freya had the feeling that they might be very dangerous indeed.

'Well,' she sighed, 'I just hope you're right, Dot.'

The bank had a recently constructed car-park, carved ingeniously from a sloping, awkwardly shaped, vacant space left by the demolition of an old-established pork-butcher's premises which had lost the battle with the supermarkets. Shrubs and trees softened its edges. Admonitory notices forbade parking there by non-customers of the bank but in spite of that it was always full when the bank itself was nearly empty. The parking in Steynton, like everywhere else, got worse every day, thought Polly.

It was a crisp, sunny day and she was content to sit at the wheel for a while, watching the last of the leaves float down from the trees, occasionally looking at her watch. It wasn't like Ginny to be so late. That's my privilege, Polly admitted with a wry grimace. They'd have finished serving lunches at the Woolpack if she didn't arrive soon, and there was quite a bit they must talk about before Ginny was due back at her boutique – not least these so-called memoirs of their mother's, which they wanted to discuss in peace and privacy. They'd also arranged to go and look at the house in Ingham's Fold after a quick sandwich. Polly knew she could trust Ginny to give her a frank opinion, and she'd know just whether, or how, it could be fixed up to best advantage. That was one of the perks of having someone like Ginny, always so calmly certain of herself, as an elder sister.

Where was she? Polly looked again at her watch and the dire possibility struck her . . . had the time they'd agreed to meet been *twelve o'clock*, not one? Oh damn, it was more than a possibility, the way she was about getting times right! Ginny would have waited, perhaps up to twenty minutes, but not more. Knowing Polly as she did, she'd have guessed the truth and given up and gone back to the shop. Polly thought she'd better go along to Roydholme and make her peace with her sister as best she could.

She slid the key in the ignition and was about to start the engine when there was a tap on the nearside window. She swung round, reprieved, but no, it wasn't Ginny, it was someone she'd hoped to avoid in future. Tom Richmond.

He tapped again and, reluctantly, she wound down the window, whereupon he leaned his head in. 'Mrs Winslow, spare me a moment?'

Maybe it was just because she now knew he was a policeman that the words seemed to her to sound ominous, more like an order than a request, and her hackles rose. Nevertheless, she leaned across and opened the door.

'I won't keep you long.' He slipped into the passenger seat and twisted to face her. 'I only wanted to let you know that I've just moved back here to work, so it's unrealistic to suppose we shall never meet – no, let me finish, please,' he added hastily when he saw she might be about to intervene. 'I appreciate what prompted you to say what you did the last time we met, but you're wrong. What happened ten years ago is old history now. I don't bear your family any particular grudge. There's no reason that I can see why we shouldn't be civil with each other.'

She was trying not to remember her previous gauche reaction to finding out who he was. He was reasonable and pleasant, a tall man with thick, grey-blond hair and a lived-in face. No longer the stony-faced young man she'd glimpsed at the funeral of his ex-wife, grieving for his still missing daughter and perhaps for the wreck of his marriage as well, but an older, controlled man stamped with an air of authority and decision and a look of something else, not quite understood, in his eyes.

She sighed and said, looking down at her hands, 'I overreacted, I know. It's just that – I have a daughter the same age as – as Beth was. I can't know, but I can imagine – I think I can imagine – what you must have felt . . .'

She could see him doubting that, but her sympathy was genuine, even if she did feel she might be going slightly over the top when she added, 'You've every right to feel badly towards me. It was my family. She was in our care.'

'Even if I felt that, it's pointless blaming anyone. You needn't be afraid of me, I'm not harbouring thoughts of revenge.'

'Oh,' she said, with a small, embarrassed laugh, 'I hardly thought that. Well . . .' She reached towards the ignition. 'I appreciate what you say . . . I have to go, now.'

'Another minute. Do you think we could meet – have a meal together somewhere? Talk?'

The quick colour rushed to her face. She looked down at her hands on the steering wheel. 'I – don't really think that would be possible.'

'Think about it. I'll be in touch, but meanwhile – think about it.'

Out of her rear-view mirror as she drove off, she saw him standing, watching her. Immobile, a dark expression on his face. She felt her stomach lurch – whether from fear, or something else, she wasn't sure she wanted to know.

Richmond watched her drive off, despising himself for having exerted himself to win her over, simply because she might be useful in the future. He'd also lied to her when he said he bore no ill-will to any of her family. To any except the one who might have killed his daughter, he should have said.

And yet, he'd surprised himself with that invitation to her to have a meal with him, though she'd been in his thoughts ever since meeting her in the coffee bar. He'd asked about her and found she was divorced, and like himself had only just come back here to live. He'd half expected her refusal, but he wasn't giving up.

He climbed into his own car and drove through Towngate to a short street half-way up the hill. He'd found somewhere to live – or rather, Charlie had found it for him. In Albert Street, one of a pair squeezed between the Bethel chapel and a corner shop. 'It's Molly Pickles as was that owns it,' Charlie had told Richmond. 'Her brother left it to her when he died.'

Both small, Edwardian houses had been bought forty-five years ago by the corner shop's owner as wedding gifts for his son and his daughter on their respective marriages. The shop had passed into other hands when he died and had many times changed ownership. It was presently run by a Pakistani couple, but Molly Greenwood, now widowed, had lived in her house ever since her father had given it to her on her wedding day, as had her brother, Leonard Pickles, in his, until his death a few months ago. He'd been a childless widower and had left his house to his sister. Molly, a comfortable, voluble lady, was glad enough to let it, furnished, short term, on Charlie Rawnsley's recommendation, until her daughter made up her mind about marrying that dozy article of a boyfriend she was living with.

Richmond felt himself in a time warp as he wandered around the tiny premises. Stone built, with sash windows. Two up, two down, kitchen and living-room below and the small second bedroom over the stairs made into a bathroom, it had been untouched since being furnished just after the war. A beige-tiled fireplace adorned with a row of relentlessly burnished brass ornaments, a three-piece suite in rust-coloured uncut moquette with crocheted chair-backs, and a highly polished square oak dining-table with four chairs round it and a matching sideboard. The only modern additions were a gas fire and a television set of overwhelming dimensions.

The house made him feel like Gulliver in Lilliput. If he stood in the centre of the kitchen and stretched his arms out he could touch all four walls. You had to skirt the dining-table to get to the fire. He knew if he stayed much longer it would begin to give him the screaming habdabs but for the moment it would have to do. He'd thought his only problem would be keeping up the formidable standards of cleanliness – even the forty-odd-year-old gas cooker shone like new – but the problem was solved by Mrs Greenwood announcing that if he wanted her to she'd pop in every day and keep an eye on the place, as she'd been doing for her brother ever since his wife had died twelve years ago. Richmond didn't relish what he suspected could be an invasion of his privacy but he didn't doubt that his new landlady believed no man capable of doing anything other than bring in the coal and help with the washing up.

'She's a good lass, Molly,' Charlie said. 'Providing you don't tell her owt you don't want everybody in the northern union to know. Keeping her mouth shut's never been her strong point.'

Wyn Austwick made the preparations that were now habitual to her before going away. She'd always liked to see things nice and tidy, but when you owned your own place, such things became specially important. She looked round with a sense of pride and achievement. This cosy little bungalow in Cresswell Close was the best place she'd ever lived in. She might even, if things went as she planned and hoped, settle here permanently. She'd had enough of moving around, living in rented rooms, and relished being comfortably alone, with her own things round her, and having only herself to please. There might be something to look forward to in the future, after all. For an instant she had a qualm of misgiving about that and closed her eyes, but it soon passed.

She cleaned out the fridge, carefully turned off the gas, water and electricity, opened her case to put in the document she'd shown Tom Richmond. Better safe than sorry. She checked again that she had everything necessary, then zipped up the case. The door bell rang. That would be the taxi she'd ordered.

Slipping her coat on, she gave a last quick look round to see that she'd missed nothing, then picked her case up, went into the hall and opened the front door. The last person she wanted to see was standing on the doorstep.

'What in God's name are *you* doing here?'

'It won't take long to explain, but we'd best go inside, unless you want all the neighbours to know.'

'It won't do any good,' she retorted, 'but now you're here, you'd better come in and tell me what you want. Only for a minute, mind. I'm expecting a taxi.'

Councillor Bob Widdop wasn't built for walking any further than needs must. The last time he'd walked this far had been from the concourse at Manchester airport to the jet waiting to take him on holiday to Madeira. He puffed valiantly on, several feet behind the trim form of his companion, Councillor Mrs Joanna Martin, as she walked lightly this Monday morning across the rough, uneven, rock-strewn ground of the old stone-quarry workings, overgrown now with grass and weeds and therefore all the more hazardous.

'Come on, Bob,' she encouraged over her shoulder. 'Only another fifty yards, it won't kill you.'

Councillor Widdop seriously doubted this. All right for some. All right for him, if he'd been twenty years younger, the same age as Joanna, one of the new breed of councillors, one of these young, trendy mothers with a university degree and seemingly limitless energy. A share in the running of her husband's information technology firm, three young children – and she still found time to sit on the council. A member of the public works committee, and relentless in pursuing causes. He toiled on, wishing he hadn't had that heavy fry-up for his breakfast.

They gradually drew nearer the target of their morning walk: the old delph, one of the last left in the area and which, if Joanna had her way, would soon be utilised, as nearly all the other defunct stone quarries had been, as a landfill site.

'Talk about a disgrace!' she declared as she neared the rim, slowing down for him to catch up. 'Apart from being a blot on the landscape, what about the danger to children – and *how* many suicides have we had here?'

'Three in the last eight or nine years, I reckon,' Bob answered, puffing as he lumbered up to join her. He looked down into the quarry and a frisson of atavistic dread made the hairs stand up on the back of his thick neck. Why had she said that? Was she psychic, on top of everything else? At first, looking down, he thought it was a dog that had drowned.

'Did I say three? It's four now, by the looks of things,' he warned her, pointing with a shaking finger to the surface of the water and issuing stern commands to his heaving stomach.

'Oh, my God.'

After wind, rain and that first, soon-dispersed sprinkling of snow in October, mid-November had decided to be kind. Crisp and exceedingly cold, but sparkling. Beautiful, good-to-be-alive weather. Make the most of it, it can't last, everybody was saying. Meanwhile, the sky was pale blue and clear, and down below, in the shelter of the valley, foliage here and there blazed red and gold as a Canadian maple grove. The sunlight was reflected in the still, glassy water in the bottom of the quarry, with the body floating serenely on the surface.

It was a long time since Rumsden Garth had seen such activity. Frogmen and other personnel all over the place, police vehicles on the uphill road leading to the disused stone quarry, including a battered old Volvo belonging to the Home Office pathologist.

'Unidentified middle-aged female, well-nourished,' Gillian Hardy was dictating crisply into the small microphone hung around her neck. 'The body has been immersed in water –' She looked up, switched off when she saw Manning. 'Two, no, nearer three days, I'd guess, Sergeant. That's what you want to know, isn't it?'

Steve Manning, who thought himself case-hardened, averted his eyes from the bloated thing that now lay on the lip of the quarry. Drowned bodies were never pretty, and this was no exception, though he'd seen worse. 'Suicide?' he asked, for something to take his mind off it, not doubting that it was. Nobody who wasn't intent on self-destruction would have reason to scramble over the broken dry-stone wall that surrounded the environs of the quarry, then make their way across the rocky wasteland, avoiding the disused shafts and all the rest of the detritus left behind when the workings were abandoned. Apart from kids looking for excitement, there was nothing in it for anyone else, only for those seeking oblivion in the water at the bottom of the quarry, where they were unlikely to be found for some time. This one had turned up sooner than most.

'Suicide? Doubtful. There are injuries to the head, could have been caused when she went in, of course, but it's unlikely. Killed here, probably. You'd maybe have problems otherwise, getting her across from the road.'

'Not a lightweight,' agreed the sergeant, no sylph himself, thinking, Murder, by God! Here's excitement. 'But you *can* get a car in.' He pointed to the hearse bumping towards them even as they spoke, the driver apparently prepared to risk its suspension rather than face the prospect of humping the body back across the uneven wasteland. 'No means of identification, doc? No? We'll get a description out then, put an appeal on the radio,' he went on, expanding on this, being over-chatty, not wanting to look at what she was doing.

There was a shout from the far side of the quarry, where the frogmen were still searching. A DC cupped his hands and shouted, 'They've found summat else, Sarge.'

The suitcase was heavy, and when it was brought to the surface, and the strap around it unfastened, it was found to contain several rocks as well as items of clothing and a hand-bag.

'That accounts for her belt being torn,' the doctor said. Manning looked, and registered her meaning. It was evident that the suitcase strap had been threaded through the belt of her slacks before being fastened around the case, with the object of weighting down the body. The weight of the suitcase, however, had proved self-defeating, causing the belt to tear in the centre back and the body to float to the surface.

Richmond's new abode in Albert Road had what passed for a garden. A couple of square feet of earth, just about big enough to contain six floribunda roses and a bare, narrow strip easily filled by a couple of boxes of bedding plants in their due season. Bounded by a low stone wall which had once had iron railings embedded into it – long since removed for the war effort – its main function was to separate his window from the pavement.

So that when the big car drew up on the road outside, it almost seemed to have parked itself inside the front room. From it emerged the ponderous, six-foot-three form of Detective Superintendent Jackson Farr.

'I wanted to see you and I have to be in Huddersfield by twelve, so I thought it'd be quicker to pop in on my way,' he announced with typical directness as Richmond opened the door to his thunderous knock. 'It won't take more than five or ten minutes, what I have to say.'

'Time for some coffee, sir?'

'I wouldn't say no. And not so much of the bloody sir, not here, any road, just the two of us.'

He parked himself with some difficulty in one of the small moquette-covered chairs, looking like a circus elephant, waiting while Richmond brought in two mugs of coffee. 'Three sugars, all right?' Richmond hazarded.

'Aye. Still trying to cut down but it's a bit late in the day. Settling in then?' he asked, looking round with candid deprecation. 'Not a lot of room, is there?'

'I won't be here for long, I hope. It'll do until I find somewhere permanent. I'm in no particular hurry, though.'

'Right. Only one thing got with rushing!'

Jacks had been Richmond's sergeant in the days when Richmond had been a DC. None better – and one case, at least, of rapid promotion through the ranks that was justified, in Richmond's opinion. They'd always got on well, and Richmond knew, without being told, that he'd Jacks to thank for endorsing his application for the transfer back here.

'What can I do for you?' he asked.

Jacks sipped at the coffee, stretching his thick thighs towards the gas fire. Richmond sat in the chair opposite and by awkwardly angling his own long legs, managed not to entangle with the other man's size twelves.

'We've got a body,' Jacks said abruptly. 'Perfect timing, as usual, wouldn't you know it? What with Gutteridge busy clearing his desk, hopping on one foot for Friday, can't wait for his bungalow and his carpet slippers at Southport. Me, with more than enough on my plate, and short-handed into the bargain –'

'And you'd like me to start?'

Jacks finished his coffee in one huge swallow. 'You'd be doing us all a favour, Tom. If you haven't any other plans, that is.'

Richmond shook his head and grinned. 'Try keeping me away!' What plans did he have for the next couple of weeks? He could see how Jacks was placed and followed his line of thinking. Manpower shortage apart, he wouldn't want to land Gutteridge with a case he'd have little interest in, and with no hope of finishing off before his retirement party next Friday. Better have the new DCI, Tom Richmond, Gutteridge's replacement, starting right at the beginning of a case. What was all that big city experience for, if not to make use of? As for Richmond himself – the rush of adrenalin at the thought of getting back into the swing of things made him feel suddenly alive. 'When do you want me to start?'

'Today?' Jacks asked hopefully, his big face creasing into a huge smile of relief.

Richmond laughed. 'Give me half an hour. And some idea what it's all about.'

Jacks sat back. The chair springs protested ominously. He said, 'Female floater in Rumsden Garth quarry. Not suicide. Doc Hardy says she didn't drown, somebody clobbered her on the head before chucking her in. We've identified her as a woman that lives on the Clough Head Estate, name of Wyn Austwick. Why, what's up?'

A bus ground up the hill, changing gear and darkening the room as it passed the other side of Jacks's car. Richmond let the sound die away before he answered. 'Sorry, Jacks. No go. Shan't be able to help out, after all.'

'What the hell does that mean?'

Richmond had a sense of *déjà-vu*, the feeling of having been here before as he explained to Jacks just what the position was with Wyn Austwick and her connections with the Denshaw family and Low Rigg, what she'd told him that night at the Woolpack. Jacks listened in silence, with the concentrated interest that was his hallmark. 'Same old story, isn't it?' Richmond finished. Personal involvement. Conflict of interests. On your bike, Richmond.

Jacks prised himself out of the armchair. Despite his bulk, he was an active man who never sat still for long, who liked to be on the move. Here, there was nowhere for him to move to, except four paces round the dining-table and back to his chair.

He went twice round the circuit, then perched dangerously on the chair arm and sat deep in thought for several minutes.

'Yes,' he said at last. 'If what she said to you is right, there might – *just* – be a connection. On the other hand, it's more likely she was feeding you a load of codswallop. No, you hang on a minute,' he said as Richmond opened his mouth to intervene, 'just answer me this. The truth, mind, no callifudging. Did you put in for this transfer here on purpose to sort out who did for Beth?'

Richmond thought carefully about what he should say. 'I won't deny I thought there might be –'

'Did you, or did you not, Tom?'

'Yes, but –'

'I bloody knew it!' Jacks exploded, ignoring the qualification. Richmond stayed quiet, leaving him to let off steam, feeling the adrenalin pump through his own veins, knowing for sure now that the answer to one case lay in the answer to the other. Let Jacks suggest what he wanted, Richmond knew that Wyn Austwick hadn't been spoofing.

'Soon as you applied, I knew it!' Jacks was continuing. 'All that claptrap about stepping stones to further promotion and –'

'That's true.'

'Aye, well, that's as maybe. And it's no use, is it, me telling you to forget it? But I will, any road. There's no mileage in that sort of thinking, Tom. You know I can't recommend reopening the case, much less put you on it.' He paused. Richmond began to speak, but Jacks stopped him. 'Shut up and let me think.'

Two minutes later, he said, 'I want my head examining, but I need you on this investigation, this Austwick murder. So get on with it – and officially, if I hear you're looking for further evidence about Beth, you'll get your arse kicked. Off the record . . . well, lad, we both know what we thought of the balls-up that was made of it. I was seconded down to Lincolnshire at the time, but I heard plenty.' It was heartening to Richmond to know that others had felt the same way as he did, would have been even more so to have known it at the time. But men had their jobs to think of. 'So –' Jacks stopped and pointed a finger like a pork sausage – '*so*, as long as I don't hear about it . . . Understand me, Tom?'

Richmond only just stopped himself from jumping up and

grasping his hand and thoroughly embarrassing both of them. He contented himself with a grin. 'Understood – and thanks. You'll not regret it.'

'Not so bloody fast! I'll be the one that ultimately carries the can, think on. This is my neck as well as yours, so I'll still be keeping my hand on the tiller,' he said, never one to shy away from a mixed metaphor, and as if there was any chance of him doing anything else but keep tight control. Jacks as a sergeant had always done that, why should Jacks as a superintendent be any different?

She'd lived on the Clough Head Estate, three doors away from another semi-detached bungalow with a Whiteley and Horsfall To Let sign in the garden, presumably the one Richmond had been offered and declined. Hers was at the end of the road, a quiet avenue of identical ones, set horizontally against the steep rise of the hill, with small sloping gardens back and front. Outside, paintwork and windows sparkled, inside it was unimaginatively furnished, but impeccably clean and tidy. The gas and water had been turned off, the fridge cleared out of all perishables, and the neighbour who lived across the way, an elderly woman walking with a zimmer frame, stated that Mrs Austwick had on Friday asked her if she'd like what was left of a pint of milk and some tomatoes since she was off to Torremolinos for a holiday. She hadn't said what time she'd be going and Mrs Dalton hadn't actually seen her leave because she herself had been picked up at ten and taken to the day centre, where she'd spent the day with other elderly and disabled people. Only the two houses opposite had any sort of view of the murdered woman's house – Mrs Dalton's and her neighbour, but there was no joy to be got there as the neighbour had been at work, like Wyn Austwick's neighbours.

The task of sifting through the dead woman's belongings was made easier by the neatness of the bungalow, though its impersonality was sad. Except for one framed snapshot, that of a smiling young man astride a motorbike, cradling his crash helmet, there was virtually nothing personal about the place.

The small second bedroom had been made into an office, furnished with a state-of-the-art computer and printer.

Richmond told Manning he could have the pleasure of running through the stack of disks later, pleasing the sergeant, who was something of a computer buff. Together they went through the papers and documents neatly filed in one of the deep bottom drawers of the large desk, finding her financial papers, tax documents and bank books, as well as research papers from each of her former projects. But of the concert programme she'd shown Richmond that night at the Woolpack, there was no sign.

Manning whistled when Richmond pointed to the size of her monthly building society repayments. 'What did she do to be able to afford that?' he asked, obviously thinking of the hole his own much more modest repayments made in his salary.

'According to what she told me, she didn't make it from these.' Richmond indicated the bookshelves ranged along one wall, one of them containing about a dozen light romances by someone called Bryony Thorpe.

'She wrote books?' Manning asked, with all the awe of one who took two days to write a letter, after two days thinking about it.

'Either that, or she was Bryony Thorpe's number one fan – but yes, I think they're hers. I met her once, briefly, and she told me she was a writer.' And Manning could make what he liked of that. It was substantially true, and disposed of any questions about his previous knowledge of Wyn Austwick, as far as Manning was concerned. But what interested him more than the romances was a set of nearly a dozen uniformly bound volumes in red leather on the next shelf, all accredited on their spines to different authors. 'Recognise any of these?' he asked Manning, who at first shook his head, then exclaimed in amazement as one or two names sank in. 'James Holdsworth! Harrison Priestley! And get a load of this – Willie Muff! Stone me, who'd have thought he could string two sentences together?'

'He probably didn't,' Richmond said, and explained why. 'Somebody once had this bright idea and they're cropping up all over the place now, these sort of outfits – willing to edit or write and publish the books for you.' Their success, he felt, said as much for the need people seemed to have for contact with their roots as it did for what Wyn Austwick had described as a big ego trip. As an ego trip, it didn't come cheap, he decided, cogitating on those business accounts. After production costs from the printer she'd employed were deducted from the hefty outright payment, she'd been left with a very decent profit by any standards, most of which had gone into the bank, along with a number of other sizeable, as yet unexplained, regular cash deposits. There were also some large standing orders to the name of Brentdale which, together with those big mortgage repayments, seemed to explain why she had maintained only a small balance, despite what she'd been making.

'You can see why she stopped writing romances!' Manning said, still entertained by that other row of books and the notion of their so-called authors. 'Would you credit it? Old Muff! Used to have a so-called antique shop – junk shop, more like – and a market stall, till he retired on the proceeds. Sold anything and everything. Should be some interesting reading in that, it might tell us a lot we've never been able to prove about his activities.'

'What about these others, who are they?'

There was always one officer, somewhere around every police station, someone who was locally born, with inbred knowledge and an encyclopaedic memory. Here in Steynton, it was Steve Manning. A raw but promising young cadet when Richmond had worked here before, he was developing into a natural successor to Charlie Rawnsley. He was a big lad, Manning, his uniform holding him in like a corset. A tight cap of curly hair, rigorously barbered, fists like York hams. Not easily roused, but when he was, like a bull elephant. Salt of the earth, the soon-to-be-retired Gutteridge had informed Richmond, worth his weight in gold dust, which had to be considerable.

'James Holdsworth's an ex-mayor,' Manning answered. 'Harrison Priestley had the furniture emporium on Market Street, retired now, left his son to run it.' Still chuckling, picking up another volume, he read out: '*A Million Miles of Carpets*, by Harold Brackenroyd. No longer with us, old Harold. Died last year. But here's one the wife'll be interested in – Margaret Whitfield, her old headmistress at the Girls' High!'

'We're going to need to talk to these people. Something has to account for those cash deposits. She mentioned she had to have access to a lot of confidential documents in the course of her work,' Richmond pointed out.

He could see Manning getting hold of the idea, then shaking his head doubtfully, not liking it.

'Putting the screws on would be a good way of supplementing her income.'

'On Willie Muff, maybe. But the others – whiter than white, all of them. No way.'

'The money was coming from somewhere.'

'They couldn't *all* have had something to hide.'

'Supposing she came across the occasional one or two who had? She could soon have made herself a tidy sum. Blackmail's a dodgy business, though. All right if you like living on the edge, but you never know when you might meet the worm that turns. We can't discount any of them without talking to them, Steve.'

There were seven books altogether on the shelf, and presumably another in the making, too – the as yet unpublished family history of the Denshaws, nothing relating to which had turned up so far. She'd told him she'd made notes, and there was a rough, far from complete, handwritten outline. He couldn't find anything else, but maybe it was on disk. Manning could have the rest, but Richmond decided that was one he'd save for himself. The hint she'd given him could mean that someone in the Denshaw family, too, was ripe for blackmail.

The sergeant, shuffling through a pile of what appeared to be scrap paper, said suddenly, 'Before we start getting excited about that idea, take a look at this.'

It was a letter, or rather a short note, undated, with no address at the top, written on a piece of paper torn from a lined scribbling pad, the biro having been pressed down so hard that it gave the impression of having been engraved. 'Dear Wyn, Expect me Friday night, but don't expect me to go away empty handed this time.' Signed, Trev.

'The bloke in the photo?' hazarded Richmond.

'Nah. Trevor Austwick, husband of the deceased, can't be anybody else,' Manning said, gratified.

'The grieving widower?'

'Don't know about grieving, but I heard tell he'd got himself hitched – just before he went down, I think it was. Armley jail. Armed robbery, five years if memory serves me right . . .' He stopped, did a few mental calculations. 'Meaning that he's been out some time if he's been a good boy, though that's doubtful, for a start. And if he hasn't, he must be due out about now.'

'"*This time*",' Richmond repeated, reading from the note. 'Looks as though demanding money with menaces might run in the family.'

8

The outlook from her bedroom window, down into the valley, across the town and up to the opposite moors, never changed, except when it snowed. The same eternal prospect had dominated her view for forty years, the grey huddle of urban sprawl spreading up the sides of the hills from the valley bottom, the timeless sweep of the hills which Freya had once thought would drive her so mad with boredom she didn't see how she could stand the sight another minute. Ironic that she'd welcomed this dreary landscape at first as an escape; the contempt with which she now regarded it, the stoic endurance it had forced upon her, was the price she'd had to pay for security.

My life's been nothing but a series of escapes, she thought bitterly. Ever since she'd taken flight from the poverty of those early years. She'd been born Freda Cassidy, and her mother had died when she was still a child, leaving her to the care of her Irish father, a railway worker in Swindon. Only that hadn't been the way it had worked out. She'd been the one who'd done the looking after, caring for her adored dad as if he were the child and she the parent. A lovely man, even when he'd drink taken, or when he gambled his wages away before bringing them home, which was mostly, since his gambling was compulsive. Poor Dad, he hadn't been able to help himself. After her mum had died, since there was no one else to do it, she'd managed the house as best she could. There was always escape into a world of fantasy, her father never averse to aid and abet her. One day – one day, he promised her, he'd come home rich – and she could have everything she wanted for the rest of her life, trifle every day and wine to drink like a lady, servants to make the beds and never have the washing up or the laundry to think about again.

But, Michael Cassidy, gambler and eternal optimist, you were a born loser, Freya thought with a tolerant smile. Until that glorious day when it happened! He'd won nearly a thousand pounds on a horse, which in those days was a lot of money, to them unbelievable riches.

'There we are, me darlin', and didn't I always tell you?' he declared, waltzing her around the room. The brogue always came out more strongly when he was excited. To celebrate, he'd gone on a two-day drinking binge which had resulted in a drunken, fatal stagger into the path of an oncoming lorry.

That was when she'd made her first actual escape. Shocked and bereft, she'd still known instinctively what to do: she gave up her hated job serving behind the counter in Woolworth's, took a train ticket to London, and with her father's winnings, plus what the contents of the rented house had fetched, enrolled with a model agency.

It was what they'd all dreamed of at that time, the girls she knew – dazzled by the current cult that held up a beautiful face and figure as being the acme of any girl's hopes, by the reputed, so-called glamour of the life. Fame, riches, adulation, wearing super-elegant clothes, their faces on the front of every women's magazine, Heaven itself. She could tell them a thing or two, now! But I wasn't fooled, even then, she thought, with a twist to her lips. Too much had already happened to me for that, things to be grateful for, in retrospect. Teaching her to look at the world shrewdly through those great violet eyes she'd been blessed with. She'd always known she wasn't clever, but clung to her strong sense of survival, and the innate sense of knowing she might have something to offer.

She'd been tall and gawky, but that was not seen as an impediment, and the model agency had immediately recognised her potential; she was accepted and taught to make the most of what assets she possessed – to emphasise her height and slenderness, her good bone structure – and to be thankful for her undoubted stamina. She'd been taught things she'd never forgotten – how to use make-up so that she seemed beautiful, to walk and posture and strut, parading and showing off fabulously expensive creations to clients on whom they would never look so good. From the moment she was launched on to the fashion world, she'd never looked back. She'd worked for Dior, Balenciaga, Hardy Amies, and the rest. The camera loved her, and her face, its haughty expression soon hardly recognisable even to herself, regularly looked out from the cover of *Vogue*. Freda Cassidy was told to call herself Freya Cass.

Oh, the wonderful years that had followed! The bright lights and the glamour and becoming a household name, as well as the darling of the fashion press. It was only later that she'd seen how tightly the life had gradually enmeshed her in its toils. She was in demand everywhere, money, money, money, the getting and spending of it dominating her life. The life was sordid sometimes, the continual mad pace was gruelling, but possible because one knew one would be young for ever – until the slow realisation dawned that youth didn't last, that everyone grew older.

Escape again, this time in the form of Laurence Denshaw.

He was considered a difficult man, Laurence, but other people didn't see the tender side he showed to her, an understanding of which she knew no one else would ever have believed him capable. If he'd lived longer than the short twelve years they'd had together, helping her to bridge that gulf, that chasm, that no man's land between herself and the people who surrounded her, she wouldn't be sitting here now, at her bedroom window, filled with regret. He'd been twelve years older than she was, but she'd never imagined he would die so comparatively young, she had never quite forgiven him for leaving her with the long, long rest of her life to live out as Freya Denshaw.

After his death, she'd felt too apathetic for any more serious bids for escape: only her little sorties down to London. Condemned by the terms of his will and the demands of her children to live among the hills that were always in front of her, behind her, surrounding her, imprisoning her, she'd understood how one might, quite easily, die of boredom. Ironic to think that she'd once thought that coming here would be a beginning, when in reality it had been an end – the end of freedom, of that glittering life she'd made her own. Shallow and ephemeral that life might have been, but it was vibrant and amusing – unlike this life, conditioned by the hard landscape of sad, grey-green, silent moors, rocky outcrops, and the deep valleys through which the busy industrial life flowed.

Dot Nagle, arriving to help out after Laurence died, had been a lifeline, despite everything. Someone who spoke the same language, a robust personality who could snap Freya out of her depressions – though she could be a great trial at times, especially when she told Freya things she didn't want to hear. She'd been proved quite right about the Austwick woman. Freya now bitterly regretted the impulse that had made her say yes to the woman's request. An impulse, that's all it had been, anything to relieve the eternal ennui. But what it had turned out to be was something quite other. Nothing she could do about that now, events must take their course, she was almost resigned to it. The woman was dead, gone, murdered. When she'd heard that on the radio an hour ago, she'd been stunned. And now she was even more afraid.

She desperately needed to talk to Dot, but Dot wouldn't be back until tomorrow. She'd set off, first thing, to attend the funeral in London of some ancient relative, someone she'd never seen for years. She'd been doubtful about going, but Eddie had egged her on, no doubt hoping there'd be something in it for her.

Freya plucked at her petit point (the last of a set of eight seats for the dining-room chairs, though they were rarely used), unable to avoid the hated sight of her hands with the wrinkles and liver spots. Her face she could keep looking comparatively young, with creams and massages and skilful make-up, and becomingly arranged hair, but there was nothing she could do about her hands. Or about the wretched stiffness and pain in her knees and feet . . . She levered herself from her high-seated orthopaedic chair and made her way to the bedside cabinet to check that Dot hadn't found her stash of tablets. One day, when she could no longer bear it, they'd provide the final escape.

Suddenly unable to be alone with herself any longer, she grasped her stick and began the painful journey downstairs.

Eddie Nagle looked up from leathering down the Rover when Freya came out into the yard. Sloppy as he was in other directions, it was a point of honour with him to keep anything he had to do with – his car, or his dogs, even his clothes, for that matter – clean and in good nick. She was leaning heavily on the silver knob of her cane, silver hair sleek and elegant, wrapped in the full-length mink coat she'd had for years and never wore when her daughters were around, because they didn't approve.

He leaned insolently against the bonnet, arms folded, legs crossed at the ankles, waiting, watching her hobble across the uneven flags in the yard. He didn't go over and give her a hand. He hated to touch her, to feel the old bones like a bunch of dry sticks under the skin.

Despite the temperature, he was wearing only a pair of tight jeans and a snow-white singlet which showed every ripple of his taut, compact, muscular figure. He was very proud of his physique and worked out regularly to keep in shape. He knew his appearance was against him, his square, shiny bald head, his thick, rubbery lips, and the menacing, rolling gait he'd culti-vated. All to the good. People shrank away from him and he enjoyed that, seeing them afraid of him even before he'd said a word. It gave him a sense of power. Besides, not everyone avoided him. There were plenty women his blatant sexuality appealed to.

Freya stopped within a couple of yards of him, noticing the bruise on his upper arm, hoping that it hurt. 'I want to go for a drive,' she said peremptorily. 'How soon can you be ready?'

'Ten minutes.'

They never addressed each other by name, never willingly at all if it could be avoided. 'I'll be in the morning room, then,' she said, and turned to make her slow way back to the house.

He slapped the wet leather into the bucket, rinsed it, and with one quick twist, as if he were wringing the neck of a chicken, screwed it as dry as a piece of blotting paper.

'Where do you want to go?' he asked, when they were ready to start off, Eddie in the driving seat wearing the leather jacket which was as far as he'd go in the way of concessions when he drove her, Freya sitting in the back like a duchess.

'Anywhere, I don't care.'

He was accustomed to this, she never stated any preference. He understood she couldn't be bothered to say where, didn't really care. He knew she simply wanted to get away from the house. Sometimes, when he was feeling well disposed and had time to spare, he drove her out along pretty, tree-lined valleys to places like Knaresborough, or Bolton Abbey. When he wasn't, he took her to the top of the moors and the big, windy spaces where there was nothing to see except more moors, and ugly, industrial towns huddled in the bottom. On these occasions, she'd refuse to get out of the car and simply order him to drive back home. She knew he'd done it on purpose to annoy her. But she never reprimanded him.

He decided this was one of those days, and drove her towards Huddersfield and through the busy town and eventually up to the top of Holme Moss, pulling the car off the road, facing a long descending view down into the valley with glimpses of pewter-coloured reservoirs tucked in between the hills. Like a petulant child, she refused to look at it, but turned her head and stared at the television masts on the other side of the road. He half turned in his seat to face her and said, in the Estuary-speak she hated, 'I think it's time you and me had a little talk.'

Her face drained of colour under the make-up.

He grinned. He was pleased to see Mrs bloody Denshaw jump when he barked.

He'd been thrown in at the deep end, plunged right into a murder inquiry, and commiserations for it came from all sides, but Richmond preferred it this way. For one thing, the frenetic activity this demanded helped to cover up the awkwardness of being a new boy in a new job, when nobody had quite got your measure and you weren't yet sure of yourself. For another, total immersion was the watchword he'd set for this investigation, especially in these crucial first days – and with nobody waiting for him at home, no reproachful glances to contend with, he meant to work if necessary round the clock.

Having made do with a cup of coffee for breakfast in his impatience to get started, he'd begun to feel hungry by mid-morning, after the briefing meeting where he'd already set his mark on the investigation, established lines of inquiry and seen tasks allocated. So he welcomed the biscuits and a pot of tea – thick, Charlie Rawnsley tea that he'd better get used to again – brought in by a young DC, a bouncy, good-humoured sort of young woman called Sally Jenner.

'Don't think I make a habit of this, sir,' she warned him, smiling, putting it on his desk as he was booting up his computer, loading the disk bearing the label 'The Denshaws of

Steynton' he'd found among Austwick's other disks. 'I'm only doing it because you're new and I want to get in your good books.' Cheeky, testing him.

Her grin was infectious. She had a round, open face, a generous bosom and nice legs. He smiled back. 'Thanks, I like to know where I stand, Constable.' Letting her know he'd understood, setting limits beyond which she wouldn't go.

'Oh, and I've brought this as well. What we've been able to find out about the victim. It's not much, so far,' she said, leaving him with a neatly typed report which she placed on his desk next to the three-inch-thick paper-stuffed folder which contained all the official documents to do with Beth's disappearance, the inquiry, and the subsequent discovery of her body. In it were recorded verbatim reports, details of every interview, every question put, every answer received. He noted the lack of hard evidence, the failure to trace the blanket she'd been wrapped in, or the pillow. He'd already read it through several times. He was very nearly word perfect.

Dan Brearley had gone about it in the wrong way from the first, in Richmond's opinion. Bully boy tactics weren't likely to have cut much ice with the sort of people he'd been dealing with. He'd been convinced from the first that Peter Denshaw had murdered Beth. Fair enough, the obvious solution usually was the right one, and policemen did develop an instinct for a killer. But Brearley had gone against all accepted wisdom, formed his theories and sought facts to prove them, and when this hadn't worked he'd been stymied, and willing enough when Isobel had made her 'confession' to accept it as an answer, and have the case closed. After all, the Denshaws still had a high profile in the area, somewhat lower than it had been at one time, but still not to be disregarded.

The file would have to stay where it was for the time being. There was as yet no reason to requestion those who'd originally been interviewed in connection with his child's death, questions that had failed to reveal the truth then. They were unlikely to change their testimony now – not yet, at any rate. But he'd chosen to go up to Low Rigg himself this morning to see Freya Denshaw and talk to her about her work with Wyn Austwick. Unproductive maybe, or maybe not. If anything turned up through it, well and good.

He picked up the report WDC Jenner had left and absorbed what it had to say about Wyn Austwick, then willed himself back to the computer and began accessing the Denshaw file, hoping he wouldn't be interrupted, but not sanguine about it. The station outside his door was humming like a beehive as the routine of a murder inquiry got under way, doors banging, printers clacking, telephones ringing, an excitement generated by the sort of crime rare in Steynton, where murder, if it happened, was usually the result of a pub brawl or a domestic, grown out of hand.

Half an hour later he sat back, accepting disappointment. He'd learned considerably more than he wanted to know about Freya Denshaw and her glamorous career, but damn all about the Denshaw family history, except what was surely a matter of public record – unless that part of it was still to be filled out for the proposed book. Had it ever been finished, it would have turned out to be ill balanced, or overlong. But there appeared to be no plan for its completion. The notes stopped abruptly, just before Christmas, ten years ago . . . that Christmas he'd spent alone, when Beth had come to him for New Year . . . He stared at the blank screen, unseeing . . .

The door opened and Manning came in. 'He's hopped it.'

Richmond blinked, still back in his fractured past. 'Who has?'

'Trevor Austwick. He came out on licence from Armley about a month ago, but he hasn't reported to his probation officer for two weeks. He's a bad lad, he is, and right. Sent down for armed robbery, as I said, and got five years because he had previous form. Did the whole stretch – he'd likely have been released earlier, except he was as bloody-minded in there as he was out here.'

'Pull the stops out to find him, Steve. And here, have a read of this.' Richmond handed over the report Sally Jenner had brought in.

'"Winifred Austwick, née Seaton, born 1952 in Consett, Co. Durham,"' Manning read aloud. '"Father a miner . . . both parents died early . . . family dispersed, no connections there now. Nothing more known until she moved into the Clough Head Estate five years ago –" that'd be when Trev went down, I reckon.'

'Read on and you'll see there's been bad blood between them seemingly, at any rate she'd filed for divorce. But we haven't come across a will, and since he's still her next of kin, he'll come in for a tidy bit – unless he's the one who topped her.'

'No justice, is there?'

'Unlikely he'd risk it, though, isn't it?'

'That note he sent her didn't sound very conciliatory. More like he was out to touch her for what he could get. Maybe they had a row and he clobbered her. It'd stack, he's not noted for his forward thinking, and he has a very nasty temper.'

'All the more reason for getting hold of him. Meanwhile, how've you been getting on with the budding authors?'

Manning moved his backside off the corner of the desk and went to sit opposite Richmond. 'I've been at it since yesterday and I feel gutted.' He looked it, his face settling into despondency. He'd obviously hated the task that had fallen to him. Community policing was all very well, but you could get too involved. 'You were right, blackmail was the name of her game – with two of them, so far, but that's enough to be going on with. She did try it on with Willie Muff, but he told her to get knotted. He's been in enough hot water for that sort of threat not to bother him. But he's been spreading the word not to get involved with Austwick, so it looks as though her days here were numbered anyway, if you see what I mean.'

'What about the others?'

'Harold Brackenroyd's dead and I doubt she'd ever have got much change out of him anyway, he wasn't a Brackenroyd for nowt! Harrison Priestley denies anything of the sort, but he would – I've been asking round, though, and it seems he has a little bit on the side, tucked away in a flat in Hebden Bridge. He'd be terrified of his wife getting to hear. So I think we might count him in for a contribution.'

'You said two. Who's the other?'

'Oh aye. Margaret Whitfield.' Manning looked down at his shoes and sighed. 'Headmistress at the Girls' High, very respected figure in the town. She lives with her sister. Who turns out *not* to be her sister, if you see what I mean. Austwick was getting four hundred a month from her, can you believe!' He stopped and said awkwardly, 'They're good women, what they do's their own business – but not a haporth of sense between them! If they hadn't tried to cover up, reckoning they were sisters . . . folks don't automatically assume two women sharing the same house are lesbians – not round here, anyway, not yet.'

'Would that sort of thing really matter to anyone if it came out?'

'Probably not – but it would to them, Miss Whitfield especially, she's that sort. Spent her life instilling moral sense and good behaviour into her girls . . . The speculation alone would kill her.'

And that was what blackmail was all about, of course, preying on the fears of people who had secrets, real or imagined, which they lived in dread of being exposed. Hush money, conscience money, guilt money. Trying to cover up like that, Margaret Whitfield had automatically put herself at risk. While Austwick was ostensibly helping her write up the school's history, she was ferreting out some nice little juicy personal details at the same time, which was how it would work out with her other victims. 'I dare say she and Priestley won't be the only ones,' Richmond observed. 'Which means a lot of people won't be sorry to have seen the back of Mrs Austwick. Including Miss Whitfield.'

9

There were no daffodils in November, but sometimes an unexpected bonus like this arrived: another golden day, when the deep intensity of the light made the distant hills look teal blue and the air was like chilled wine. This time, Richmond didn't stop his car in the lane outside the stone gateposts and sit there; this time, there were no thousands of blowing trumpets in the garden simply to sit and stare at, as on the one and only time he'd ever passed Low Rigg.

Correction. No one ever *passed* this house – the unmade-up road soon petered out into nothing more than a stony footpath up to the top of the moor, and there were better ways of getting up there. Neither had the daffodils been the attraction. The truth was, he'd gone there on purpose, driven by some masochistic need to picture Isobel and Beth as part of the family who lived here. Consumed with jealousy of all these unknown people, and with self-hatred because somehow, without meaning it, he'd failed both wife and child. This time, however, he drove right up to the flagged frontage, left his car and walked directly to the door. Out of the sun, it was sharply, bitterly cold. Snow was predicted and couldn't be far off.

There was a modern bell, inviting you to ignore the heavy, old-fashioned iron knocker beside it. He pushed it, heard it ring and looked around while he waited.

It needed attention, obviously, this place. Not so much the house itself – the windows were stone mullioned, the door was of ancient weathered oak, and although the low, stone-tiled roof dipped somewhat, it was sturdy enough. But grass sprouted in the gutterings, a seedling tree grew in a gully between the gables, and the sun on the window panes showed them smeary and in need of a clean, the flags in front of the door were grouted with weeds, and unswept. The sloping garden too, was uncared for, wild and overgrown, an untidy straggle of untended herbaceous debris, mostly dead michaelmas daisies by the look of it, competing with more weeds. Moss furred its flagged paths, a sundial lay toppled on its side, the centuries-old dry-stone wall surrounding the garden had finally collapsed in places.

He'd prepared himself, but hadn't expected the upsurge of emotion brought on by the sight of this garden, where Beth had last been seen, playing in the snow.

He hadn't expected Polly Winslow to answer the door, either, but she it was who stood there, framed in the darkness of the large hall behind her. Strangely subdued and pale, the deep rich colours she wore seeming a little dimmed, even her hair having less bounce and shine than he remembered.

'Oh,' she said, 'it's you,' then flapped a hand in apology. 'Forgive me . . . It's just that I was expecting . . . We're all at sixes and sevens this morning.'

'I'm sorry if it's inconvenient, Mrs Winslow. I wanted a brief word with your mother. In connection with the death of Mrs Wyn Austwick,' he added, in case she thought he was pursuing his own concerns.

'My mother?' She caught her breath and stared at him. 'You'd better come in,' she said at last, stepping back and holding the door open wider. 'I don't think you can have heard. My mother died last night.'

Momentarily, what she'd said didn't register, but then the shock of it hit him. 'No, I hadn't heard. I'm so sorry.' And he was, for the woman in front of him, understanding now why it was she appeared so – diminished was the only word he could think of. Sorry for her, yes, but also bitterly disappointed for himself, which told him how much he'd been hoping from the interview, and aware that yet another door had closed to him in his search for the answer to why Beth's short life had been ended so needlessly. 'I'll make myself scarce, come back later.'

'You couldn't have known. Please come in. I really think you ought. There's something you should know.' There was an edge to her tone that intrigued him, over and above the natural distress one would have expected at such a time. 'Wait in here, if you will, my brother-in-law will know what to do,' she added oddly.

Almost before he knew it, he'd been ushered inside and left alone in a large, shabby room, sunny and low-ceilinged, with panels whose white paint was cracking, tatty yellow silk curtains and a ceiling painted yellow between the beams. An enormous, ancient radiator added to the heat given out by a piled-up leaping fire in the huge stone fireplace – you'd need to chuck whole bucketfuls of fuel into a grate that size to make any difference, and it looked as though that's exactly what had been done.

In the corner by a window stood a large grand piano, spread with a silk shawl and covered with dozens of slightly tarnished silver-framed photos. He caught his breath, still shaken by that vision of Beth playing in the snow, half afraid he might see her ghost – silver-blonde hair, tip-tilted nose – sitting reluctantly at the piano stool.

'Why do I have to practise scales all the time, Daddy? I want to learn to play "White Christmas", like Miss Crisp, at school.'

('White Christmas'? Good God, what have you started, Miss Crisp?)

'Fact of life, sprog. Can't have one without the other.'

He averted his eyes, turned away, concentrated on the rest of the room. Cluttered with a haphazard arrangement of furniture – two huge, comfortable-looking settees covered in some worn, indeterminate fabric, chairs of all shapes and sizes, various tables and an exceedingly tall, breakfront bookcase, all of which were obviously old and almost certainly valuable. Scattered around on the seating were piles of beautiful cushions, glowing in embroidered silk and needlepoint. A large tapestry frame with a half-finished piece of work stretched on it stood in front of a chair and footstool. Threadbare rugs covered a stone-flagged floor that was time-smoothed and polished by the passage of many feet. Hanging incongruously over the mantelpiece was a large, blown-up, modern-framed colour photograph of Freya Cass in her heyday, modelling a stiffly off-the-shoulder ball gown.

He scarcely had time to take in the fashionably nonchalant pose, the throwaway grace of the long, elegant figure carelessly displaying a fortune on her back, before Polly Winslow returned, followed by a big man bearing a tea tray whom Richmond immediately recognised as Leon Katz. He'd hardly changed at all from the smooth, good-looking, solidly built young lawyer Richmond remembered, though he'd lost some of his hair and gained a lot of authority. Behind him came a tall, fair, generously proportioned woman, beautifully dressed in black, carefully made up. Polly introduced them both shortly: 'My sister, Ginny, my brother-in-law, Leon Katz.' A heightened atmosphere seemed to come into the room with them, a sense of words of some sort having been exchanged before they entered.

Katz remembered Richmond, too. 'We've met. Leeds Crown Court, wasn't it?' He proffered a large, warm handshake.

His wife offered tea. 'You might as well join us, Mr Richmond, at the moment we're drinking it as though there's no tomorrow. The universal panacea.' She had an attractive, husky voice. She sounded slightly ironic, calm, in control. The two women were not much alike – Ginny with her slow-moving elegance and Polly, every movement quick and impulsive. But they bore that elusive, underlying family resemblance, always difficult to define, and both, in their different ways, had inherited their mother's grace.

'I'm sorry,' he said formally, 'I couldn't have chosen a worse moment –' He wished to God he wasn't here, or that he hadn't come alone, could have anticipated this and brought Sally Jenner with him. A woman helped, at times like this, knew what to say other than sorry. He'd never been good at sympathising, himself.

'On the contrary,' Katz interrupted authoritatively, waving him to a seat. 'Please sit down.' He himself settled into a wide Georgian wing chair. Every inch the lawyer, calm, well-tailored, carefully non-judgemental. 'So, you're here in connection with the murder of Wyn Austwick?'

'That's right, checking up on her movements – I understand she was working with Mrs Denshaw on a family history. It was only a matter of when Mrs Denshaw last saw her.'

If any of them wondered why a chief inspector was undertaking such a menial task, they didn't show it.

'Well, none of us here ever met the woman,' Katz said, 'so you'd be wasting your time with us! Dot Nagle would tell you, though I doubt she's in a position to answer questions at the moment. She's been with Mrs Denshaw for many years, and she's naturally very upset by what's happened.'

Nagle. Dot, and her husband, Eddie, the housekeeper/companion and the handyman, thought Richmond, slotting them into place from the old case notes he'd been reading only a few hours ago. 'I can see them later, then, if necessary.'

'They don't live in. They have one of the cottages down by the Moorcock.'

Richmond nodded, waited. No one said anything more. 'What's this something you thought I should know, Mrs Winslow?'

Katz smoothly intercepted. 'I think I can answer that. It's simply that Mrs Denshaw had made up her mind not to pursue the matter of this book with Mrs Austwick – and my sister-in-law has the idea the decision may possibly be indirectly relevant to your inquiries.' He arched an eyebrow at Polly, and Richmond sensed dissension.

'In what way relevant?' he asked, speaking to her. Never mind Katz.

'When Freya told Mrs Austwick of her decision, she became very abusive. Not surprisingly, that upset my mother very much. Then, last night, she died of a stroke.'

'I can see that something like that might have distressed her. But how do you think this affects the inquiries into Mrs Austwick's death?'

'Isn't it obvious?' Quick colour came into her face. 'The woman didn't exactly go out of her way to make friends, if she treated all her clients like she treated my mother!'

'Are you implying one of her other clients killed her?'

'Would that be so surprising? In the nature of things, she was given access to a lot of private family matters, and if she chose not to be discreet –'

'Polly.'

Polly looked at her sister, took a deep breath and subsided, though looking very much as though she would like to continue.

'Did she threaten Mrs Denshaw in any way?'

'Not that we know of,' Ginny replied quickly.

The air was full of what wasn't being said. Richmond let the silence go on, sipping his tea and looking out of the window towards a group of near-leafless elms, and the huddle of ragged-feathered crows (or were they rooks? He never knew which were which), their empty nests now exposed, wedged high up in the forks of branches that were limned black against the cold sky. Behind him, the mechanism of a big, mahogany long-case clock, its hood within an inch of the ceiling, whirred and then bonged out eleven strokes while he speculated on the cause of the tension between the three of them.

Katz was frowning, tapping his fingers on his chair arm, watching Richmond in a cautious, lawyerly way. He must know who I am, Richmond thought, other than as the police officer he remembered through seeing him from time to time in court. If nothing else, Polly would surely have given warning that the man on their doorstep was not only the officer investigating Wyn Austwick's murder, but also Beth's father. She, too, was now gazing out of the window, perching on the arm of the deep old settee where her sister sat as if, having said her piece, she was deliberately distancing herself. The light lit her hair, which Richmond saw now had lost none of its gloss. That had been a trick of the light as she'd stood in the doorway of the dark hall. It gleamed in the strong sunlight like a polished conker.

'Do you smoke, Mr Richmond?' Katz asked suddenly.

Richmond shook his head and the lawyer brought a pack of cigarettes from his pockets and lit one. 'Neither do I, except in emergencies.' Richmond finished his tea, reached out to put the empty cup and saucer on the table next to him, expecting to be enlightened as to the nature of the emergency, but nothing was forthcoming.

'And that's all you wanted to tell me?' he said eventually.

'Isn't it enough?' Katz asked.

Polly suddenly went to sit on the needlepoint stool which had been in front of the embroidery frame, pulling it up to the fire, hunching her arms around her knees. Stifled enough in the suffocating room to wish he could remove his jacket, Richmond shifted uneasily when she shivered and leant forward to pick up the long iron poker lying on the hearth, prodded the fire and the whole edifice that had been built up fell in a blaze of flame and smoke. A wave of heat and a strong smell of sulphur pervaded the room.

He wondered where to begin sorting out the lies. Or perhaps the half-truths, which virtually amounted to the same thing. He'd only been told what he was bound to find out, anyway. He spoke to Polly again, whom he guessed to be the most vulnerable of the three. She, at least, looked so shiningly honest and sincere, he wanted to believe her; but he was damn certain that what he'd been told was a long way from the whole story, and she was no more immune from suspicion than the rest.

'Why do you think your mother decided to abandon the project?'

'Does that matter?'

Her question was followed by another irritating silence, orchestrated by the crows outside, setting up a raucous quarrelling, engaging themselves in furious activity around the elm branches. She looked at him with those amazing lustrous eyes, and after a moment added, in a low voice, 'I think now that it was because she knew she was dying.'

Well. He felt, suddenly and strongly, that if it had been up to her, he would have been told the whole truth and not simply what it was they thought he should know. The idea created a return of the instant empathy he'd felt between himself and this woman, right from the start. He was so aware of it that he couldn't believe it wasn't stamped on his face. But such feelings had no place here and now, possibly ever. He sharply returned his mind to what he'd just been told, and what it might mean, in what way Freya's abandonment of her memoirs might impinge on the matter of Wyn Austwick's murder.

'I agree, I think she knew, too,' Ginny said suddenly, as if capitulating. 'She wanted us all here, especially my brother, she quite desperately wanted to see him. Unfortunately, he was at a diocesan meeting and didn't get here until it was all over. She collapsed and died before the doctor arrived. He said it was a stroke.'

Richmond's mind swung back to his conversation with Wyn Austwick at the Woolpack, and her claims. That night, she'd sworn she'd told no one – apart from Richmond himself – of whatever it was she'd discovered regarding Beth's murder, had promised she wouldn't contact Freya again until she'd spoken further with him, until he'd had time to reconsider his refusal to recommend that the case be reopened. Well, he didn't hold any brief for Wyn Austwick's probity. It seemed more than likely that Freya's refusal to go on with the book had caused Austwick to reveal what she regarded as the damning evidence she had unearthed, the proof she claimed she had.

So that if Freya *had* known she was dying – and who was to say this wasn't possible? – or even if she'd only been afraid that she was, it could explain why she'd been so desperate to see her son, the Reverend Peter, the original prime suspect. In order to warn him about the woman? But she'd been dead several days before Freya's collapse. There had been plenty of time for her to have warned him already. Time enough before that for him to have silenced Austwick.

'Did your mother do anything yesterday that might have caused her to be so upset? Where did she go? Who did she see?' he asked.

'No one, as far as I know,' Polly answered. 'She asked Nagle to take her out for a drive, that was all. After she came back, I went to pick my daughter up from school and while I was out she walked down to post a letter – there's a box by the Moorcock. It's not far, but it's a good pull back up to the house, and it was very difficult for her to walk. She should've asked me to post it for her, obviously the effort was too much for her – she looked exhausted when I got back.'

'Perhaps it was important enough for her to want to catch the post.'

'I can't think of anyone who she could be writing to who was *that* important – she hardly ever wrote letters, anyway.'

'I need to speak to Mr and Mrs Nagle. I can come back if Mrs Nagle isn't fit enough to talk, but what about her husband? Is he around?'

'Not at lunch time,' Polly said drily. 'He'll be at the Moorcock, where else?'

Richmond stood up and thanked them all for their time. He took his leave and Katz saw him to the door. 'Terribly upsetting, all this. My wife . . .'

'She seems to be taking it very well.'

'Oh yes, Ginny copes with most things. But so does Polly. She means well, but she can be very outspoken.'

Richmond took this to mean he wasn't to take too much notice of what she'd said.

'If we can be of further help, don't hesitate.' Katz offered the warm handshake again, maintaining eye contact. A likeable enough man, or one accustomed to making himself agreeable when the occasion demanded it, Richmond thought as he was about to get into his car. His key in the lock, he heard someone calling his name and saw Polly at the door.

'Mr Richmond! Mrs Nagle will talk to you. She's in the kitchen.'

When he reached the door again she said, 'I'm sorry, we weren't much help in there. It's just that you're not – well, not the usual sort of policeman, are you?'

'Perhaps your experience of policemen isn't very extensive.'

'That wasn't what I meant. I'm sorry – sorry that it's had to be this way, I mean – you having to come here like this . . .'

'It's my job.' His expression said he didn't have to like it. They looked embarrassed, not knowing what else to say, until he added, 'Why don't we stop apologising to each other, Mrs Winslow? We don't seem to have done anything else since we met.' Mrs Winslow, Mr Richmond! How ridiculous it sounded. And he thought, what the hell do I mean by *that*?

She smiled suddenly, the first this morning. A pale imitation of the one he remembered, but he immediately felt better for it, and smiled back.

'Come on, then,' she said. 'Mrs Nagle. She's a tartar, but not if you stand up to her.'

He followed her out of the bright cold sunlight, plunging into the gloom of the hallway and on through the rest of the rambling house. She walked ahead of him, warning him where the floor levels varied and where to duck his head under great oak lintels, herself quick and sure in the familiarity of a house she'd grown up in as a child. God, what a home for children to be brought up in! He pictured them – the two little girls, one fair and placid, the other brown-haired, like quicksilver. The brother, artistic and sensitive, or that was how Isobel had seen him. And in the background, that other child, the one he hadn't yet met, the one called Elvira Graham, whom none of them had mentioned, but with whom Wyn Austwick, according to her diary, had had an appointment after she came back from holiday. What part did she play in this family? It seemed important to him to know: she'd been there on the day of Beth's disappearance, had been the last person to see her.

He stumbled a little and she warned, 'Careful.' Away from the yellow and white room, the whole house was dark and draughty, all unexpected nooks and shadowy corners. Two uncarpeted staircases with wide shallow treads and carved newel posts, several more vast fireplaces. Tiny windows where you least expected them, sometimes high up on the wall, beamed ceilings. He suspected the house might be an architectural treasure, but it would take more than that for him to want to live in it. Even number 4, Albert Street seemed suddenly to have acquired all the characteristics necessary for a very desirable residence indeed.

In one dark corner, at the foot of one of the staircases, a small Christmas tree had been set up, ready for decorating. Brightly coloured glass baubles and tinsel spilled out of a box alongside. Five weeks to Christmas. Her child – Polly's child, Harriet – was obviously as impatient for Christmas as Beth had always been.

He'd bought a tree for her for that last New Year she'd spent with him, a last-minute purchase, a left-over, an ailing creature whose needles dropped like rain. She'd professed to love it and he'd held her while she ceremonially put the angel on top. It had stayed there, leaning at a drunken angle, until weeks after she'd disappeared. He'd carried the tree outside at last, angel and all, and set fire to it in the garden. He'd been sweeping up pine needles until the day he finally left the house.

At last, a long, draughty passage ended with a door leading into a cavernous kitchen. Somewhere, in all that dark labyrinth behind them, must lurk a dining-room. How did they ever manage to have a meal that was even half-way hot?

The woman whom Polly introduced as Dot Nagle was standing at an ironing board, a small, skinny woman, in her early sixties, he guessed. Very pale but heavily made up, scarlet lips compressed into a thin line, punishing a pile of linen with a heavy old-fashioned iron. Perhaps it was this that gave him his first impression of suppressed anger. Later, when he'd learned how close she'd been to Freya Denshaw, he decided he might have been mistaken, that it could have been sorrow she was suppressing, that drew the plucked eyebrows together and kept the lipsticked mouth tight, like a slash. But then, her whole being was one of held-in emotion. She had tightly permed grey hair, and a belt round her narrow waist that looked fit to cut her thin form in two.

The kitchen itself was wonderful to behold, a jumble of ancient and modern. A free-standing oak dresser so huge it must have been made *in situ*, now a repository for a chaos of plates, pots and all the oddments for which life has not provided obvious resting places. Under the window, a stainless steel sink of industrial dimensions, next to it a microwave oven and a gleaming, state-of-the-art electric cooker. The question of the dining-room was resolved by the presence of a long oak refectory table, set with table mats and cutlery. The room seemed not to have been decorated since the years when cream and eau-de-nil were the *de rigueur* colours for kitchens, half a century ago.

The faint sound of the front door bell penetrated into the kitchen. Polly jumped. 'That'll be – excuse me, Mr Richmond.' She was gone, disappeared with the swish of her skirt and the memory of her perfume.

'The undertaker,' Dot Nagle said, resolutely ironing.

She professed herself willing to answer questions, speaking through the smoke from the cigarette dangling from her lips. Richmond didn't need to lead in. She lost no time in telling him that she wasn't in the least surprised that woman had got herself killed. 'Asking for it, she was, meddling in things that didn't concern her.'

'So you didn't hold with this collaboration?'

'Is that what it was, then? Pouring money down the drain, more likely. If Freya wanted to write her life story, that was one thing, but –' She coughed and took the cigarette out to tap off the ash, then decided to stub it out in an ashtray balanced on the top of the stove. 'There's things that should be made public and things that are private. Let somebody like her into your life and you'll never have it to yourself any more.' That chimed in very much with what he'd thought of Wyn Austwick himself, and Richmond was glad to see that his impressions hadn't been due to simple prejudice. 'All right if them you're writing about are dead, they don't care,' she went on, scarcely pausing for breath, 'but what about the living? What was it to her how long I'd been here? What Eddie and me were paid? Why we came here? Insinuating . . . Oh, I've met her sort before!' She stamped the iron down on to a rumpled pillow case without smoothing it first, thereby creasing it still further, but didn't seem to notice.

'What sort of insinuations, Mrs Nagle?'

'I warned her, but she wouldn't listen,' she went on, ignoring the question. 'She was always wilful, Freya.' At last hands and voice came to a stop. The passage of the iron was halted as she stared bleakly out of the window, until a smell of scorched linen made her switch it off. She threw the pillow case back into the laundry basket, pulled out one of the chairs from the table and sat down heavily. 'You've caught me at the wrong time. I can't think straight, not yet, not when she's lying cold upstairs.'

Richmond didn't say that he preferred to catch suspects at such times. It might not be pleasant for either party, but when people were off their guard, questioning them then often brought forth the truth that they might otherwise have kept hidden. It wasn't happening now, though. She was keeping her lips buttoned as tight as her interlocked fingers, laced together, as though holding her very thoughts in. He was pretty sure Dot Nagle would be able to tell him much more about this family's affairs than the family members themselves, if she so chose, but she wouldn't, now. He'd lost her. She vouchsafed no further personal opinions, confining herself to practical details, such as the last date Mrs Austwick had been here – a week before Freya had died.

It would have to do for now. He'd tackle her again, later. He knew panic when he saw it. And panic like that didn't go away.

The sun had gone in behind banking grey clouds as Richmond eventually reversed his car in the limited space left available by the arrival of what he saw to be the undertaker's hearse. As he emerged from the gates of Low Rigg, he smelt in the air the snow that had been forecast.

10

'You're sure you'll be all right, Polly?' Ginny inquired search-ingly, zipping up her boots. Leon, firm, kind, unshakeable, had stayed on with them while the undertaker finished his grisly business. After Freya's body had been borne away, Leon had recommended a stiff drink, but both women had opted for coffee and sipped it in a sad silence after Leon's own departure. Now it was Ginny's turn to go. 'You look a bit off colour, I must say,' she added with some concern, as she stood up.

Polly smiled. 'I'll be fine. It's been a shock, that's all. For all of us.'

'You haven't looked a hundred per cent for a day or two, though.' Ginny put a sisterly arm around Polly's shoulders and hugged her.

'I'm OK,' Polly repeated, with an effort. 'And with all there is to be done, it's better if I make a start.'

'If you'd wait until the weekend, we could do it together. It's a miserable business to tackle on your own, and you know how chaotic Freya's things are likely to be.'

Polly was tempted, but resisted it. 'You've got your hands full enough, and since I'm at a loose end, I might as well. You know me.' As someone who naturally needed plenty of physical activ-ity, getting things moving had always been her reaction to stress. 'And don't forget,' she added drily, 'I've had a lot of experience of doing this sort of thing lately. The thing to do is keep your mind on practicalities. Besides, we don't want to leave those papers lying around any longer than we have to.'

'Sonia did offer –'

'I know, but she's better occupied looking after Peter . . .'

'Poor Sonia.'

The picture of Peter accepting comfort from Sonia, however, seemed an unlikely one. More probably, he had closeted himself in his study, shut Sonia out, denying her the solace of being needed. But poor Peter, too. Their mother's death had been such a body blow to him. Not only her dying: the fact of his own absence from her bedside was weighing heavily on him, he was wearing the guilt for it like a hair shirt.

It was a terrible thing when death, rather than drawing together those who were left, tore them apart, Polly thought. Dissension had already arisen. Why hadn't they interrupted his meeting with an urgent message? he'd demanded passionately, refusing to believe that they hadn't appreciated how ill Freya really was. Maybe he had some justification for feeling upset, maybe they should have persisted until they reached him. He and their mother had always been so much in accord, he'd always been the favoured one. Polly didn't really like to admit that maybe they hadn't tried too hard to get him because Peter, despite his calling, would have been no use at all to any of them. He'd always gone to pieces in a crisis.

'There's not a lot anyone can do to help Peter, there never has been, he doesn't encourage it,' Ginny said, firmly putting him aside, confident in her elder sister knowledge of her brother. 'He's his own worst enemy, we all know that.'

But Polly had lately felt she didn't know anything about her brother at all. They hadn't been really close, even as children. He'd never had much time for young sisters, which was normal enough, but that apart, he'd always been introverted and dreamy – though not moody and totally withdrawn into himself, subject to outbursts of rage as he was now. Ginny had been closer in age to him; she'd mothered him and stood up for him, but even she had never understood him.

What had happened to all that artistic promise he'd shown as a young man, before he'd astonished everyone who knew him by throwing it all away to enter the Church? Though perhaps no one should have been surprised at that. He'd always been inclined to – self-righteousness, she supposed. Actually, a bit of a prig! But such a dramatic reversal had been so unexpected. Mind-boggling, really. If he'd suddenly found a vocation, that might have been understandable, but if he had, it was not obvious. Certainly, it had brought him no joy.

Ginny stood up and walked to the door. 'OK then, love, do what you can here, and don't worry about Harriet. I'll pick her up from school with the twins. You'll come down later? No silly ideas about staying here the night?'

Polly was more than willing to promise that, having no wish

to stay here alone, with shadows and ghosts at every corner. Philip didn't count. He'd shut himself up with his music, deaf to everything else, his usual way of coping with any kind of stress. So Polly promised. 'And Ginny – I'm sorry. Maybe Leon was right and I shouldn't have said anything. Me and my big mouth.'

'Forget it – but just don't say any more. Not until we *know*.' She flipped a big black wool serape around her shoulders, gave Polly a quick hug before settling into her low-slung car, swinging her elegantly booted legs sideways. Polly watched her drive away. Ginny, so dependable and sensible, the elder sister, the calm centre of this unstable family. Wishing she too could compartmentalise her feelings so successfully, she went to make herself a mug of coffee and took it up with her to her mother's bedroom, determined not to put off the task she'd set herself, otherwise she might not start at all.

It took a positive act of courage to push the door open and enter her mother's room, to force back the notion that Freya would still be there, in the least forbidding, the best room in the house – beautifully proportioned, with a low ceiling and a long row of mullioned windows which gave a wide panoramic view right over Steynton to the moors on the other side of the valley. A huge, chilly room nevertheless, unless warmed by the large capacity electric fire set on the old hearth, which Freya had kept constantly turned on to augment the barely adequate and wildly erratic heating system. Polly switched the fire on. Beautiful as it was, this room had always dampened her spirits and now, with the chill of her mother's last hours still laying cold fingers along her spine, she welcomed the heat as much as Freya had done.

As children they'd never been encouraged to come in here. Nor really wanted to, Polly thought sadly. Freya hadn't ever been the kind of mother to snuggle up to in bed, while she read them stories. The only times when they were tolerated here at all were when the collection of clothes with designer names were taken out for their occasional airings, to be shown off – most of them dating from the fifties and no doubt now worthy of places in a museum – to look at, to admire, perhaps to touch, but never, ever, to play with as dressing-up clothes, as little girls loved to do.

Freya herself had always passed a good proportion of her time here in her bedroom, and lately more so, either spending the whole day in the heavy, dark oak bed, for which she'd embroidered a sumptuous silk coverlet, giving audience from there. Or from the high orthopaedic chair, somewhat reminiscent of a throne, where she sat sewing. As in the yellow room downstairs, there was a large standing tapestry frame where some needlepoint or other was always stretched. And it was here, too, where she'd worked at that wretched book with Wyn Austwick, at the long oak table that had served as a desk, extending along one wall.

Freya had never been a tidy person, only so far as her clothes were concerned, and Polly knew she could leave the disposal of the immaculate contents of the drawers and cupboards containing them to Dot. It was the range of cupboards flanking the chimney breast on either side which compelled her attention. Here she knew Freya had kept the scrapbooks, the untidy pile of newspaper clippings, the albums of photographs, tattered old fan letters, all the memorabilia connected with her cherished past. Polly expected to find what she sought there – the files and cardboard boxes, their contents sorted into some kind of order by Wyn Austwick, the raw material for the proposed book, even perhaps a rough draft. But as she flung open the cupboards one by one, she found them quite empty – nothing remained in them but a bulging cardboard box, the lid secured by an elastic band. She pulled it out roughly and the perished rubber of the band snapped. Hundreds of old photographs cascaded to the carpet. There was absolutely nothing else in any of the cupboards.

For a moment, she was nonplussed. Had Wyn Austwick taken them all away? She turned to the dressing-table drawers, the shelves of the wardrobe, but found nothing except exquisite silk underwear, immaculately kept dresses, rows of shoes, suits and coats. It was only when she looked in the deep drawer of the night table that she found anything, and it wasn't what she was seeking. Right at the back, hidden behind a pile of folded handkerchiefs, her hand touched a brown glass bottle with a child-proof cap. Full of the sleeping pills which Freya had occasionally needed. She'd had a prescription for years, there was a bottle of them beside her bed now, alongside the foil packs of pills for her arthritis and her blood pressure. That bottle was half empty. The full bottle, concealed behind the hankies, told its own story.

Oh, Mother.

Tears which she still couldn't shed gathered in a hard lump in Polly's throat. Regrets, an indulgence she normally forbade herself, flowed over her. She sat on the edge of the bed and grieved at the waste, the *separateness* of Freya's life, and tried to remember if there were times when she and her mother had ever been close, as a mother and daughter should be. But she found only that cool, untouchable centre she'd never been able to reach. What hurt more than anything was the fact that she had not had an inkling of what had been going on in her mother's mind, that she was finding life unbearable. But Freya was Freya. Ordinary standards didn't apply. She would always be what she had made herself into, what the public remembered her as: Freya Cass. Her inner life was her own secret.

But even Freya – how could she, how *could* she, have kept silent about that little girl's death for so long?

Polly shivered in the still cold room, suddenly wanting an end to this, aching to hold her own child in her arms, to feel an affirmation of life.

It was then she heard the footsteps approaching. Slow, dragging steps, barely noticeable if it hadn't been for the give-away creak of the ancient floorboards. Goose pimples lifted the hairs on her arms. Not for the first time in her life, she was afraid in this old house.

Slowly, the door opened, and Dot Nagle came in. For a moment, as taken aback at seeing Polly as Polly was to see her, she stood in the doorway with her shoulders sagging, naked emotion on her face. Then, taking command of herself with a visible effort, she straightened her spine, wiped the sadness from her face and moved forward with almost her usual briskness, the highish heels she always wore to give her more height clipping on the polished boards between the old rugs in the familiar way, until she came to the photographs on the floor. She took in at a glance the open cupboard doors, the empty interiors. She looked at Polly, sitting on the embroidered counterpane.

'I burned them,' she said.

'What?' For a moment, Polly was disorientated, not understanding what she meant.

'The papers. She told me to, yesterday. Before I left to catch my train, she told me to clear it all out – everything, all that old

103

rubbish. Everything except those family photos, we agreed it wouldn't be right to destroy those – and the professional ones, she gave them to me. I put everything else in the boiler.'

Only then did her eyes light on the bottle, still clutched in Polly's hand. She stared, searched for and found the other one on the night table. Her breath caught in her throat with a harsh, rasping sound. 'She – she didn't – she couldn't have . . .?'

'No, look, the bottle's full. It was hidden away and I think she might have meant to use it sometime, when the pain grew too bad, but it wasn't necessary. It was a stroke, Dr Simmons saw her . . .'

She couldn't help feeling pity for the other woman, sensing how deep her loss was. If anyone had ever understood Freya, it was Dot. They'd been inseparable for over forty years, their lives had intermeshed in a way that had made them closer than blood relations. To Dot, losing Freya would be like losing half of herself. Polly wished she could help her in some way, but even a warm hug was unthinkable. Dot was as resistant to emotional contact as ever Freya had been.

'If only I'd been here!' Dot said fiercely, as though her very presence would have forced death to back off. 'I've never stayed away overnight for years, I knew I shouldn't have gone, she wasn't herself and it was just a funeral, after all. And the old bugger only left me a cracked jug,' she added with a spurt of grim humour. She half bent to pick up the photos, then straightened. 'What brought it on? Eddie says he only drove her up to the top of Holme Moss, it couldn't have been that.'

'No, it couldn't. Her blood pressure was so high a stroke could have happened any time, the doctor said. But walking down to post that letter didn't help.'

'What?' Dot asked sharply, drawing in her breath. 'What letter was that?'

Polly spread her hands. 'No idea, but no doubt we shall find out, from whoever it was sent to. Leave those photos, Dot, I'll see to them.'

'All right.' She was staring at her shoes, her hands clasped so tightly the knuckles showed white, for the moment miles away. Then she blinked and nodded her newly permed tight grey curls. 'What about supper? Could you eat any?'

'I'm staying with Ginny tonight.'

Suddenly, the warmth and ease, the soft comfort and affection in Ginny's house seemed like the best and most desirable thing in the world. Low Rigg, full of draughts that blew old miseries around, was insupportable. And then, tumbling into her mind for no reason at all, came the question Ginny had been asking recently. To which Polly's answer was that she'd never felt the need for another man, not since she'd finally sent Tony Winslow packing. Tony had been more than enough for a very long time. Just at this moment, however, she'd have given a lot for a broad chest to lean on, arms around her belonging to a big man with thick, greyish fair hair, a strong face, an awkward manner and haunted eyes. She felt a rush of heat, and something like a *frisson* of fear, then sighed and deliberately shut the picture of Tom Richmond from her mind.

When Dot had gone, she looked helplessly at the mess on the floor, then knelt down and began to gather the photos together.

Family photos, Dot had said, but they were mostly of people Polly didn't know. Ancient sepia ones of ladies in shirtwaists and their hair in buns, men in homburg hats and suits with waist-coats, narrow trousers stopping short an inch above their shoes. One she did recognise was of her elegant grandmother, in a head and shoulders pose, her dark hair shingled, with the front in a dip held back with a slide, a beaded blouse and a long rope of pearls around her neck. Laurence, serious and unsmiling in wartime uniform, and someone with a daredevil grin and his RAF hat at a jaunty angle whom it took her several moments to identify as Philip. A few early childhood ones of herself and Ginny and Peter . . .

The group photograph was unusual among all this, an informal snap taken on a seaside holiday, which must have been the last one they ever took together – regular holidays were not part of Polly's childhood memories. She didn't remember Filey at all, but 'Filey, 1972' was written on the back. 1972, the year after their father had died. The family and a young, pert-faced, dark-haired Dot. Freya lounging in a deck chair, looking glamor-ous in designer beachwear. Philip, in shorts! Elf as a baby, sitting between Ginny's legs with a furious, scarlet face, wielding a tiny wooden spade, all ready to demolish the sandcastle she herself, a chubby-cheeked four-year-old crouched down beside it, had evidently just painstakingly constructed. Peter, ten years old, even then wary, sitting self-consciously to one side and scowling at the camera. No one looked particularly happy. How they'd all changed physically since then! Even Freya, whose life had been dedicated to keeping herself looking young. Polly studied the faces carefully; knowing that it was telling her something she had realised, subconsciously, for years.

She looked at it for a long time before slipping it into her bag.

When he left Low Rigg Hall, Richmond had no intention of going to seek out Eddie Nagle. But Beth had been very near to him in the big house, and now he felt emotionally wrung out and in need of a drink. With Mrs Nagle's tirade against Wyn Austwick still ringing in his ears as he drove slowly down the few hundred yards of unmade-up road to where the swinging sign of the Moorcock hove in sight, he suddenly changed his mind and drew up outside.

The pub, occupying a corner where the road curved sharply, was squeezed in at right angles to a row of old cottages with low sweeping roofs, which he guessed was where the Nagles lived. Once inside, he discovered it with pleasure to be one of the dwindling number of old inns which had escaped the depredations of relentless modernisation. It boasted a small but spotlessly shining bar, a bare, stone-flagged floor, unplastered stone walls, not a horse brass in sight, the ceiling between the old beams pickled to a rich, tobacco brown, and the only ornament an undistinguished stuffed bird in a glass case on a shelf. The ubiquitous heaped-up, scorching fire, cratch-back chairs, benches and strong oak tables, and that was that. One single drinker and no landlord in evidence.

'You'll have to shout,' the customer informed Richmond, then did it for him. 'Shop, Susan!' His hand went out to gentle the trembling his raised voice had aroused in the elegant greyhound quivering against his leg.

Richmond's half-pint having been pulled by a young woman who came in drying her hands on a tea towel, who accepted his order and his payment with a nod and nothing more than the usual civilities before departing, he moved to one of the benches by the fire, near the shelf with the stuffed bird. 'Moorcock. Male of the red grouse, *Lagopus scoticus*,' he read, settling himself and stretching his long legs to the fire.

'Chatty piece, that Susan,' his fellow customer commented. 'Like all the natives, you'd fink they was charged for every bloody word.'

'Not from these parts yourself, are you, Mr Nagle? I take it that's who you are?' The nasal tones, the glottal stops, would have dubbed the man a stranger, even if Richmond hadn't expected him to be there.

'And you're up here about that woman found at Rumsden Garf quarry,' retorted Eddie, whose powers of deduction – or possibly his experience of the police – evidently equalled Richmond's own.

Richmond showed his warrant card. Watched the other man carefully store up the name, the rank. 'You knew Mrs Austwick?' he asked.

Nagle pulled on his pint, smacking thick, blubbery lips. Richmond had met bruisers, chuckers-out at night-clubs, punch-drunk boxers more prepossessing. Not over-tall – Richmond could have given him half a head – but his tight jeans showed impressively muscled thighs, the sweatshirt was stretched across well-developed pectorals under a leather bomber jacket. He was sporting a wonderful black eye, just turning from purple to greenish-yellow. 'Depends what you mean by know. Only met her when she come up here to do that book. Fixed her starter motor for her once, used to turn her car round for her. Not a lot of room to manoeuvre up there and the ladies never seem to get the 'ang of it, know what I mean? But we wasn't hardly what you'd call mates.'

'How long have you worked for Mrs Denshaw?' Since the beer – not his first and probably not his second – appeared to have loosened the other man's tongue, there seemed no point in not taking advantage of it.

'Since I married Dot, so that must be over twenty years, Gawd 'elp us.' He grinned to indicate a joke but all the same, Richmond wondered. The Nagles did seem an oddly assorted pair, and he must be a good ten years younger than she was, possibly a lot more.

'How d'you find the life up here? Bit quiet, isn't it?'

'Say that again, but it suits me OK. I had enough racketing round the world when I was in the Marines. I got me job down the 'ealth club, plus general 'andyman at the big 'ouse, used to drive Mrs D around. All keeps me occupied.'

With plenty of spare time, Richmond assumed, deducing from what he'd seen at Low Rigg that Nagle's handyman duties couldn't exactly weigh him down. 'What are you going to do now?'

'Dunno, rightly. No chance to talk about it yet, me and the wife. She's took it real bad, see. Her and the old girl was like that.' He extended one thick finger on top of another, to indicate closeness. 'I've always wanted to breed dogs,' he added thoughtfully.

'What's stopped you?'

'Capital, mate,' was the reply, indicating a train of thought that led directly from Freya Denshaw's death to expectations of benefiting from her will. He rose and called into the back for another pint. The silent Susan came in, and watched Richmond as she pulled it. She was dark-haired and brown-eyed, and would have been pretty if she'd allowed herself to smile. Too young to have been here at the time of Beth's disappearance, he noted automatically.

'You need capital to do it right – professionally, know what I mean?' Nagle continued, coming back with a brimming tankard. 'There's big money in the right sort of dogs, but you need to lay it out first. Go on, she's all right –' as Richmond reached out to stroke the greyhound – 'wouldn't hurt a fly, Lady wouldn't, soft as a boiled turnip.'

Richmond felt the small bony skull beneath the velvet skin. The dog lifted a paw and laid it, light as a feather, on his knee. 'She used to be a champ,' Nagle said, 'but she's no bloody use to nobody now. Greyhounds have a pretty short working life. Don't know why I keep her, that's the trufe. You'd never believe how much she eats. Bloody useless, aincher, dog?'

The dog turned from Richmond and looked up at her master with liquid eyes. Nagle ignored her, then cuffed the side of her head gently, with obvious affection. ''Armless, though. Funny, that, being Wyn was dead scared of her – and she didn't like Wyn, neiver.'

Richmond noted the familiar use of the Christian name. 'When did you last see Mrs Austwick?'

'Last week, I reckon. She said she was off on 'er 'olidays to Spain and wouldn't be up here for a couple of weeks.' He swilled down his beer in one last draught. 'What's she been up to, then, getting herself topped?'

'That's what we're trying to find out.'

The irony was lost on Nagle. 'Sad. But say lah vee, as the Frogs say.' He stood up. 'I'm off now. All that beer. Anyfink else you want to know, you won't have far to go to find me. Only live next door.'

'That's a rare old shiner you have there. You want to take care of it.'

'You should see the other feller,' Nagle said automatically, winking his good eye.

As the pub door closed behind him, the landlady entered again, and came from behind the bar to collect the empty glasses. A rich, savoury smell of cooking issued from the kitchen.

'Any chance of some food?' Richmond asked.

'Soup all right?'

'If that's what I can smell, yes.'

'Five minutes,' she answered, smiling. He'd assumed correctly. She was pretty. Plump and pink-cheeked, a right bonny lass, in local parlance.

In less than five minutes, she was back with a steaming bowl of soup, so thick with meat and vegetables it was a hearty meal in itself, plus crusty brown bread and a generous pot of butter. She set the food carefully before him. 'That'll stick to your ribs. Get it down while it's still hot, nothing worse than lukewarm soup.'

She watched him while he tasted it and found it lived up to every bit of its promise. 'This is excellent.'

'All right, is it?' She nodded, satisfied, and went to wash the empty glasses. When they were dried, she busied herself with polishing the bar counter, rearranging the bottles behind it, while Richmond savoured the delectably blended flavours of smoky ham, haricot beans, carrots, celery and onions. After a while, she spoke up: 'You want to watch that there Nagle. I heard what he said about not knowing that woman, and it's a barefaced lie. They were in here a lot, dinner times, and sometimes in the

109

evenings as well. Never mind what he said, they were thick as thieves.'

Richmond swallowed the last spoonful of his soup and sat back, replete. 'Did you ever hear what they talked about?'

'Well, I don't know.' She was uncertain, aware that she'd laid herself open to that. 'They just seemed – well, matey. You know, laughing and joking and that. Except for Friday – no, Thursday night, it'd be.'

'What happened then?'

'Having a few words, if I'm any judge. We get crowded in here of a night, especially in winter. There's a bit of a garden at the back, but only for summer. We do bar meals and that and we're usually pretty busy, gets a bit noisy, like. So I didn't actually *hear* what they were talking about. They just seemed – not all that friendly.'

Richmond saw what she meant about crowded. A couple of dozen in here and they'd be pushing the walls out. 'I can see why you're busy if that's a sample of your food,' he said, as she began clearing his dishes, 'You do the cooking yourself?'

She seemed pleased and told him she did, and then, as she took his payment, she said, 'Maybe I've been talking out of turn, but . . . there's something about him that doesn't half give you the creeps, that Nagle, I mean. You notice his eyes?'

Richmond had. Grey and flat. Cold, empty. 'How do you find him and his wife, as neighbours, Mrs . . .?'

'Hoddinott. Susan.' She screwed up her pretty face. 'Hard to say. She's all right, I suppose, when you get to know her. But him? I'd rather have his dog. This one, anyway.'

'He has others?'

'Used to have a pit bull terrier, horrible thing it was, till it savaged a little lad down in Rumsden and had to be put down.'

On the upper floor of Low Rigg Hall, Philip Denshaw had what it had amused Freya to refer to as his executive suite. It was far from grand, however, comprising a small sitting-room, an even smaller bedroom and a bathroom. But it suited him, gave him all he needed in the way of comfort. When he had come to live here, after Laurence's death, selling his own house and almost its entire contents, he had first made sure he could get his piano in, his music books and all his paraphernalia for listening to music. Then he'd had it painted white, installed a couple of comfortable chairs and bookshelves, and that was that.

He sat back in a chair that had, over the years, accommodated itself to his shape, listening to a Radio Three concert, the score open on his knees, not reading it, however, but watching through half-closed eyes the small, silent figure perched on the arm of the opposite chair.

'I'm almost sorry she's dead,' Elf said suddenly. 'Almost. You'll miss her. You thought a lot about her, didn't you?'

The words cut brutally across the third movement of the Bruch Violin Concerto and Philip's eyes flew wide open. He wondered what on earth had given her that idea, it had never occurred to him to believe that anyone could view his relationship with Freya in that light. Everything they'd ever been to each other had been a matter of expediency. But he supposed he would miss her being there. He hadn't yet allowed himself to think of the changes on the way.

Her death had caused all sorts of strangenesses – that he should be talking to Elf for one thing, like this, when they hadn't spoken anywhere nearly so intimately for years. 'That's a terrible thing to say,' he rebuked, genuinely repelled. 'You'll miss her, too.'

'Me?' Elf looked sardonic.

'She was very good to you,' he reminded her gently.

'And never let me forget it! Everything she ever did for me I had to be grateful for, every minute of the day.'

'That's a cynicism that doesn't become you.'

Her chin went up, she looked out of the window, watching the noisy, bad-tempered crows. 'One thing I've always wondered,' she said, turning back to face him. 'Did you ever tell her about – that day? In the garden?'

Shocked to his conventional core, colour rising to his pale cheeks, he stared at her. 'Of course not! And I don't think it's a subject we should discuss, either.'

'I don't suppose you do. You never want to face anything unpleasant, do you, Philip? You've always hidden behind someone else, somebody's always made out for you, let you off the hook –'

'Elvira. Do you realise who you're speaking to?'

She looked at him then, her little pixie face creased, her ageless black eyes curiously blank. 'Oh, yes. I never forget that. And I don't forget what you thought you saw, in the garden, all those years ago –'

'You'd better not go on.' Abruptly he reached out to the radio and turned up the volume, but the exquisite violin cadences were now too loud and screamed on his taut nerves. He adjusted it back and her voice rose above the music.

'– what you *thought* you saw. There was nothing wrong about it, it was quite innocent, until you came and destroyed that innocence.'

'It wasn't innocent as far as Peter was concerned!'

'Peter wanted to *paint* me, that's all!'

'In the nude? An eleven-year-old girl?'

'He just wanted to paint me, standing near the pink rose. He had this idea – part of it was in full flower, part just coming into bud –'

'Be quiet!' The colour had left his face. He realised he was shaking and with an effort lowered his voice. 'It was – depraved.'

She stared at him, unblinking, ignoring the naked pain in his eyes. 'Are you sure that's what you felt? Or maybe you were just jealous? You've always liked little girls, haven't you, Philip?'

'How dare you?' This was unbearable. His heart was jumping. His eyes had filled with tears. 'How *dare* you say that – to me, of all people?'

'Look at it, Philip, face it. You've made other people what they are by what you've done. Or what you haven't done –'

'What I haven't done? I've done *everything* for you!'

'– retreating into your own little world. Look what's become of all of us. Me, and Peter. Especially little Beth.'

He was breathing so heavily his voice came out in a rasp. He snapped off the radio, his pleasure in that particular piece ruined for ever. 'Exactly how much more do you want from me, Elvira?'

'I think I want justice, at last. For want of a better word.'

He was suddenly unbearably weary, filled with sorrow for what might have been, remembering the delightful child she once was, consumed with overwhelming pity for her. For the soft, vulnerable, unprotected creature beneath the brittle shell. Pity for himself, too. 'Don't you really mean revenge?' he asked softly, sadly.

'I don't know,' Elf said, looking suddenly, desperately sorry. Sometimes she couldn't think what came over her. Sometimes, she really hated herself.

Outside, the first snow flurry came in on the wind.

11

Friday, 13th November had lived up to its reputation for being unlucky, as far as Wyn Austwick was concerned. That was almost certainly the day she'd been murdered, and you couldn't get much unluckier than that. Glancing at the autopsy findings, Richmond saw that no more precise time of death could be arrived at: the pathologist could only confirm her original opinion that the body had been in the water for approximately three days, would go no further.

Reading through the rest of the report, cutting through the medical jargon, a picture emerged of the victim being attacked by a right-handed person wielding a heavy blunt instrument; she had apparently received a blow to her left temple which had caused her to fall, in the process catching the other side of her head on something sharp-cornered. Both wounds had caused bleeding, but which of them was the crucial factor in her death was at this point academic, since the pathologist indicated the strong probability was that she had died within minutes of being attacked. But that wasn't all, as he found a moment later when he received a call from Gillian Hardy herself. Always a conscientious woman, she told him she was ringing as a follow-up to her report. Had he read it through, yet?

'Not quite. It just landed on my desk a few minutes ago.'

'She was in trouble, as you'll see if you read on. In addition to the fatal injuries, there was an abnormality . . . the uterus –'

'I hadn't got so far,' Richmond intervened hastily. 'Serious?'

'She was going to need treatment, but chances of recovery in these cases . . . possible. If you get there in time, that is . . .' Guarded, like doctors everywhere.

'Would she have known?'

'Hard to say. Probably no severe pain yet, but not very comfortable, certainly. A diagnostic operation would have confirmed. She should've been seen already, but you know how some people react to illness – they shut their eyes to the problem until it's too late. Don't want to know, pass it off as being nothing, a temporary hiccup that'll go away if they ignore it or have a good holiday to tone them up . . . that sort of thing.'

'I do know,' Richmond said feelingly, being more than a little inclined that way himself.

'I can say I found no traces in her blood or her organs of drugs, but that could depend on the time of day she took her medication, if any. It's debatable whether she'd have been given anything. If she had, and she'd been due to take it around the time she was killed, the previous dose could already have passed through her system . . . Well, that's it. I just thought you ought to know.'

'Much appreciated. Thanks. What bearing it'll have, if any, I'm not sure, but thanks all the same.'

'You're welcome.'

He sat thinking for a moment or two after she'd rung off, then picked up the phone again and spoke to Sally Jenner. 'Find out who her doctor was and see what he can tell us, will you?'

While he waited for the answer, he reached for what had come through from Forensics and Scenes of Crime. The reports were necessarily incomplete as yet, but he'd asked for quick results, and couldn't grumble at the speed with which they'd sent all that had so far been gathered and analysed. There seemed no doubt that she'd met her death in her own home, and that her assailant was probably someone she knew, or at any rate someone she'd let into the house, since there had been no indication of forced entry. No mystery either about the sharp-cornered object against which she'd fallen: this had been a wooden, rectangular telephone shelf, attached to the wall in the narrow hallway of the bungalow by fancy wrought-iron brackets. An attempt had been made to clean blood off the table, the walls and the carpet – on the face of it successfully, but the Scenes of Crime team had taken the place apart and stringent forensic tests had extracted microscopic traces of blood from the carpet fibres, and from underneath the table, where the blood had flown upwards. A search of the house had yielded nothing likely to have been used as the murder weapon.

A tidy murderer, as tidy as his victim, just to make things more difficult.

An opened pack of black polythene bin liners had been found in a kitchen drawer, and the officer in charge of Scenes of Crime was of the opinion that her body had been taken out of the house wrapped in one of them. 'That's where he wasn't so tidy,' he'd reported at that morning's briefing. 'The rest of the bags were stuffed any-old-how back into the drawer, with a corner of one sticking out. He slipped up there. Panicky, maybe.'

'Lucky, though,' Richmond said glumly. To have had such a quiet area, a road running down the side of the house where a car could have been parked to help him get away. No one around to see when a body was dragged out of the house, and finally driven away to Rumsden Garth. Where there was little that could be expected in the way of tyre tracks from the flinty surface of the approach to the quarry, either.

But all was not gloom. Arriving at the last page of the forensic findings, Richmond found a nugget of gold. Maybe the killer hadn't been so lucky as all that, after all. For among the dust particles carefully vacuumed up from the carpet in the hallway and painstakingly sifted through, there had been discovered a scattering of short, grey dog hairs. For all he knew, there could be dozens of breeds of dogs with short grey hairs. But only one breed interested him. Greyhounds.

The telephone rang again. This time the call was from the legal firm of Rowlands, Marshall and Trimble, requesting an appointment for Mrs Marshall to speak with someone senior. Her secretary implied that it was on a matter of some urgency, but having just returned home from a winter holiday in the Azores, Mrs Marshall found the rest of her day was fully booked. She had time free the following morning, however. Accordingly, Richmond made an appointment to see the solicitor at her office for nine thirty the next day.

In the incident room, two constables had been sweating over travel agencies and airline manifests with no result whatsoever as to the murdered woman's holiday intentions. As yet, there was no indication that she'd booked an airline ticket to anywhere, let alone evidence of hotel accommodation. Maybe she'd intended to cross the Channel, taking her own car, and drive to wherever she was going in Spain, that was possible. She'd been all ready to set off, with her case packed – only a small suitcase, not much in it. Her large leather shoulder-bag had been stuffed inside. Wallet, purse and credit cards intact, but no sign of a passport, there or in the house. So had she been intending to go to Spain at all, in fact? Two people thought she had – Mrs Dalton, and Eddie Nagle, since she'd told them so, but she might have changed her mind, or said Spain because it sounded grander, when she was really going somewhere unadventurous in England.

The young DC, working on his first murder case, wasn't impressed by the importance of the task he'd been allotted: he felt his undoubted powers of deduction could have been better employed than in knocking on doors, questioning those neighbours not already seen. All of whom, so far, professed to have seen or heard nothing, to have had no more than a passing acquaintance with the dead woman. Most of them were out at work all day, the rest seemed to consist of geriatrics – elderly, housebound, immobile if not bedridden. God, thought Thompson, hoarse with shouting above TV sets turned up to full volume because the owners were deaf, God, I'd shoot myself first.

Old Mrs Dalton, across the road from the victim's bungalow, peeping from behind her lace curtains, had seen him knocking on doors. She hobbled to her own front door and called out to him. 'I've remembered something,' she said as he came up the path. 'Come in and have a cup of tea while I tell you. I've just mashed.' He'd already refused tea four times, but decided it might be prudent in this case to accept, and was glad he had when it came, hot, strong and sweet and accompanied by mince pies.

'I make a few at a time to freeze for Christmas. Go on, help yourself, have a couple while they're still warm,' she said, pushing the plate across to him in the trim little kitchen, neat as a pin and smelling of spicy Christmas baking. Still game, she was, despite the handicap of the zimmer frame. 'I just remembered, when they brought me back from the day centre at about quarter past four, there was a car at the end of the avenue. There wasn't hardly any room for Jim – that's the ambulance driver – to turn round.'

What colour and make was it? Good heavens, how was she

supposed to know that? Even before she had cataracts forming on both eyes, she'd didn't know one make of car from another. It was late afternoon, the light was bad. 'But it was a funny little car – like a Dodgem – you know, them with a pole up the back at the fairground.'

Could well be a Ford Ka. They *were* a bit like Dodgem cars, thought Thompson, suddenly very chuffed with the old girl. Nippy little motors, his girlfriend was hankering after one.

'Would it be the murderer?' she asked eagerly. Thompson, mindful of warnings about scaring the elderly by exaggerating the amount of crime there was around, assured her it was unlikely, though he hadn't the least idea. She looked disappointed.

He thanked her and, nicely full of mince pies and hot tea, knocked on the door of the other half of the semi-detached bungalow where Wyn Austwick had lived, relieved at last to find the door answered by someone in his own age group.

Mrs Austwick's immediate neighbours were a young couple who worked in the same insurance office and came home together, usually arriving about six. But on Friday night they'd called at the DIY supermarket to pick up some paint and wallpaper – that's why they were at home now, they were taking part of their holiday entitlement to do some decorating before relatives came to stay at Christmas. On Friday, they hadn't reached home until around seven. Ian Macallan had been hanging his coat up in the hall when he'd heard a crash, followed by further unidentified noises, from the house next door.

'Sounded like she was throwing the furniture around!' he said. They'd been surprised, because sounds from their neighbour were rare. Except sometimes, they'd heard her singing. They'd heard she was a member of a choir.

'We never had any trouble with noise, kept herself to herself,' his wife added, a trifle wistfully. Perhaps she'd have liked a show of friendship, a wee Scottish lassie far from home.

Thompson felt inordinately pleased with himself. All this was going to earn him Brownie points. Sounds like that, he was sure, could mean only one thing. His euphoria was only slightly deflated when he learned they hadn't seen any sort of vehicle parked nearby. So what about the car Mrs Dalton had seen earlier?

Chief Inspector Richmond, in the incident room when Thompson arrived with his new information, didn't seem sanguine about the outcome of that one. Four fifteen? Dusk, not yet dark, but still risky to be hauling a dead body about. 'Impractical, too, getting a body into a little Ka – if that's what it was,' he added, with a funny look on his face. 'Someone parked there with a perfectly legitimate reason, no doubt, but get the ambulance driver – he should remember it.' He changed his tune, however, when Thompson reported what the neighbours had heard. Even went so far as to say, 'Good work, Thompson.'

Sally Jenner came into the DCI's office, triumphant. 'Well, we've found out why she didn't make any holiday arrangements, sir! She was registered with the Coledale and Salter practice, on Dr Salter's list. He'd recently referred her to a specialist at the Infirmary, who'd recommended an immediate hysterectomy. She was booked in for Friday evening, to prepare for her op the next day, but of course she didn't turn up.'

'Didn't they try and find out why?'

'They did. They rang her two or three times but couldn't get any answer, so they gave up. Apparently people do that – just don't turn up, get cold feet, I suppose, and who can blame them? Then somebody saw in the paper that she'd been murdered, and that was that, as far as they were concerned.'

Richmond swore. 'A phone call would have helped,' he said, unfairly attributing sympathy with police problems to the overworked hospital authorities. 'But what was all the secrecy for? Why did she lie about going on holiday?'

Sally said slowly, 'Embarrassment – over female stuff like that? Men especially – sorry, but it's true! – don't want to hear about it. Or scared stiff? Talk about something like that, you make it happen. Pretend you're going to do something else, right to the last minute, you don't get the collywobbles about it.'

'We-ell . . . If you say so. But I don't think she was the sort to know what embarrassment meant. Nor easily scared, either.'

Did the feminine mind really work like that, did anybody's? He hadn't liked this woman when they'd met, liked her even less now, knowing more about the way she'd screwed up other people's lives . . . but he could almost find it in himself to feel sorry for her.

Manning was about to demolish a theory put forward by his superior. He'd have to employ tact, which wasn't his strong point. 'As far as the murderer being among Austwick's former clients, sir – I think we'd better forget it,' he began cautiously.

He'd now finished interviewing the rest of those whose names were on the spines of the books on Wyn Austwick's shelf, he told the DCI, had managed to speak to all but one of them, an eighty-two-year-old, retired mountain climber known as 'Birdie' Wren, who'd achieved a certain amount of national fame. But since he was now in a wheelchair and reported to be far gone with Alzheimer's, any blackmail attempts subsequent to the writing of his memoirs three years ago seemed unlikely. The rest of Austwick's customers, as far as Manning could ascertain, had led such apparently blameless lives as to have given no cause for pressure to be put on them. Either that, or they'd been more careful than either Margaret Whitfield or Harrison Priestley when allowing their collaborator access to personal information. Priestley, after vigorously denying making any payments to her other than the lump sum for the book, had finally come round to believing it was wiser to make a clean breast, especially as he would now be better off by several hundred a month, and in addition had a cast-iron alibi for the time of the murder, which no one could fault: like Margaret Whitfield herself he had, for the whole of Friday evening, unquestionably been present at the pre-Christmas Fayre at the Girls' High School where his grand-daughter was a pupil and he was a governor.

'They seem to be the only two she was squeezing,' Manning said.

'Two's not a bad score, considering what she was getting from them. Sideline them for the moment.' Richmond wasn't at all put out, since in Wyn Austwick's case he'd never completely taken on board the idea of an overpressed blackmailee turned killer.

He wouldn't discount anybody yet, though, not at this stage, however unlikely, but the more he thought about it, the more certain he was that this murder went straight back to that

meeting of his with Wyn Austwick at the Woolpack. And everything that stemmed from that thought put the murder squarely
back to Low Rigg. For one thing, that concert flyer with the
scribbles on the back which she had flashed about that night was
still missing. There'd been no trace of it among the Denshaw
files. He thought it inconceivable that she would have destroyed
it – though her murderer might well have done so.

And Eddie Nagle, owner of a short-haired greyhound, also
had connections with Low Rigg.

It wasn't until after the sort of supper Ginny considered
impromptu – loads of delicious things bought in from the delicatessen, washed down with a bottle of chilled white wine, and
another to follow – when the children were at last tucked up in
bed and safely asleep, that they began to talk. Or rather, Polly
did. Her feelings were fermenting inside her like a shaken bottle
of fizzy pop which might go off any minute if she didn't let the
cork out.

'I still say we should have told him everything. Tom
Richmond, I mean. Apart from being a policeman, he has a right
to know. Anyway, I don't think we fooled him for a minute. He
guessed we were keeping something back.'

Leon lounged in the big, squashy velvet armchair, his legs
stretched out, his shoeless feet resting on the matching pouffe.
Having discarded Leon-the-lawyer by stepping out of his formal
clothes into slacks and sweater, he now wore his Leon-the-
husband-and-family-man look. And with it an entirely different,
less starchy, more relaxed persona, making him seem ten years
younger. 'Come on, love, I explained all that,' he reminded
her.

'Well, explain it again,' said Polly, 'because I still don't see how
you, of all people, could recommend lying to the police.'

'Lying?' Leon repeated, picking up his glass of golden wine
and squinting through it appreciatively. 'Lachryma Christi,' he
murmured, picking up the bottle and reverently reading from
the label. 'What an utterly appropriate name.'

'What?'

'Hmm,' she said when he'd translated. Drinking Christ's tears seemed to her to be profane, to say the least. She thought perhaps Leon had drunk more than enough of it.

'Every word we told him was the truth,' he said.

'Haven't you ever heard of lying by omission? And you a lawyer?'

'But we know it was Freya who was lying, don't we? All that guff about Beth that she gave you before she died was sheer nonsense, wasn't it?'

Polly stared at him, eyes dark and sombre. 'What exactly are you saying?'

'Come on, think about it,' he said, more gently. 'Is it really feasible?'

That had been the problem for her all along, ever since Freya had chosen, at last, to break the barrier of silence. No, admit it, feasible it was not.

'I suppose it could have happened that way,' Ginny said. But, knowing her husband, it was a question more than a statement.

'No, love, it couldn't, and the police already know it couldn't,' said Leon, suddenly very serious, and proceeded to tell them why.

'Which poses the simple question,' Ginny said into the silence which followed, 'why on earth *did* she say it, then?'

'I think we could all hazard a guess.'

Polly turned cold inside, not needing to guess. She'd been sure of it ever since hearing what Freya had to say. 'She was protecting Peter? After all? Oh God.'

When was all this going to end? Horror that had started with an innocent child's murder and repeated itself with the murder of one neither innocent nor young. But not deserving to die, for whatever reason she'd been killed. How long they sat there, the three of them, Polly didn't know, but whether it was true courage or only the Lachryma Christi talking, she began to feel a surge of the same sort of rebellion she'd felt only once in her life before. And that had ultimately resulted in a permanent break with Tony. This is no sort of life, she'd thought then, for me or for Harriet, so why put up with it? Admitting at last that there was no changing Tony. But this was different, surely they could somehow get out of this bind now, put an end to the secrecy and silence that had for too long run like a dark stream beneath the surface of life at Low Rigg Hall? There had been enough lies and evasions in this family.

She rummaged in her bag for the photograph which had been lying in the bottom, reproachful as an unanswered letter, ever since she'd found it, waiting for her to do something about it. She glanced at it, felt again the same tremor of something half submerged as she handed it over to Ginny. 'Remember this? I don't.'

Ginny made a wry expression when she saw what it was, then laughed. 'Vignette of the Denshaw family! Truth embodied in the camera! Lord, I haven't seen this for years, but I remember Filey. Not the most successful holiday. This must have been taken on the one warm day, it was freezing most of the time. The sea was arctic.'

'Who took it?' Polly asked.

'Philip set it up on a time switch. Look at Peter, sulking! He wanted to take it so's he wouldn't have to be in the picture. All hell broke loose a minute later, when she knocked your sand-castle down,' she said, pointing to Elf, furious-faced, wielding her tiny, threatening spade.

It suddenly occurred to Polly that the answer to a good many questions might lie with Elf – or even with Ginny. But an unaccustomed caution kept her silent. If Ginny had said nothing, she'd have her reasons.

'More wine?' Leon poured what was left of the bottle into his own glass when the others refused.

'She was a right little horror sometimes,' Ginny said, still looking at the photo.

'What do you mean, was?' asked Leon, only half joking.

'Is, then. No, that's not fair. It's just an act she's put on for so long she can't give it up, now. She used to be a lot of fun, as well.'

'We weren't always very nice to her,' Polly said, 'at least I wasn't.'

'Children aren't nice. That's a myth created by those who haven't any,' said Leon, every bit as much a doting parent as Ginny.

'Maybe I was jealous,' Polly said. 'I'd always been the baby until then, I suppose, had my nose pushed out of joint. But my memory doesn't go that far back.'

'Mine does, though. I remember the day she arrived, poor little soul. Everybody being very sorry for her because of what had happened to her parents. And Dot – even Dot – spoiling her like mad.'

They exchanged significant looks. 'Hard to think of Dot in those terms! But yes – I think I do remember something about it. I wondered why everyone was cooing over her when she looked just like a little monkey to me.'

'If you two are going on a trip down Memory Lane, I'll leave you to it.' Leon drained his glass, stretched his long legs and stood up. 'I've some reading to do for tomorrow, anyway. Give me a shout when you're ready to go up, Ginny. 'Night, Poll.' He pressed a light kiss on her forehead, ruffled her hair and said, 'Don't *worry* about it.' He picked up the empty wine bottle and went out.

Efforts to trace Trevor Austwick had so far proved fruitless, but even if he was found, Richmond couldn't see him being so stupid as to have murdered his wife in order to inherit what money she'd left. Regular habitués of Her Majesty's prisons, like Trevor, learned a lot to help them in their future careers outside. He could probably have graduated with honours in criminal law by now. At any rate, he couldn't fail to be aware that no one could ever be allowed to benefit from his crime. But if he was innocent, and his wife had left no will, as her next of kin, he would automatically inherit a not inconsiderable amount of money. Of course, knowing she'd applied for divorce, he could conceivably have supposed she might at any time make a will which excluded him, and have murdered her before she could do so, but Richmond thought even Trevor, with his abysmal record of violence and lack of success in getting away with it, might have appreciated this was a less than brilliant idea. Even allowing for the fact that he was prepared to pay the price of the ludicrously few years in jail such a crime would have earned him. On the other hand, what about the threatening tone of that note he'd written her, warning her that he intended making her a visit? And why had he disappeared?

'If he's gone to ground,' said Manning, 'could be a long time before we find him.'

'We haven't got that long,' Jacks had growled. 'He can't have vanished into thin air. If he's innocent, why hasn't he surfaced before now? With the prospect of all that money coming to him?'

Richmond arrived at the solicitors' offices for his appointment the next day to find confusion reigning. Behind the desk in the reception office, a little blonde girl was distractedly sorting through a snowstorm of paper. Short, spiky yellow hair, big eyes brimming with tears, she resembled nothing so much as a drowned baby duckling. Richmond coughed to attract her attention. She turned and looked at him, blinded with tears.

'Sorry. It's just that I've lost a conveyance. I had it earlier. I've been looking everywhere and I daren't face Mr Trimble if I –'

'*Sophie!* Ask the gentleman what he wants, he's not interested in your muddles,' instructed a bossy voice he recognised from the previous day's telephone conversation, issuing from a smart, dark-haired woman in horn-rimmed glasses. She was tapping on a word processor at the back of the office and spoke without glancing round or breaking step.

Richmond smiled at Sophie and identified himself.

'Oh!' His name and rank having placed him, the Queen Bee at last looked up. 'She's expecting you, Chief Inspector Richmond. Ring through, Sophie.'

Sophie looked even more distracted as she searched for and at last found the intercom beneath the blanket of papers, swallowing hiccups as she spoke into it. Switching off the machine, she said, 'She'll be out right away. Oh God, I *know* it was here half an hour ago, wasn't it, Mrs Blackburn?'

'So you say.'

'Forget about it and it'll turn up, always does,' Richmond advised, by no means sure he was right, but remembering the despairs of youth. Eve Marshall's office door opened and he moved forward quickly, hiding the chaos from her.

He remembered her well: clever and smart, small, dark, blue-eyed, and still a beauty in her late fifties. The intervening ten years had brought more grey hairs, but her eyes had lost none of their sparkle and her personality none of its energy and forthrightness. She came straight to the point and handed Richmond an envelope, across which was written, 'Only to be opened in the event of my death.'

'It was posted to me on Monday, addressed to me personally, with a covering letter. I only heard of Freya Denshaw's death when I returned yesterday.'

So here it was: the letter Mrs Denshaw had gone out to post after she returned from her drive with Nagle. It was quite short. A signed confession from Freya Denshaw to the murder of his daughter, Beth.

'I had told the child she was not to play the piano with oil paint all over her hands, she must go to the kitchen and ask Dot Nagle for something to clean it off. I left her alone in the room and when I came back, there she was, still practising her scales, without having made any attempt to clean herself up. I was very angry with her, I raised my stick and she must have thought I was going to strike her. She backed away, tripped over the rug and fell. She banged her head against the piano and lay quite still. I shook her and she didn't move and I realised she was dead. I am very sorry for what I did, I was entirely to blame, and no one else was involved.'

The room was very quiet. Richmond handed the letter back without speaking.

'It's a fairly astonishing document, don't you think?' Eve Marshall said.

'In more ways than one.' She raised her eyebrows, and he went on: 'For one thing, the post-mortem showed the child's skull had been fractured, not by a fall, but by several blows. And even if she was lying about that and *did* actually hit Beth, someone else was involved – unless we choose to believe Freya Denshaw drove her down to East Park through the snow and concealed her under the bandstand herself.'

'I don't think that would have been possible, even ten years ago she was too crippled by arthritis. I'm not even sure she ever did drive, come to that, she's always had that man of theirs to chauffeur her around.'

'Then this confession was pointless. It raises more questions than it answers.'

Mrs Marshall offered more of her excellent coffee, refilled her own cup when he declined the offer and thought for a while. 'I remember the circumstances of this case well.' She hesitated, then said gently, her blue eyes full of sympathy, 'You were the DC Richmond who worked here years ago, weren't you, and Beth was your daughter? I'm so very sorry. This must have brought it all back again.'

Of course she remembered his own connection with the case. There were not many people in Steynton who wouldn't, given a jog to their memory.

'Thank you.' He swallowed, the last of the digestive biscuit he'd nibbled like sawdust in his throat. 'I will have some more coffee after all, if I may.' She pushed his replenished cup across the desk and he added two generous spoonfuls of sugar, stirring it and letting her take her time to pick up the conversation.

'If I'm being unprofessional and uncharitable in what I'm going to say . . . well, I'll risk that, in view of the circumstances,' she began eventually. 'Mrs Denshaw, as you know, was a successful professional model before she was married. It's a mistake we fall into with women like her to think that because they're so beautiful, they're not – well, let's say not well endowed in the brains department. But in Freya's case, I'm sorry, but it happened to be *true*. She was shrewd enough, where her own interests were concerned, but I don't think I'd be maligning her by saying she wasn't, I'm afraid, all that clever. There's a difference.'

'Indeed there is. You're saying –'

'I'm saying this letter's typical. We – the firm, that is – have acted for the Denshaws for decades, and I've known Freya Denshaw personally for nearly thirty years. I think she acted on impulse in writing it, as she invariably did. She never thought beyond the moment, just made quick decisions in order to put the problem out of her mind. That's not as unusual as you might believe, either,' she said wryly. 'Added to which, she'd grown a little confused lately. She was over seventy and maybe the drugs she was taking for her arthritis . . . but there I'm only guessing, I wouldn't know about that. I used to try to persuade her to take her time, think things through, but she was a very stubborn woman.'

He had an idea that this last was referring to something specific, but if so, she was not proposing to tell him what it was, probably not considering it relevant to this particular occasion. Not for the first time, he took a dim view of the caution of lawyers and bankers when it came to the affairs of their clients, living or dead.

He requested a copy of the letter, which Mrs Marshall had handy, having anticipated the request, though in his view it changed very little. As a confession it held about as much substance as Isobel's had done. Both were designed to clear someone – the same person, he was in no doubt, in both cases: Peter Denshaw.

What was it about this man that attracted such protective instincts in women? Richmond had only ever seen the Reverend Peter from a distance, never met him, never wished to, but clearly an early meeting between them was becoming inevitable. And when they did meet, he couldn't yet be sure that he would be able to comport himself with dignity and restraint, old-fashioned words which didn't fit the way he felt. But he knew their paths had to cross, sooner or later.

The outer office was calm and tidy again as he emerged from Mrs Marshall's inner sanctum and Sophie gave him a sunny smile. 'I've found it! I'd put it in the wrong file, that's all.'

'Good,' he said absentmindedly, his mind already making the transition from what had just passed to the coming interview back at the station.

'Filed it under C for conveyances instead of W for Williams.'

'Logical, in its way.'

'It's not the sort of logic we use in this office,' said Mrs Blackburn severely, over her specs, catching the remark. 'It could have stayed there for ever.'

If ever a man seemed conscience-free it was Eddie Nagle, occupying the hard plastic seat in the interview room as if it were the most comfortable chair in the world, and looking as though he was prepared to stay in it all night, just to be obliging.

None of the questions he was asked fazed him for more than a moment. He had an answer for everything, though Richmond could have sworn the one regarding the presence of the dog hairs on Wyn Austwick's carpet came as a distinct surprise, if not a shock. 'You know how it is, Lady's friendly with everyone. Must've brushed against her.' He stretched his fleshy, Mick Jagger lips in what he must have imagined to be an ingratiating smile, which only made Richmond think what he might be capable of, with his fists like hams, square head as menacing as a battering ram, an undoubtedly mean disposition.

'I thought you said your dog didn't like Mrs Austwick?'

'Well, it's all relative, innit? I mean, she's been trained up to be very polite, Lady has, she wouldn't go for her nor nuffink. Tolerates all my friends, know what I mean?'

'Oh, she was a friend, now, Mrs Austwick? Well, she would be, wouldn't she, all the places you've been seen together. The word is you were a lot more than that, Nagle, never mind you said you hardly knew her.'

'All right, I might've said that – you have to be discreet when you're a married man an' all.' He smiled again, revealing magnificent, predatory teeth, his eyes cold as a lizard's. He was sweating all the same, Richmond noticed, greasy beads of it pearling the shiny, hairless scalp.

'So you *were* having an affair with her?' he said softly, wondering how any woman on earth could ever fancy a man like this.

'Wouldn't go so far as that. Bit of a fling, more like. A bit of 'ow's-your-farver now and then, nobody knows, nobody hurt. But we hadn't been seeing each other for weeks – and I wasn't wiv her that Friday night. Friday the fir'eenf – no way! Superstitious I am, once had a dog that ran . . .' He caught Richmond's eye and halted his reminiscences. 'I was right, it *was* dead unlucky, that Friday. We had a darts match, see, the Moorcock against the Black Bull, down in Rumsden, and we lost. Credit where credit's due, though, they was the best side,' he added magnanimously. 'Stands to reason, wiv your PC Stalley playing for 'em. Real 'ot-shot, Dick is.'

He sat back, enjoying his triumph.

Richmond watched him coldly, refusing to let him see he'd hit his mark. 'What time did this match start?'

'Seven. And we didn't leave till going on for eleven. So I couldn't hardly have been there, and killing Wyn Austwick at the same time, could I?'

On the face of it, no. The pathologist's estimate could not be so exact, but there were the noises heard by the Macallans to fix the time precisely enough. The taxi she'd ordered had also been traced. The driver had knocked on the door at seven fifteen as ordered and, receiving no answer, had finally gone away, not best pleased.

'You're up a gum tree with that one, mate,' Nagle added with a smirk.

Richmond was very much afraid he might be. There was no justification for keeping him, the only chance was to have a go at his car, his clothes. He didn't have much hope. He could not imagine Nagle laying himself open to a murder charge by not having got rid of every single item of clothing he'd worn, or by not cleaning his car within an inch of its life. And there remained the question of his being short of a motive . . .

But who needed motive when passions were aroused? *I don't know what came over me* – the sorriest, most abject phrase in the world.

A violent man, Nagle. A thug. His records had been turned up and showed he'd been in trouble more than once. When he was in the Marines he'd nearly killed a man in a fight, served his time for it in a military prison, been court-martialled. A sudden spurt of blind rage against her, yes, you could believe that – but wasn't he a man to use his fists in that case: a punch in the stomach, a slap around the mouth, hands round the throat? An assertion of male superiority, aggression personally expressed – in the worst kind of way.

But . . . Violent as the attack had been, the use of a blunt instrument – which hadn't yet turned up – didn't suggest that kind of killing, it suggested a certain distancing, a wish to avoid close contact. Or the fear of it . . .

But supposing *Nagle* had been the accomplice Freya Denshaw had needed ten years ago, supposing she'd paid him to get rid of Beth's body when she was afraid Peter had killed her? And supposing Austwick had found this out?

Blackmail, of the sort Austwick employed, presupposed the availability of money. It seemed unlikely Nagle would have access to anything like enough of it to satisfy her. But there were other angles. And on his own admission they hadn't been seeing so much of each other. Susan Hoddinott, at the Moorcock, had seen them having words the night before she was murdered. It could easily have been a simple quarrel, gone too far.

But Richmond went back to the question he'd asked Austwick the first time he'd met her – why had she been so keen to have the case reopened? And he remembered the pure spite he'd seen on her face then. Maybe revenge had been the name of her game. And maybe she was hoping to get it by having Nagle's part in Beth's murder exposed. It wasn't something he found any difficulty in believing.

But it still didn't explain how Nagle could have been playing in a public darts match at the same time as Wyn Austwick was presumed to have died.

12

It was going well, they were through the industrial estate without having met any other vehicle – no suppliers making night-time deliveries, nobody going home from late shift. In two seconds flat, Little Jimmy had opened the Yale and the three of them were through the door of the plumbers' and builders' merchants, no bolts and security locks on, no alarms ringing, just as the lad had said. He'd worked here, sweeping the floors and making the tea, for six weeks and swore the job would be a piece of cake.

Going too bloody well, Skinner muttered under his breath, but nobody took any notice of him, he was always a right bucket of cold water. But sweating like a pig he was now, you could smell him a mile off, a rank, farmyard smell. Over and above that other smell that hit them as they stepped inside: the layers of stale cigarette smoke that the old bloke serving behind the counter had churned out for years, chain smoking and fugging the place up like a kipper factory.

'Christ, it's disgusting! You'd of thought they'd all've popped their clogs with lung cancer years since!' That from Little Jimmy, still high on his last fix, jumping as if he had a hot wire coiled up inside him.

He was tall and thin as a lath, half a head above Skinner, and that said something because Skinner was *big*. Trev, at five-ten, felt like a midget between the two of them. He groped inside the sports bag, reassured at the bulk and weight of the sawn-off sitting in there. Then nearly staggered as Jimmy nudged him and jerked his head, grinning like a Cheshire cat, to where there was a small display of home safes incongruously on show in the midst of all the gold bathroom fittings and pastel-coloured suites. This tickled him in view of what they were about to do and he began to laugh like a drain, lifting the counter flap for the others to pass through, inclining his head like a butler. 'After you, me lord.'

'Shut it, will you?' Skinner said, but Jimmy only laughed

more. Give him his due, he was the best peterman in the business, even stoned out of his mind he'd have that safe in the office cracked before you could say lovely lolly, but he was a right berk. A bloody liability and no mistake. The sooner they were out of here the better.

They stepped through the opening behind the counter into the stock room and then into the glassed-in office where the safe was.

Security was a laugh here. Jimmy twiddled about with the knobs and in about two seconds flat the door flew open. Even Skinner laughed as he scooped the contents – the day's takings and whatever else there was – into the Head bag. After that they were off, ducking under the counter again and towards the door. As they reached it, all hell was let loose. Pressure pads under the floor, the lad hadn't told them that. Burglar alarms coming at them from all sides.

'Move it!' Little Jimmy yelled, knocking against a display of heavy chrome fittings, sending them clattering into a porcelain washbasin with a thundering crash, tripping over a stack of facing bricks and knocking over a double-glazed patio window, which gave a crack like a pistol shot. Outside, into the Cortina. In less than two minutes they were on the main road.

'Where you bloody going?' yelled Skinner as Trev, breathing hard, but unfazed, slowed the car to a more sedate pace and turned into the parking lot of the pharmaceutical company offices.   -

'Keep your mouth shut and just look as if we know what we're doing!'

Trev parked the car neatly in one of the dozens of vacant parking slots. Two police vehicles, sirens going, screamed past on the road, and Trev, the adrenalin still pumping, killed the engine of the Cortina. 'You friggin' mad, or what?' Skinner shouted.

'Have faith, have faith, I know what I'm doing.'

'Could've fooled me!'

Faith was what Trev himself never had when anyone said nothing could go wrong, experience having taught him otherwise. The lad who'd told them there were no burglar alarms wasn't too bright in Trev's opinion and he'd sussed out the options himself, just in case. He'd found this place, plenty of parking after office hours and no barriers, no regular security patrols: they'd only be one out of all those cars coming and going all night. Who was to say their business wasn't legit – until it was too late? By then they'd be long gone, car abandoned, loot in the sports bag. The all-night sports centre was just round the corner. Look cool, walk in, have a work-out maybe, a shower and a double hamburger and chips, with a chocolate fudge sundae after – God, he was ravenous! He began to have that feel good factor, not seeing any flaws in his reasoning. 'What's up with Jimmy?' he said into the back seat.

'Well out of it,' Skinner replied disgustedly. He began to shake Jimmy, but already another car was turning in, followed by another, blue lights flashing. They hemmed in the Cortina and Trevor bitterly watched the story of his life unfold yet again as several lads in blue poured out.

While Trev was sitting morosely in a police station interview room not a hundred miles away from Steynton, cursing the stupidity that had made him overlook the fact that security would consist of someone monitoring the premises on a television screen somewhere in the building, with direct communication to the police, and facing the prospect of yet another stretch inside, the Denshaw family were sitting on Freya's tapestry-seated chairs, the embroidery glowing in the dingy splendour of the little-used dining-room at Low Rigg. Half-warmed by an unsuccessful fire, lit for the occasion, that kept belching out smoke, they were assembled there for a dinner called by Philip and cooked by Polly, since whatever desire Dot had ever had to cook had deserted her. She was sitting hunched over the fire, in the kitchen, as if she hadn't a home of her own to go to, drinking endless cups of tea, while the family ate in the dining-room.

Everyone was there – everyone except Elf, who'd made out she was too busy. Ginny and Leon, Peter and Sonia, Polly – and Philip himself. It was a subdued gathering and, apart from the wine, which Leon had brought, it was an undistinguished meal, based on pasta with bottled sauce from the supermarket. Polly could cook when she put her mind to it, and the salad was pretty good, but she, like Dot, couldn't summon up the will to concentrate on food in the unsettled interval between her mother's death and her funeral. Polly and Sonia cleared the plates from the main course and then Sonia surprised everyone by producing a chocolate cake she'd bought at the WI stall in the market. 'I didn't imagine you'd want to be bothered with making a pudding, Polly, and Peter does so love them.'

'Bless you, you're an angel!' Sonia blushed.

'Who else but Sonia would have thought of puddings at a time like this?' Peter remarked ungratefully, but he didn't refuse when a large slice was put in front of him.

'Nobody,' replied Leon, 'and I for one will do it justice.' He smiled at Sonia, whose eyes filled with tears at the unexpected kindnesses coming her way.

By the time Ginny had made coffee, and Polly was wondering what the point of this gathering was, Philip was ready to enlighten them. 'I dare say what I have to say will come as a shock to you,' he began portentously. 'How many years is it since I came to live here?'

'You should know.' Peter wasn't used to wine with his meals, and he'd had three glasses of Leon's excellent claret.

'Let's see,' Ginny calculated, 'it's what – twenty-eight years? – since Father died. So it must be –'

'Twenty-five years – twelve months after your Aunt Joan died, to be exact.'

During that year, he'd lived alone, a middle-aged widower, in the cold and sterile house on the other side of Steynton – detached, four bedrooms, two bathrooms and two garages, fitted carpets and toning floral curtains throughout – which his wife Joan had considered appropriate to one who'd been born a Brackenroyd. It had evidently been a year too long.

'I'm sorry if this is going to be a shock,' he repeated. 'It was never my wish that it should be kept secret, but Freya insisted.'

'That what should be kept secret?' Peter was acting like an ill-mannered adolescent, but at least the wine had shaken him out of the morose silences he usually fell into at any family gathering.

Philip went on as if he hadn't heard. 'I dare say you'll all be as shocked as Freya was to learn that when your father died,

135

he'd left her virtually without a penny, nothing except the house – his share of the family inheritance, as you know.'

He had certainly succeeded in gaining their attention. Shock in various forms did indeed register on every face at the table, but no one spoke and he went on in his pedantic way. 'It would have been unthinkable to allow Low Rigg to go out of the family – even supposing a buyer with a fortune to spend on doing it up could have been found. She managed for some time but it wasn't easy. Eventually, we came to a somewhat unusual agreement, your mother and I: if she turned the deeds over to me, and allowed me to move in, I would make her a monthly allowance, adequate for her to live on. Knowing Freya and her extravagance, I knew better than to buy it outright. It will, of course, come to you children when I'm gone.'

For a wild moment, Polly wondered if he and Freya had been lovers – that photo of the dashing young flight lieutenant! – and that other one, the solemn, rather humourless face of her father, an enigma to the end, seemingly. But no, that couldn't be, she thought, while Peter, breaking through the shock, voiced harshly what they were all, in their various ways, thinking. 'May I ask what was in it for you?'

Sonia gave a little gasp of shocked reproach but Peter ignored her.

'Me?' Philip smiled gently and let his gaze linger lovingly on each of their faces in turn. 'Why, I found myself something I thought I'd never be fortunate enough to have. I gained a family, didn't I? All of you,' he added with a tinge of sadness for the one who had elected not to be there.

There was a small silence. Another eddy of smoke billowed out into the room and Sonia coughed. Then impulsively, Polly reached out her hand and put it over her uncle's. She was surprised to find how cold his was, that it was trembling slightly. You forgot, sometimes, that he was an old man. To her, he'd always seemed ageless. It wasn't so much, she thought, that he'd stayed young-looking, as that his years had caught up with the way he'd always looked to her: elderly, rather shapeless, slightly balding. Somewhere between the handsome young RAF officer he'd once been and her first recollections of him, what hair he possessed must already have turned from fair to white.

She'd always thought of him as simply a pleasant, slightly

ineffectual man who needed little except his music to keep him happy, and though she'd suspected he would have loved to have had children of his own, she hadn't realised how much. It was salutary to think how lonely he must have been, and to realise that his reserved nature had masked a practical ability to deal with both his problem and Freya's in a sensible and useful way, that for once in his life he hadn't opted out.

But Peter, at least, wasn't seeing it that way, hearing only what he wanted to hear. 'My mother did *that*? Gave away our inheritance?'

'Your mother,' Leon intervened coldly, looking suddenly very fed up with Peter, 'your mother did much worse than that.' And he proceeded, in a few crisp words, to inform Peter what had passed between his sisters and Freya on the night she died.

Peter listened with mounting anger, which quite suddenly, inexplicably, drained away, leaving him looking defeated but not, Polly noticed, either surprised or shocked. He lowered his head and stared at the tablecloth, then raised it and turned his eyes from Ginny to Polly, and back again. 'Why didn't either of you see fit to tell me this?' he asked at last, in what sounded very like despair. 'After all, it concerns me more than either of you.'

Before waiting for an answer, he levered himself against the table with the heels of his hands, pushed his chair back and lumbered from the room. Sonia, with a distracted flapping of her hands, rushed after him. No one else followed.

A moment later, Philip stood up unsteadily. He was white as lard, except for two hectic spots of colour high on his cheek-bones. In a trembling voice he said, 'I don't feel well. I think I should be better in bed. Help me upstairs and send Dot to me, if you will. Ask her for my usual nightcap.'

There had been no reason to stay on at Low Rigg. Once undressed and in bed, sipping the hot drink Dot had made for him, Philip seemed to have recovered himself and Polly had gone back again to Garth House with Ginny and Leon for the night. By half-past seven the next morning she had seen to it that Harriet was ready dressed for school in the new uniform which still gave her immense satisfaction, sent her down for breakfast and then showered and dressed herself. Judging the weather by a glance out of the window, she pulled on layers of warm woollen clothing, long boots. She was fastening her hair back with a big tortoiseshell slide when she heard the telephone ring downstairs. A couple of minutes later, Ginny put her head round the door. 'It's Tom Richmond, the chief inspector. He wants to see you down at the police station.'

'Me?' Polly's heart plummeted. It was the summons she'd been expecting for nearly a week now, but hoping against all expectations would never come. 'Wonder what he wants to see me about?'

'I wonder.' Ginny glanced at her curiously, but she obviously hadn't slept well, either, and was now too occupied with the business of overseeing breakfast and school departures to probe too much, for which Polly was truly thankful. 'At your convenience, he said, when I told him you were doing the school run. He seems quite nice, really, for a policeman. Hurry up, or the coffee will be cold.'

In the usual scramble that accompanied preparations for work and school, Polly's preoccupation remained unnoticed, or at any rate unremarked on. She didn't think Ginny could have mentioned the call to Leon. Never a communicative man first thing, he buried his head in the newspaper while he drank his usual cup of tea and ate one slice of toast, shouted at Sheba, one of the boys' mongrels, who'd illicitly insinuated herself into the kitchen and was shedding hairs all over his dark suit, deposited hasty kisses on his offspring and his wife and left. Ginny followed fifteen minutes later, miraculously transformed by several cups of coffee and make-up into her usual model of elegance.

Polly drove the three children to school and then turned the car on to a side road, a quiet, tree-lined cul-de-sac of substantial houses behind long front gardens, where no one was around to remark on a woman sitting in a car at that time in the morning, staring out of the windscreen at nothing in particular. She wondered what on earth she was going to say to Tom Richmond that would sound convincing. He wasn't a man to be fobbed off easily, that was already very clear.

A dustbin lorry turned into the road ten minutes later, forcing her to move. The situation wasn't going to get any better by sitting here worrying about it, anyway, she thought, letting in the clutch. There was only one possible answer – to tell the truth. But after Philip's bombshell and the restless night which had followed, she felt ill equipped to deal with the consequences of her own impetuous action.

'Please don't worry about what I told you,' Philip had said when she'd gone up to his room to convince herself he was all right before leaving him. 'None of you will be deprived of your inheritances. Postponed, that's all. When I'm gone, you'll all receive equal shares of whatever I have to leave.'

'Philip, let's not think about that just now. You're not going to go for a long time yet. More important is what Freya told us.'

'Never mind that, either,' he interrupted, and he'd looked so distressed that Polly obediently fell silent. 'But I have to say that I think Leon was right. Best to keep it in the family. It's all nonsense, just the sort of nonsense Freya was capable of.'

But keeping quiet about it hadn't been very sensible as far as Peter was concerned. And then, Leon's telling it that way had been a mistake, Peter's reaction was just what she'd feared, and what worried her. She'd rung him before she left Ginny's house this morning, but there'd been no answer.

'All this, you know, it needn't make any difference to anyone,' Philip had continued. 'Things will go on just the same . . . except that you'll all take whatever furniture and so on your mother left to you, naturally, and –' he let his voice quaver, take on a pleading note, playing the old man now for all he was worth – 'and I hope that you and Harriet might choose to live here, Polly.'

Which had been an added reason for her sleepless night. As a child and a young woman growing up in Low Rigg, she'd taken the house for granted, accepted its cold and draughty corners, groaning pipes and creaking floorboards, it was just somewhere she lived, but after the years away – college and then marriage with Tony – she'd come to be uneasy with it, its remoteness, not just in terms of distance, but its separateness from the warmth and busyness of other people's meaningful lives, down in the valley. Recently, this uneasiness had grown into distaste, as much for its associations as for itself. A tragedy had played itself out here and it had left its mark, had changed it for ever as far as she was concerned. The idea of committing herself to living here, with only the Nagles and Philip for company, was something she found difficult to contemplate without dread.

But, consideration for Philip apart – and emotional blackmail from the old was hard to resist – she had to have somewhere to live. There were some nice new houses being built on a good location only a few miles out of the town, previously too expensive even to consider. It would be dishonest to deny that since her mother's death the possibility of now being able to buy one of them had crossed her mind. Well, that was not to be, and she knew the young couple who owned the nice little house in Ingham's Fold were anxious for her to make up her mind. Houses were selling with difficulty and it wasn't fair to them to keep them in suspense.

'It's not bad,' Ginny had said candidly, 'but too cramped. You'd be fighting your way out in three months.' Polly remained undecided, which probably said it all, she thought, joining the slow-moving queue of traffic through the town centre.

It was a dark, raw, cheerless morning, the roads skaty from yesterday's snowfall, which had quickly turned to slush, then frozen, following the miserable weather pattern of the last week. The sort of weather they might expect from now on. Polly hated winter. She drove carefully, progress was slow and she was able to see that the lighted windows of the shops were already decorated, stacked with presents, displaying Christmas fare. Piles of small fir trees lay on the pavements outside the greengrocers' shops. Men employed by the council lighting department were working from a tower on a vehicle, stringing fairy lights and Santas between the lamp posts. She hadn't dared to contemplate Christmas yet.

While he waited for Polly Winslow, Richmond read through the notes of last night's interview with Trevor Austwick. Apprehended last night, in pursuit of an armed robbery at a plumbers' merchants near Sheffield. He and Manning had driven over there as soon as they heard. With the absolute certainty hanging over him that he would be going back to where he'd come from for some time, Trev, caught red-handed in one thing, was ready to co-operate in the next, in the hope of mitigating his sentence, though that wasn't Richmond's province and of no immediate concern to him.

Swearing that the note he'd written had referred to the *previous* Friday, Trevor admitted that he'd gone to the bungalow then to try and get some money from the old bitch. All she'd stumped up had been a lousy fifty. Reminded him she'd filed for a divorce, that his days of getting easy money from her were numbered. Said she was going away and wouldn't be back for some time, so it was no use pestering her. Thrown him out, with a promise that she'd call the police if he didn't leave her alone.

'She refused you money then, so you went back to try your luck again the following week?'

'No, I bloody didn't!'

'Maybe you got a bit rougher with her than you intended and she ended up dead.'

'I never went back, I've told you!' Trevor shouted. 'I can prove where I was, Friday night.'

He'd produced a list of several mates who swore he'd been playing cards with them on the evening of Friday the 13th, and a lady with whom he'd spent the night. An alibi so thin, with names such as he'd given to support it – it just had to be real.

'All I wanted was a couple of thou' till I got back on me feet, but not her! She was a right cow, I tell you, that one, for all she could write books. I want my head seeing to for ever getting tangled up with her.' A thought occurred to him even in the midst of his troubles. 'How much did she leave?' he asked, his eyes lighting with greed.

It would have given both police officers a great deal of pleasure to tell him that she'd left it all to the cats' home, but life was never so obliging. However it stuck in the gullet to admit it, it was quite likely that this lowlife would find a substantial sum waiting for him when he came out. Nevertheless, Manning extracted what satisfaction he could from giving Trev a few nasty moments. 'Forget it, sunshine. The way you're carrying on, you're never going out be outside for long enough at a time to worry about that.'

13

Polly was shown immediately into Richmond's office, which wasn't what she would have expected for a chief inspector. A dismal sort of room, painted an unfortunate shade of yellow in a failed attempt at cheerfulness, the fluorescent lights turning the colour to margarine. Chairs with wooden arms were covered in grey and beige tweed which fell short of giving either pleasure to the eye or comfort to the body. A row of dark green metal filing cabinets was lined up against one wall. On Richmond's desk a small modern computer sat surrounded by a mass of paperwork, a three-inch-thick file and the coffee she'd been offered and declined. She could feel against her leg, right through her long skirt and her boot, the heat from a radiator going full blast, yet one of the windows was opened several inches at the top, making the room stuffy and draughty at the same time.

A young woman detective who was introduced as DC Jenner sat disconcertingly just out of her range of vision, presumably ready to take notes. Richmond himself looked less awkward, more at home in these official surroundings, totally absorbed with the task in hand, but even grimmer. He had a foolscap pad ready to make notes, and a silver biro in his hand. When she thought of the ways in which she'd imagined them meeting, she could feel the heat in her face. She studied the uninspired pattern of the carpet tiles on the floor.

He'd pushed a pile of papers he was working on to one side as she came in, and wasted no time in getting to the point, to her relief plunging straight into the matter, without polite preliminaries or prevarications. 'Mrs Winslow,' he began formally, 'it's come to our notice that you visited Mrs Wyn Austwick on the day of her death. That is, Friday, 13th November. Is that correct?'

Half of her would have liked to deny it, but obviously someone had seen her, or her new Ka. That stroppy ambulance driver who'd bawled her out for parking badly had taken her number, she'd bet her life on it. She'd no alternative but to agree.

'I asked you previously when you'd last seen her and you denied ever having met her. Why didn't you say you'd been to her house?'

She forbore to say it was Leon who'd denied any meeting between them and Mrs Austwick, because she'd gone along with it after all, and she'd no wish to antagonise him with what he might see as smart-alec remarks, but she didn't welcome feeling like a schoolgirl caught out in a fib. She wouldn't have refused to give an account of her movements if she'd been asked to, it was just that she'd hoped to avoid her idiocy coming to light – though it had seemed right at the time, and perhaps it hadn't been so daft to try and do *something*. Stupid, though, to blame yourself, to be unable to swallow this illogical feeling of guilt. She tried to relax her body, feeling its rigidity must be apparent.

'I thought it would only confuse matters.'

'The only confusion that arises is when people don't see fit to tell us the truth,' he said austerely. 'What time did you get there?'

She'd met the three children out of school and left them with Ginny at the shop, then driven up to the Clough Head Estate. 'Just after four, I think.'

'And what was the purpose of your visit?'

This was more difficult. She shifted her position while she thought how to put it. Behind her, the policewoman sniffed and blew her nose. 'Well, we told you on the morning after my mother's death what the situation had been with that woman. I began to think, we don't *have* to put up with her abusing my mother like this!' Suddenly, the same red-hot anger she'd felt when she'd first learned what had been going on, the rush of adrenalin that had carried her along then, was now beginning to make it easier. 'After all, Freya had a perfect right to stop that wretched book, if that was what she wanted to do. She'd honoured the contract between them and already paid Mrs Austwick what she owed her, so that was no problem. By the time it got to Friday, I decided to go and see her and have it out with her, and tell her that if she persisted in annoying my mother, I'd make a complaint to the police.'

'What was her reaction?'

'She . . . I'm afraid she just laughed. She told me to get on with it.' Polly tried not to show the rush of humiliation as she relived that put-down. He was bound to misinterpret the subsequent anger she still felt.

He didn't say anything for a while, just watched her coolly. The silver biro flashed as he twirled it round. 'Didn't it occur to you that there might be more to it? That your mother was being subjected to something other than abuse?'

He knew. Of course he knew. How could she have believed he wouldn't, somehow, have found out? Instinctively, she drew herself together, crossing her arms across her chest and rubbing them. Richmond stood up and shut the window. 'Sorry if you feel a draught. We get a lot of smokers in here,' he said, the first natural remark he'd made since she entered the room, and his tone was one shade warmer, the look he sent her as he came back to his seat might even have been interpreted as sympathetic. 'I'll tell you what I think . . . I think that when your mother spoke to you before she died, she told you the real reason for what must have struck you as Mrs Austwick's rather strange behaviour. Am I right?'

After a moment, Polly agreed that he was. She realised her voice was shaking. Take deep breaths. Several deep breaths. 'She'd hinted that she'd found, among my mother's papers, something extremely damaging to her. She was threatening to go to the police with it.'

He didn't, as she expected and feared, ask her what this was. 'So what did you do? When Mrs Austwick refused to take you seriously?'

'What could I do? I just left. To be honest, I felt shaken, incapable of arguing with her. I'm not used to dealing with people like her, I didn't really know what to do.' He must think that feeble, she thought it pretty feeble herself.

He went on watching her, tapping his fingers on the desk. He appeared to come to a decision. 'I know this is difficult for you, so I'll help you out. You told me your mother had posted a letter on the day she died –'

Her stomach lurched. 'Has it turned up?'

'Yes, it was sent to her solicitor, Mrs Marshall, and she felt it necessary to inform us of the contents. I'd like you to look at this photocopy and tell me if that was substantially what your mother said to you.'

She reluctantly did as he asked, read the document he handed to her. Recognised Freya's large, loopy handwriting and felt an enormous sense of relief that she wasn't going to have to repeat her mother's dying words, which had grown less and less credible to her as time went on. 'Yes, that's what she told us, more or less word for word. Do you believe it?'

'Do I believe your mother wrote it? Yes. But do I believe she was telling the truth? Not as it stands. It's not possible that this was the way it happened.'

He began to explain how a post-mortem examination could, by revealing on which side of the head brain damage had occurred, demonstrate whether a head injury had been caused by the head meeting an irresistible object, as in a fall, or conversely by the head being hit with a hard object. However –

He stopped and unnecessarily squared up the papers on his desk, so that she couldn't see his face. She thought of the implications of that 'however': that perhaps such deductions hadn't been possible in Beth's case, for obvious reasons. The child had been dead, after all, for four months. Polly closed her eyes for a moment against a picture she'd never been able to bear contemplating either, ever since Beth's little body had been found.

– however, he continued, looking up, expressionless, the autopsy had also revealed not one single skull fracture caused by a fall, but several injuries consistent with being hit, repeatedly, by some heavy object with a blunt, rounded end. 'Your mother, of course, would not necessarily have known about the autopsy's findings, but events could not possibly have happened as she said.'

This was what Leon had already explained to her and Ginny, and it had been insupportable to think what this inevitably implied. She tried to steady herself, not to let her imagination run away with her. If this was hard for her, think of Richmond himself – it was this man's child, his and Isobel's, they were talking about. His child who'd been murdered. She felt him watching her and knew then for certain that it wasn't primarily Wyn Austwick's murder he was concerned with, not first and foremost, not in his mind and his heart, and she was suddenly

145

afraid. But, though she didn't have much idea about police rules and procedures, it seemed unlikely to her that he'd be allowed to delve too deeply into a case – and a closed one at that – in which he'd had such a strong personal interest.

It occurred to her that this wouldn't necessarily stop him.

She said very carefully, through stiff lips, 'What you're saying is that Mrs Austwick held this over my mother – that my *mother* repeatedly hit Beth until she died?'

'We've no means of knowing that, have we, Mrs Winslow? What I do say, since it appears your mother was disabled by her arthritis even then, is that someone else must have been involved in the removal of her body.'

'She could never have hit a child deliberately! Whatever she says in the letter – whatever she was pretending – I doubt if she even raised her stick. I cannot recall one single instance when she ever lifted a finger to any one of us – and we were normal children, we must have given her cause to get angry from time to time.'

She didn't feel it necessary to add that Freya's displeasure had always been expressed differently. A cold, disapproving silence, to shame you, to make you shrink inside. A silence you remembered, long after a smacked bottom would have been forgotten. Withdrawal of parental approval, far more devastating, just as cruel in a different way.

'Then if she was lying we can only assume that she did it to protect someone. A person close to her, it must have been. You'd have to love someone very much to admit to murder in order to save them, wouldn't you?'

At last. Out in the open. 'You mean Peter. My brother.'

'Not necessarily.'

But she knew he did. And Peter had thought so too, last night, when he'd rushed away from Low Rigg, unable to bear what his mother had taken it upon herself to do. 'Listen,' she said, suddenly angry, 'my brother went through hell ten years ago. Nothing was proved against him, but it's screwed up his life. It's haunted him ever since. I'll ask you one question, Chief Inspector. Why should my mother have written this letter if it isn't in some way true? The case has been closed for ten years. This only throws out even more suspicions, puts Peter under more pressure. Why would she risk that?'

'As I've said, it was unlikely she would have known what I've just told you about the post-mortem. I can only assume she expected the document Mrs Austwick was threatening her with to turn up among her papers after she died, and knowing that it would implicate the Denshaw family in some way, she was prepared to take the blame. I have to tell you we haven't yet found any such document.'

'You mean it doesn't exist?'

'No, only that we haven't found it.' He pulled the thick file towards him and opened it at where a marker had been inserted between the pages. 'I see you weren't there, on the day Beth disappeared?'

'I wasn't living at home then, I was at teacher-training college.'

'Yes, of course. I see the permanent household at that time consisted of Mr and Mrs Nagle in addition to the family – your mother, your uncle, Philip Graham Denshaw. And Elvira Graham . . .' He paused. 'She's not technically a member of your family?'

'We've always regarded her as such. She came to us as a baby, when both her parents were killed in a pot-holing accident in North Yorkshire. There were no other relatives to take care of her, so she came to live with us.'

'Elvira Graham, yes. I see. Graham,' he repeated. 'Does that have any significance?'

Significance? Graham? What did he mean? And then she saw. It suddenly seemed to have become very hot in here.

'Open the door,' Richmond instructed the WDC. 'It's got rather warm in here since we shut the window. Are you sure you wouldn't like some coffee, Mrs Winslow? I can have some fresh sent in.'

She shook her head. 'No, thanks. I'm fine.'

'Are you sure?'

She'd let him relieve her of her red coat and bright scarf when she came in even though, draped as she was in layers of soft dark materials underneath, she knew she'd look sallow under the fluorescent lights. But she now felt a tide of colour sweeping up her neck, helpless to control it. 'What *exactly* do you mean, significant?'

147

'I'm asking if your uncle could be related in any way to Elvira?'

She had to break the silence at last. She felt a sense of outrage, coupled with a strong desire to kick herself for her own – perhaps deliberate – obtuseness. 'He used to make a lot of her when she was a child, but he likes children, anyway. They really don't have much of a relationship now.'

'Is that so? What happened to change it?'

'It happens, as you grow up, you change.' She shrugged, too casual in an effort not to give anything away.

But she knew it was more than that, though all she could be certain of was that their estrangement had something to do with Peter. That summer, before Peter had dropped out of art school, Elf and Peter had been as thick as thieves. And then, suddenly, it was all over. Over between Elf and Philip, too, that trusting friendship Elf had never enjoyed with anyone else. And a coolness between Philip and Peter that never seemed to have been resolved.

'OK, maybe being named Graham is just a coincidence,' he said easily.

'What does it matter, anyway? What's it to do with Mrs Austwick's murder?'

'I don't know there's any connection at all – but it's my job to collect all the bits and pieces I can and one day, who knows, one of them may be the missing piece I'm looking for.'

One of those bits and pieces had been Elvira Graham's name, jumping right out at him, staying with him, ever since he'd begun to reread those reports. She had been the last person to see Beth alive.

'I helped her to build the snowman,' her statement had read. 'I went indoors to find a hat and scarf and so on to finish it off while she rolled the snowball for the head. It was about quarter past two. Her stepfather, Peter Denshaw, was due to pick her up any moment. It took me longer than I thought to find the things, and he was late. He had just arrived when I got back with them, but Beth had already disappeared.'

'May I go now?' Polly was already half-way out of her seat.

'Yes, for the moment.'

'You do believe me – about Mrs Austwick? Whatever it looks

148

like, whatever you believe, I didn't harm her when I went to see her.'

He allowed a small smile to appear. 'That wasn't my purpose in bringing you here. But since you are here, I can tell you that she may have been alive after that.' He looked down at his foolscap pad, still blank. 'Unless, of course, you returned later.'

She said with dignity, 'No. I swear I didn't.'

'Well, I hope you're telling the truth this time. As it is, I could charge you with obstructing police inquiries, but I won't.' He stood up to end the interview. 'DC Jenner will have your statement typed and then you'll be asked to sign it. Thank you for your time.'

He held out his hand and, after a moment's hesitation, she took it. He was scarcely aware that he held hers fractionally longer than necessary.

'Good morning, Mrs Winslow.'

And what else isn't she telling us? he asked the empty room after Sally had escorted her out. The feel of her hand, small and warm, in his palm, stayed with him, her scent lingered faintly on the air. He hoped it wasn't the smell of treachery.

Would it matter, he thought, if it was? Yes, it would. It would matter a lot. Damn this to hell! Polly Winslow was a complication he could do without.

He sat for some time after that, trying to put his thoughts into order, then picked up the photocopy of the letter Freya Denshaw had written to return it to its file. And thought again of something that had lodged in his mind when the drowned duckling in the solicitors' office had found her lost conveyance, and had been eluding him ever since. Too many things chasing across his mind. He passed a hand across his face, troubled. He wasn't sleeping well, and he desperately needed clarity, the kind that comes from good sleep. He fell into bed at night, poleaxed from lack of it the previous night, but it didn't prevent the dreams. The recurrent dreams he'd suffered for months after Beth's body was discovered, which had eventually stopped, only to return since he'd come back here. Nightmarish fantasies, hideous with demons, which he couldn't remember when he woke up, thrashing, sweating, feeling on the verge of calamity . . .

He poured himself some vile, stewed coffee from the jug keeping hot on his desk, and slugged it down, thinking Polly had been right to refuse. The bitter brew puckered his mouth, but he felt better from the jolt it gave him after drinking it, and got to grips with what it was that had been escaping him. Forget it, it'll come to you, he'd told the duckling, advice which hadn't worked for him. But solid concentration, now, eventually did. He sent for Manning and instructed him to have someone go through Austwick's files again.

'We've been through them twice.'

'Go through them again. Every single one. Not only those that seem relevant this time.'

No murderer worth his salt would have left that paper lying around. On the other hand, Austwick hadn't struck him as the sort to leave anything to chance. There'd be a copy, somewhere. He'd had someone go through the papers in the Denshaw files minutely, and got Manning to prove his expertise on the computer by endeavouring to find out if she'd transferred the information on to disk, and thereafter disguised it in some fashion, but with no results. But perhaps it wasn't as complicated as that. If you wished to hide something, as the duckling had proved, the best way was simply to file it in the wrong place.

And of course, there it was, eventually. Hidden in the Whitfield file, clipped together with other papers relating to events at the Girls' High School, a mere programme, nothing to excite comment, unless you realised what it was, scribbled on the back. It was what he expected – a poor photocopy, since the original, as he remembered, had been written in pencil. Nothing but a scrawl, in Freya Denshaw's distinctive loopy writing. Three attempts she'd made, the last one making it clear that the document had evidently been destined not as a letter at all, more a sort of promissory note, to the effect that Eddie Nagle was to be paid a stated annual sum of money by Freya Denshaw. 'For services rendered', she had written in one of the drafts, before prudence had intervened and she had crossed it out. He thought it unlikely he would ever see the original again: and this rough scribble could hardly be classed as hard evidence. But it had demonstrated Freya's intentions, and services rendered were, by definition, actions which couldn't be revoked, a matter of history. And in view of that letter she'd left, it seemed pretty conclusive what those services were.

'Well, there you are.' Manning handed it over, scarcely troubling to conceal his surprise that Richmond should consider such rubbish at all. Flimsy evidence indeed, around which to construct a theory, but it was a starting point. Richmond had worked with less before. 'Let's have him in again,' he said.

Polly sped through the archway which spanned what had once been the gates of Roydholme Mill, then across the shopping concourse, hoping Ginny wouldn't see her: no time to chat. Red coat and hair flying, wings on her feet. Across to where the lift ascended to the flats above, hoping that Elf – sorry, Elvira – would be, as she sometimes was, home for lunch, and that she'd be in time to catch her. Much rather here than at Steynton Fine Art, which intimidated Polly, for reasons unknown.

The lift hummed to the top floor and opened in the corner by a window, high, high above the town, the blue-carpeted, recently vacuumed corridor stretching before her with polished wood doors opening off it at intervals, all bearing neat name-plates. In an alcove, a bank of flowering pot plants with a picture above them. A hushed, air-conditioned, privileged ambience, a far cry from the mill's original purpose, that world full of deafening machinery, flying dust and fluff and the overpowering smell of greasy wool. Polly paused for a moment to look out of the window. Had the operatives working here, when the place had occupied its true function, ever had time to gaze out over this long perspective of the valley, narrowing between the steeply sloping hills, the river like a slash of silver below, disappearing into the distance? Of course not, how fanciful! Mill owners had not been inclined to encourage idleness or to remind employees of a sweeter world outside by leaving their windows transparent: clear double glazing was part of the reconstruction and transformation that had taken place.

She'd brought wine with her that Leon might have approved of, though not Lachryma Christi, there might be tears enough without that. And handmade chocolates, of a make endorsed by

Ginny – ridiculously expensive, priced at so much *each* – to show good intentions. A pause for thought there: when had she started feeling that necessary? Conscience? Why Elf, when she didn't go bearing gifts to *Ginny*, not all the time? Followed by a wish, too late, that she hadn't done so now.

Elvira. She would try to remember.

No answer to her first, or her second, ring. Damn!

She made her way back to the concourse and went to Ginny's shop. 'Here,' she said, thrusting the wine and the chocolates at her sister. 'Another load of sin on your hips.'

'What have I done to deserve this, you sadist?'

Polly laughed and kissed her cheek. 'Call it a thank you, for having me and Harriet. May I use your phone?'

Elf was at the gallery. 'Come and have some lunch with me,' she said immediately, and when Polly hesitated, added, 'It's from Alessandra's, she always sends enough for an army.'

'In that case . . . be with you in five minutes.'

Alessandra, an Italian mama owning her own restaurant and delicatessen round the corner from the gallery, delivered sandwiches or appetising pasta dishes on request. Weighing fourteen stones herself, she believed Elf needed fattening up, consequently the dishes she sent round inclined heavily towards carbohydrates, butter and cream. Polly's mouth watered. Food had not been a priority recently.

Delicious smells greeted her as she went in via the back premises. The inner door into the shop was firmly closed, lest peasant odours of garlic and onion should waft into the studied elegance of the gallery. There, now that it belonged to Elf, everything, apart from the gilded sign outside, was neutral or a muted grey, not to detract from the works of art: pearly grey paintwork, charcoal carpet, perspex columns topped with sculptures, glass cases containing more, smoke grey walls against which pictures hung in gilded frames. Less of everything, but in better taste, and correspondingly more expensive. Polly wondered who bought it all. The populace of Steynton was not on the whole well heeled, whatever its taste might be. But executives with highly paid jobs in Leeds and Bradford, and sometimes further afield, were seeing the advantages of commuting from Steynton, which was beginning to have a lot to offer besides easily accessible, unspoilt countryside: good schools, fashionable dress shops, London-trained hairdressers . . .

Elf cleared a space on a table otherwise occupied with a newly arrived work of art and some of the packing materials it had been despatched in. It was bronze and tortuous and Polly forbore to ask what it was supposed to be. They ate farfalla with mushrooms and smoked salmon in a rich sauce, and spoke of arrangements for the funeral, about Polly's search for a house, about Harriet's new school, but skirted wider issues.

The food was wonderful. She'd been right about the cream, Polly thought, demolishing most of what there was with gusto, while Elf toyed with the rest. No wonder she was so thin. She was doing her hair differently these days, her well-shaped head shown to advantage by the sleek, pointy short cut, like a boy's. So neat she was, so well put together. Beautiful suit. Italian shoes. Looking not at all as Polly felt by comparison, dressed from somebody's ragbag.

There was a difference in Elf herself, too. She was less prickly and defensive nowadays, but around her there was still tension, as if she were holding her breath.

As a child, Elf had been regarded as a handful: impish and mischievous, nothing more really, though Freya had chosen to see it as badness. Difficult, yes – smiles and dimples when people laughed at her antics, kicking her heels and screaming when they found her too much – but never bad. Rightly regarded as a pesky little sister when she wanted to tag along, but great fun when she wasn't bent on being a demon . . . Until she reached her teens. When, with devastating suddenness, she'd changed, become withdrawn and edgy. Finally, she had seemed to reach some sort of compromise with herself, but it was still a case of allowing you to get so far, and no further.

Now she looked as assured and successful as she undoubtedly was, attested to by this gallery, previously owned by Lance Armitage, for whom she'd worked. Where had the money come from to buy it? The question had been a topic of unending family speculation, with Armitage as a possible lover well to the forefront of the scenario.

Polly wondered how any of them could possibly have believed that, realised they probably didn't, had guessed the truth, that she was the only one naïve enough not to have realised it was quite on the cards that it was Philip who'd stumped up. Belatedly honouring his responsibilities, perhaps. She could hear Ginny: *'Oh, Poll, haven't you always known? But no, you wouldn't, you never stop long enough to listen, do you? You never notice anything.'* Admit it, it was often true. Even Tom Richmond had figured it out: Philip *Graham* Denshaw, Elvira Graham. But why the secrecy? Philip had been a free man shortly after Elf was born, when his wife had died. Polly could make a guess at that one, anyway, and the answer wasn't one she cared for. She was wondering whether she dared ask Elf directly – no, she dared not, not yet, anyway! – when she was asked which she'd prefer of the dozen or so herb teas on offer, and the moment was lost.

While they sipped the blackberry and nettle brew – not half bad, really – Polly examined an unframed picture leaning against the wall. Disturbing, not something she'd want to live with, but she looked at it for a long time. It hadn't been here on the last occasion she'd visited. 'It's Peter's, isn't it?' she hazarded.

Elf answered with barely concealed amusement, topping up her cup. 'Don't tell him, he'll never know, he's hardly likely to come here and see it.'

'I didn't know he was still painting.'

'It might be one of his old ones – I found it in the basement with some others when I took the gallery over. It's not the sort of thing Lance Armitage usually bought – they probably didn't sell straight off, and he thought he'd made a mistake buying them.'

'It's time you made it up with Peter,' Polly said abruptly, wrongfooting herself right at the start of what she'd really come to say.

'I expect it is. But it takes two.'

Spiky as ever. But, since her head was still intact on her shoulders, Polly further grasped the opportunity. 'Elf – I've always wondered – you used to be such friends. What was it that happened between you two, and Philip?'

Elf shrugged, her face closed. 'If we could leave Philip out of this.'

But Philip couldn't be left out. There it was, the three of them, in that broken, triangular relationship that had never been explained. And there was Elf, maddening, infuriating as ever. Subject closed.

OK. If that was how she wanted it. But for the time being only, Polly vowed.

'Philip's partly why I came,' she said, letting it go. 'I wish you'd been there last night. He's not well . . .' Explanations followed, tinged with guilt because they'd all owed a debt to Philip they'd never recognised. Or had they? *'Gaining a family'* – that was what he'd said, hadn't he? Fine sentiments indeed! Polly was beginning to find them a little hard to stomach in view of what she now suspected – knew, really – to be true.

'So,' she finished, 'I'm afraid my mother left us nothing. But we're all to share what Philip has to leave . . . the four of us.' There was a silence. 'I – hope you weren't expecting more.'

Someone tried the shop door, went away when they found it locked. Elf said drily, 'I'd have been a fool to have expected anything from Freya! As for Philip . . .' She shrugged.

'Elvira,' Polly said. 'Stop it. Life's too short for all this. A few days ago my mother died and I shall be sorry for ever for things I said and didn't say. Philip's an old man and not too well. Don't let him die without patching up your quarrel with him.'

For a moment, she thought she'd got through to Elf, but no. 'Did I say there was a quarrel? Nothing so vulgar!'

'What would you call it, then? A slight disagreement that's lasted all these years?'

'Don't be sarcastic, Poll!' But Elf looked sideways at Polly, as if wondering how much further to go, whether she hadn't already said too much. Then she took a deep breath, and plunged. 'Oh, what's it matter, now? He – old Holier-than-thou Philip – discovered Peter painting me in the nude. Shock, horror! You can imagine how he put the worst possible construction on it.'

'Oh.' Polly could see that you might, coming across something like that, especially if it was your *daughter*! If you were Philip, who'd always been, as Elf said, a bit sanctimonious. She was rather taken aback herself. 'In the *nude*? And how old were you?'

'Nearly twelve.' Elf's chin went up.

Eleven years old. God. Still a child. But old enough for Elf, always a precocious child, to know the danger. And young enough to be frightened of the consequences. 'And you told no one?' Not Freya, of course, she'd never have told Freya. Nor Dot, whose reaction might have been uncertain, to say the least. Poor little Elf, her almost-sister, trying to sort that one out, alone! 'Why didn't you tell Ginny, or even me?' she asked gently.

'You were in the middle of your mock As, and Ginny was too busy with wedding plans. Anyway, there wasn't anything anyone could do. It was all over and done with – and there'd been nothing wrong in it to begin with. He only wanted to paint me, for heaven's sake!'

'The sensible thing would have been for him to have asked permission first.' But the sensible thing would never have occurred to Peter. 'What did he do about it?'

'Oh, you know Peter, he blamed himself. Black's black and white's white with him. Examining his conscience and asking himself if his intentions had really been so innocent. Sheltering under the Church ever since in case he might be tempted again.'

'You mean he just left it like that? And committed his whole life to an act of penance?' It sounded bizarre, it *was* bizarre, unless applied to Peter. You could never judge him by ordinary standards, though perhaps it was time somebody did. It had been cruel to leave the situation like that, to leave a child to face the consequences, alone. And Philip, the old hyprocrite, was worse. Polly felt slightly dazed with everything that was being flung at her. Nasty things were emerging from the woodshed, with a vengeance. Whatever had happened to honesty in the Denshaw family? Philip, in collusion with Freya, hiding the truth of their father's will. Freya, keeping hidden what had happened the night little Beth was killed . . .

'Listen,' she said urgently. 'There's something else you should know, something we all have to talk about.'

She told Elf everything she could remember about the recent happenings, beginning with Freya's fears about what the Austwick woman might have found out, and ending with all that had transpired at the police station. 'I think Peter's in trouble. But he's got to help himself – and I can't see him doing that,' she added hopelessly. 'He's so – oh, I don't know . . . What's *wrong* with him, Elf, tell me? You always knew him better than either Ginny, or I.'

156

'No I didn't, I never have. But I *do* know he didn't kill that child, or that woman. Not Peter.' Her face suddenly looked small and shrunken.

She loves him – not in the way Ginny and I love him, she's in love with him, but she *does* think he did it, in spite of what she says – perhaps she *knows*, thought Polly with a return of that terrible premonition of impending doom which had hung over her ever since hearing about her mother's intention to publish that wretched book.

'He couldn't have done it! I *know* he couldn't because –' She stopped, almost visibly swallowing what she'd been going to say. She was very white under the clever make-up. She put a hand to her mouth; the ring she wore was too big, and slid around on her finger. The stone, which had all this time lain innermost, towards her palm, now slipped around to the front. A black opal, a pointed oval shape surrounded by diamonds, that Freya had worn constantly in Polly's youth, but which Polly hadn't seen for years. Like so much more of her mother's jewellery, it had disappeared without explanation.

'Elf, where did you get that ring?'

14

Charlie Rawnsley walked down the hill to buy fish for his dinner from the stall in the covered market where you could always be sure it was fresh from Grimsby, straight out of the North Sea. He fancied a couple of herrings, cooked the way Connie used to do them, covered in rolled oats and fried, served with a mustard sauce, but he didn't know whether Lilian would like herrings, or the smell of their cooking. A lot of people didn't. Better get a nice piece of thick-end cod.

Walking was hazardous, despite the ribbed soles of his rubber boots, snow turned to slush over a layer of ice. He watched his step, not wanting to end up as a geriatric disaster in the hospital, where Lilian Bentley had nearly found herself yesterday. She'd been shovelling snow from her front path (after he'd offered to do it for her, mind!) and she'd slipped and sprained her wrist. Lucky it was nothing worse. Broken hips weren't to be lightly regarded when you were over sixty.

But Lilian was like him – couldn't abide being beholden to anybody. He thought himself highly honoured that she'd agreed to let him cook and share dinner. 'Just this once, think on! I'll be right as a bobbin tomorrow.'

He thought she was overestimating her rate of recovery, but he was looking forward to the shared meal, and the company. She was a lively, cheerful woman with a sensible outlook on life and a variety of interests, a retired bookshop assistant who'd only recently bought the house next door. She'd recommended him several new authors he hadn't heard of before.

He bought his fish and was debating whether or not to call for a pint before making the journey back up the hill, when he heard himself hailed by Tom Richmond. 'Hey, Charlie!' They met felicitously by the door of the Crown and Anchor. 'Spotted you just as I was going to my car,' Richmond said. 'Time for a drink?'

They settled for a sandwich as well, cheese spiced with pickle. Charlie had his dinner in the evening, now. A heavy meal midday put him to sleep. He didn't mind that in the evening, dozing in front of the telly, since there was never anything but what he considered rubbish to watch, anyway. He put his carrier bag on the floor beside him, stretched his legs to the fire, took a long pull at his beer and sat back. 'Well then, how's it going?'

The pub's enormous fat tabby appeared from nowhere. Waved its tail superciliously. Considered the options and leaped on to the cushioned chair opposite, regarding them with disconcertingly unmoving yellow slitted eyes while Richmond gave the old man a succinct progress report of the Austwick murder. 'I'm probably out of line, telling you all this, so keep it under your hat, Charlie, eh?'

'You don't need to ask!' Charlie was offended. 'It'll go no further.'

'All right, all right, sorry. I should've known.'

Charlie was mollified. Retired or not, he was still a policeman, wasn't he? He could be trusted to keep his mouth shut, to give advice when it was asked, as he was pleased to say it often was, to trawl his memory, which went back before computers were thought of, for faces and facts, but otherwise keep mum.

'I wanted to see you, anyway, Charlie.' Richmond pushed his empty plate away and looked at the old man consideringly. 'What can you tell me about the Reverend Peter – off the record?'

Charlie's eyebrows shot up. Hadn't been expecting that. 'You shouldn't be asking me, I'm prejudiced.'

'Try not to be. As a good copper, Charlie, what did you really think of him? When you met him, through Isobel.'

Charlie thought. The cat jumped from the chair and decided to come nearer and take advantage of the fire, while keeping its impassive stare fixed on them.

'I wish I could give you an answer straight out, Tom, but it's not as simple as that. I never had much to do with him, you know – even when he was married to Isobel. I sometimes go to his services and listen to him preach.'

'What?'

'I sit at the back. Mebbe he doesn't know I'm there, but mebbe he does.'

'Intimidation, Charlie? Harassment?'

'I wouldn't call it either. Started out . . . I wanted to know what made him tick, if he could've done it. And then you know, you begin to think . . . Well, you and me, Tom, we both know anybody can be a murderer, given the right circumstances, whatever they might say. And being a copper, you get a gut feeling. Something in your water tells you somebody's either guilty or not, never mind evidence.' It wasn't a popular view, but one he knew Richmond agreed with.

'So what's your gut feeling about Peter Denshaw?'

Charlie sank another couple of inches of his beer, wondering whether to admit it, even to himself. 'I dunno . . . Lately . . . I don't think he did it,' he said at last.

Richmond let out his breath. 'It's not beginning to look that way, Charlie.'

'Well, I know nowt about that. He might've been involved, he might know who did it, though I wouldn't be too sure about that, either. I'm not saying he isn't capable of wanting anybody dead – what I am saying is, he wouldn't do it that way. Too bloody soft, for one thing. But he's slippy. If he *did* do it, he'd likely arrange it so's he wasn't there to see it happen.'

Neither man spoke for a while. At last, Richmond said, 'I'm down to interview him tomorrow. Jacks has got clearance from on high.'

'You mean they're going to reopen the case, officially?'

'Wouldn't go so far, yet, but they've presumably looked at my track record and decided I can be trusted to stick to the rule books and not pursue vendettas. Might not be the wisest decision they've ever made, but with all that's happened on the Austwick murder it's beginning to look like too much of a stretch to believe the two aren't connected.'

'Well, I'm buggered!' Charlie declared, shocking two overdressed women who had come in and found a seat at the next table. But Charlie didn't notice. He was looking as gleeful as if he himself had been asked to return and take charge of Steynton nick. The two men sat grinning at each other like fools.

One of the women bent down and stroked the tabby, cooing over it, even went so far as to attempt to lift it on to her knee. Outraged at the liberty, it yowled and slipped from her grasp, pointedly turned its back on them and immediately began weaving itself round Charlie's legs.

Charlie was too chuffed with Richmond's news to notice what was going on, until the cat, with lightning dexterity and speed, appropriated what was in his carrier bag and ran off with it in its jaws, leaving nothing but the bag itself behind. He shouted and jumped up and chased after the animal but it was on home ground and had disappeared down a passage before he reached the door.

'Dang and blast!' he said, returning, his language severely moderated in deference to the two cat-loving ladies, who were trying not very successfully to hide their laughter, and looking very much as though they'd like to applaud the animal's feat. 'That there fish cost me three pounds, eighty pee! I'd best be off and see if I can't get some more – Sid's usually sold out and shut his stall up by half-past one.'

The incident effectively put an end to further conversation and the two men parted outside the pub, Richmond still smiling and thanking Charlie for his advice.

'Nay, don't thank me, lad. It's only an opinion, and I could be wrong.'

The fish man was still there, the cod wasn't. Only rock salmon left, and no wonder. Catfish, we used to call it, and that's all it's good for, thought Charlie, calling down maledictions on the thieving tabby and opting for a couple of pork chops from the butcher.

Trudging home again, he wondered what had made him say that to Tom about Peter Denshaw. Not that it was likely to get the Reverend off the hook if he'd done this other murder, and not that Charlie's opinion mattered one way or t'other. It was just that admitting it like that, bringing it out into the open, he'd surprised himself. Fair bowled himself over, in fact, never having thought he could bring himself to speak out in Denshaw's defence. But having done so, a grudge he'd nursed for ten years had suddenly ceased to hurt quite so much, like a boil that had been lanced. Leaving, in the space occupied for so long by pain and dark thoughts of revenge, that other question which had also tormented him: 'If not Peter Denshaw, then who?'

The trouble with Eddie was that you could never be sure what he was going to do. He was so unpredictable, there was no telling what he might already have done, using the only language he understood: violence. Handy with his fists, think afterwards, that was Eddie, thought Dot with unconscious irony. Strong in the back and weak in the head. And such a fool! Just think – a few dog hairs might be his undoing. If Eddie had a weak spot, it was for his dogs. He was as sentimental over them as he was about children, and that was saying something. He nearly cried every time he thought about that little girl lying for so long under the park bandstand, with her head on a pillow. He was very happy that there was another little girl about the place now.

Harriet was a great favourite with him, though he told Dot he thought the name, Harriet, was awful, old-fashioned and ugly. He'd had a terrible great-aunt called Harriet who'd smelled of cat-pee and humbugs and took her teeth out to eat. He couldn't think of this little darlin' as Harriet without remembering the old witch and so he called her Missy, the name of a favourite dog who'd won him more money than any of his others put together.

What was she going to do about him? Dot made herself some more tea in the dark little kitchen of her cottage and sucked on her cigarette, endlessly turning over all the possibilities. Nothing seemed right at the moment, but it'd come to her, she'd sort him out. She always had done, in spite of everything.

They were two of a kind, she and Eddie, with a violence in their relationship that stimulated it, kept it going. Each had a legacy from the same sort of background – a back-street, extended family, hand to mouth, day to day, where was next week's rent coming from? existence. Which was why they both wanted security, would do anything to get it and keep it. What now – back to London? But Dot had all too recently seen, when meeting her family at the funeral of the aged uncle, that most of them were now living like prisoners in tower blocks, terrified out of their lives of teenage hooligans, and half the population around them black as your hat. Or, having escaped that, they were prisoners of a different kind, living in a tight-arsed sort of way, scratching and saving, a mortgage and a semi in outer London suburbia. She'd shuddered and sworn that was never for her.

No, London wasn't the city she'd known as a pre-war and wartime child and remembered with nostalgia: the street games, the camaraderie of the Underground in the Blitz, and later, her first job picking up pins in a couture house. It was all changed.

Yet round and round in her head the problem went: what were they going to do now, she and Eddie? Together, however it turned out, she knew that, anything else was unthinkable. They'd started and so they would finish, locked together in mutual dependency, as she and Freya had been. Eddie – coming into her life when she was forty-three and he only just thirty. Eddie, a mistake in many ways, but necessary to her, for all their problems. He wanted to stay around these parts, but she thought they'd been here too long, that he'd become overfond of the easy life – a nice, cushy little number, he thought this job was, one that left him plenty of time for his own interests. Not idle, Eddie, he was never that. Always active, on the go, but doing only what suited him. Staying with her because of the promise, the carrot on the end of the stick. She'd no illusions about it.

But now, where had the carrot gone? Turned out to be nothing except the frocks and shoes, the New Look suits, the furs (which nobody wanted nowadays), the hats and handbags that Freya had left to her. Stored up from the days when she'd modelled for the famous couture houses: model gowns acquired as favours or at cost, worn once or twice, then swaddled away with a canny foreknowledge of their future worth . . . Most of them now likely to fetch a respectable bob or two if auctioned, though not Princess Di, or even Spice Girl prices, not by any means. And certainly not enough to retire on – nor anywhere near as much as she'd calculated, almost an insult, really, after giving a lifetime's service. A pittance, she thought, working herself up to a fury, forgetting that it had swung both ways. Angry at Freya, who'd always told her everything, for keeping the true state of her finances to herself. But cheering up when she remembered that it was more than the rest of them – Freya's own family – were likely to get. And don't forget the jewellery, or some of it.

Once upon a time, Freya had admired the picture of herself wearing jewels, then through necessity taught herself not to, losing interest as one by one they had to be disposed of, sold or pawned. Or were lost, disappeared, never missed . . . the ruby ring, the tourmaline one, the Victorian garnet pin, set in marcasite, the pearls – and that sapphire pendant . . . Dot had lost count, except for their value. Where Freya had admired them as decorative adjuncts to her person, Dot had coveted them, among other reasons, as future insurance.

Whiteley and Horsfall had promised to keep Richmond informed of any suitable accommodation which became available, and with Saturday morning's post came details of one of the flats at Roydholme, as the converted mill by the river was now to be called – Roydholme, without the Mill. Early viewing for this desirable, much sought after property was strongly advised.

Pity about that, it sounded interesting, he thought, swearing roundly as he banged into the kitchen table yet again while preparing his breakfast; the smallness of this place was getting seriously on his nerves and his landlady driving him nuts. Breakfast was the only time she wasn't likely to pop her head round the door, if it wasn't locked, or shout through the letter box if it was, that it was only her, come to do the hoovering, or the brasses, leave that washing up, I'll do it, Mr Richmond, and did you hear about so and so and how are you getting on finding out who's done that there murder?

Not so well that he could afford to take time off to go viewing property, Richmond thought sardonically now, angling his legs under the table and pouring himself some coffee. He read on: the owners were not in residence at the moment but a neighbour would be pleased to show prospective buyers around by appointment, weekends and evenings. Ring E. Graham, Steynton Fine Art.

It was a moment or two before he made the connection and saw a way he could in fact fit in a viewing of the flat, after all. He would check, but he was certain that E. Graham must be Elvira Graham, since he knew she lived in one of the flats at Roydholme. She had to be seen about the appointment she'd had with the murdered woman, and Richmond had no doubt he could arrange to conduct the interview himself, as he'd always intended.

When he got to the office, he rang the number given. She had a clear voice and a decisive way of speaking. 'Tomorrow morning? I have a lunch date, but I can give you half an hour,' she told him, quickly setting her own limits to the time of his visit. He agreed and gave her his name, omitting his official status.

Later that morning he sat in Jackson Farr's office, listening with him to the recording of Eddie Nagle's second interview, which Jacks had thought it circumspect to conduct personally.

The bastard didn't sound quite so cocksure this time, despite the fact that nothing had been discovered from a forensic examination of his clothes, that his car had been found to be clean as a whistle – unnaturally so, with not even the slightest trace of the mucky slush that was being tramped inside everyone else's car. Not even the normal, expected traces of himself and his wife. Perhaps he'd been less cocky due to the fact of being interviewed by the detective superintendent himself. Perhaps he was just intimidated by that impressive bulk.

After further questioning about the night of Wyn Austwick's murder, which had got him no further, Jacks was returning to the events of 5th January, ten years previously. 'I'd like you to listen to this,' he told Nagle, switching on a tape.

Into the office came the sound of Nagle scraping his chair back, his cough as he listened to the statement he'd recorded at that time. *'I last saw Beth, just before twelve, when she was going upstairs for her music lesson with Mr Denshaw before the midday meal. My wife had made sandwiches for the family but we always have fish and chips Saturday dinner time, and I'd been down into Steynton to fetch them. I knew Beth would rather have had chips, so when I saw her I asked if she'd like one, and I opened the parcel and let her have a few. She was a lovely little girl and I was very fond of her. I never saw her again. I had a sleep after we'd eaten, and didn't wake up until my wife woke me and told me Beth was missing. I helped to look for her, took the car out and drove it round for several hours, but nobody ever saw her again.'*

'I'm giving you the chance to amend that statement if you want to, Mr Nagle,' Jacks said after the tape was switched off and the new one substituted.

'Why should I? Case is closed, far as I know.'

'We've reason now to think Mrs Austwick's murder may throw further light on it.'

A massive creak that could only have been Jacks, shifting his weight, nearly obliterated Nagle's next few words.

'That's it, is it? You're trying to pin that on me, an' all! You better fink again, mate! Her mum confessed, didn't she? Mind, I can understand how you want to get somebody else for it, him being her dad an' all.' He paused. 'Richmond, I mean.' There was an unsubtle warning there of trouble ahead, of allegations of conflict of interest coming clearly across from the recording. Then the voice changed, became maudlin. 'How can you fink that, Mr Farr? I wouldn't've harmed a hair of that child's head! She was a little sweetheart.' He blew his nose loudly.

Richmond stood up abruptly, shoving his hands into his pockets, walked the length of the room and back. Times like this he wished he hadn't given up smoking. Or hadn't taken a vow never to use violence against a suspect. Christ!

Jacks's hand hovered over the machine, ready to switch off. He flicked a glance at Richmond but was apparently reassured enough to let it carry on playing. 'Leave it out, Eddie,' he was saying. 'CI Richmond's dealing with the murder of Wyn Austwick.' Silence for a moment, then: 'How long have you worked at Low Rigg?'

'Since I married Dot. 1977.'

No hesitation there. His memory had improved since Richmond had asked him that question. 'That was the date you – er – left the Marines, I see,' Jacks said. 'Still a young man! I'd have thought you'd have wanted something to stretch you, use your intelligence a bit more, like. Looking after an old woman's car, piddling around the house, not much job satisfaction there. Must've paid well to compensate.'

'Don't know about that. Like I told Richmond, I've another source of income.'

'Oh right, yes, I'd forgot, you must be rolling in it, part-time job at the health club, an' all! Unless you get a lot of winnings on the bow-wows.'

'I do all right. I'm not what you'd call greedy.'

Jacks let the silence go on. Sounds of Nagle fidgeting, blowing his nose again.

'Why did Mrs Denshaw keep you on, Eddie?' Jacks asked at last. 'We have it on good authority that you and she didn't get on all that well together.'

166

'She had to have a man around the house. Who told you we didn't get on?'

It had, in fact, been Polly, spoken to by Richmond himself over the telephone. Her voice cool at first, then warming as the conversation proceeded, its natural lilt returning. She wasn't a person, Richmond thought, who could stay angry for long, though she hadn't been entirely pleased with him when they'd last parted company. People rarely were when they were caught at a disadvantage, but he'd had no choice, had felt constrained to treat her as he would any other witness. Hadn't wanted to leave it like that, though. Which was one of the reasons he'd rung, with a question which he knew couldn't have a ready answer, which he could have made a stab at answering, anyway. But Polly hadn't needed long to think.

'I used to wonder myself why she tolerated him, because she clearly loathed him and didn't care how obvious it was. Could only have been that she suffered him on account of Dot,' she'd said, which had been how Richmond had figured it until his reading of that incriminating paper. 'Otherwise he'd have been out, long since. I think she knew that if she tried to get rid of him, Dot would go, too. Dot's very fond of Eddie, in spite of –' She'd stopped herself, then added quickly, 'in spite of him being such a dead loss.' Which wasn't what she'd been going to say in the first place, he was sure. But you could never be one hundred per cent certain over the telephone, when you couldn't see the face of the person you were speaking to, it was why he didn't like using it unless he had to.

'Somebody took Beth away from Low Rigg that day,' Jacks was reminding Nagle on the tape as it whirred on. 'If not the person that killed her. Somebody put her under that bandstand. All right, it was eventually assumed it was her mother who'd come and picked her up. But without anybody seeing her? Without her saying a word to anybody? You know what? I find that hard to believe.'

'Please yourself what you believe.'

'I'll repeat, somebody took her away. There's a difference,' Jacks went on, 'between committing murder and being an accessory after the fact, but you don't need me to tell you even that's a very serious matter. Enough to put anybody who's convicted of it away for a very long time.'

'I answered all these questions once before. You haven't got no right to go harping on what's over and done wiv.'

'We've every right, lad, if we think it has a bearing on what happened to Mrs Austwick, and if we think you know a hell of a lot more than you're letting on about both murders. Which we do. Make no mistake about that.'

'You're wasting your time! You know I didn't kill Wyn, I couldn't of. Not when I was playing darts wiv a pub full of blokes – including one of your lot.'

'That where you got that cut lip? Punch-up after losing, was it? You want to watch it, Eddie. Seeems to me you're too often in the wars for your own good.'

'I walked into a door.'

Jacks had kept him as long as he could, but Nagle knew when he'd got his teeth into a good alibi and clung on like that pit bull terrier he'd once owned.

It was going to be a long haul. But Richmond was in no doubt now as to what he believed: that Nagle had been guaranteed employment for getting rid of Beth's body; Austwick had found this out and was holding it over Freya, who believed the killer to be Peter. This would scarcely have bothered Nagle – what *would* have bothered him, though, was Austwick holding incriminating evidence of the part he'd played. So much so that he'd disposed of her. Or maybe the person who had killed Beth – whether this was Denshaw or not – had made it worth his while to do so.

How he'd done this when he was playing darts under the eye of a pub full of people, including a policeman, was still a mystery.

'I have the manager from the NatWest on the line, returning your call, sir,' Richmond was informed by the switchboard operator.

'Put him through, please.'

'Cranwell here, Chief Inspector,' said a clipped, guarded voice. 'I believe I'm at liberty now to divulge the information you requested about Mrs Austwick's affairs.'

And not before time, Richmond thought. These people had no sense of urgency in these matters. Nor was it in the nature of banks to appear too ready with information, never mind that it was at their fingertips nowadays, easily available at the tap of a few computer keys. It would have looked too easy, as if anyone could become a bank manager. 'Go ahead, Mr Cranwell, I'm listening.'

'Ahem, well . . . I hope you have time to spare.'

Ten minutes later, Richmond put the phone down, bemused but much enlightened, and within a very short time, he was back in Jacks's office.

'So she did leave a will, after all,' Jacks interrupted, grinning, when Richmond had scarcely begun. 'That little scrote Trev's not going to come in for it after all.'

'Not a bean. She made the bank executors to her will and left everything to her brother, presumably the bloke on the motorbike in that photo. Not that he's likely to benefit, poor sod. He was involved in a near-fatal motor accident about twenty years ago, leaving him paralysed and with permanent brain damage.'

Jacks hunched his shoulders, tut-tutted. 'No use telling 'em, these young lads. But if they knew what a motorbike accident can do –'

'It wasn't a motorbike accident. He was in the car she was driving. She was drunk and piled it into a lorry.'

'Bloody hell! That's some guilt to be carrying around for twenty years.'

'Isn't it? Those banker's orders represent what she's been paying to a small private nursing home ever since, run by a woman called Enid Brentdale, place near Leicester. She's left enough to keep on paying the bills for as long as he's likely to last – which they don't anticipate will be long. Anything left goes to Mencap.'

'Hope they're not counting on there being much left then. These nursing homes don't come cheap.'

'I suppose that's why she wasn't so particular where she got her money from. Funny, you know, I'd never have associated her with having a sense of duty, or a conscience . . . but there you are. She's kept him in that nursing home for nigh on twenty years, and spent weeks at a time with him even though he didn't really know who she was. I've spoken to them and it seems she was due to go down there last week, but had to cancel when she had to go into hospital herself.'

'That's why she went to all that rigmarole about Spain? Didn't want anybody to know where she was really going?'

'Search me. But I suppose it could make sense in a way. If she'd felt so guilty about her brother she'd kept him secret all these years, it could have become a way of life.'

15

For once, and for no apparent reason, Richmond slept dreamlessly, and woke to a thick yellow sky, ready to release more snow on to the world below. Only this time it looked as if it meant business, not just an inch or two falling overnight, later to melt into slush and then freeze, turning roads and pavements into skating rinks. He made himself some bracing coffee. For all he'd slept without dreams, he didn't feel rested.

He drove straight to Roydholme. Its riverside situation had very likely saved the old mill from the fate of many of its satanic companions, he thought when he arrived, though its conversion had apparently gone through without opposition. Wholesale clearance of derelict properties, and some not so derelict, had taken place around it and now it stood in solitary splendour just below the road bridge, a car-park alongside, and young, hopeful trees planted where trees hadn't stood for many a long day. A large, foursquare building, five storeys with a twin-gabled roof and rows of long windows set at regular intervals on all its four sides. Nothing beautiful about it except a certain honesty of purpose, now gone by the board in pursuit of expediency, but what of that? Finding a present-day use for it had to be better than letting it rot.

The whole of the ground floor of the original woollen-spinning mill, plus its various outbuildings, had been converted by a firm of developers into a shopping area, designed in a carefully haphazard manner, with units of various shapes and sizes dealing in a variety of products. He walked down the middle of the concourse, past the craft boutiques, the flower and patisserie shops ranged either side, a couple of upmarket cafés from whence issued a smell of good coffee, a hairdresser and, not least, Ginny Katz's knitwear shop. Though slowly gaining popularity as its reputation spread, the enterprise was still uncertain, financially shaky, Richmond had heard, mostly owing to the high rents being charged for the units, some of which were still empty. Shopkeepers were reluctant to commit themselves, cautious until they saw how things were going. If the price of the flat quoted in the details sent to him by Whiteley and Horsfall reflected other prices in the development, they had his sympathy.

There was a lift, but he chose to use the stairs to the top floor where Elvira Graham lived. He almost wished he hadn't. The extent of his puffing, by the time he reached there, was making him seriously reconsider how fit he was. The stairwell emerged into a central corridor, carpeted in a serviceable dark blue, the walls painted in a bland, neutral stone colour, with nothing to distinguish it from a modern hotel save the wood-stained, mock-Victorian front doors to each flat. He'd just about got his breath back by the time he was ringing the bell on the door marked 'E. Graham'.

She held it open after he'd introduced himself. 'Come in while I get the key.'

The winter sunlight, filtered through the snow-filled sky, cast an eerie light through the three big windows of the spacious apartment on to a spread of thick, soft carpet, on to smoothly plastered walls, tinted a pale honey colour. Her furniture was modern: comfortable chairs and sofas, a pair of low tables, dining furniture at one end, and little else apart from one or two judiciously placed pieces of metal which he took to be sculptures. One wall was dominated by a huge abstract painting in hot, vibrant acrylics slashed with black, which Richmond wasn't competent to judge, except that it seemed to him to be full of energy and not a little anger.

'The Armitages' flat is exactly like this, most of them are,' she said, noticing his appraising glance as she came back with the key. 'They've decided to live in Spain permanently now they've retired, which is why they're selling. They're over there now. Mrs A thinks it's better for her asthma,' she added, as though she might know better, inserting the key into a door two flats along from her own, right at the end of the corridor.

She was small and dark and he thought she might be clever. The slightly backward tilt of her head that some short people were inclined to adopt lifted her decisive little chin, giving her an air of alertness, or maybe watchfulness would be a more appropriate word. Nothing given away by those intelligent, almond-shaped eyes. She was dressed in a smart woollen suit in

172

winter-white, chunky gold costume jewellery and black tights. Without comment, she showed him what the flat had to offer: a good-sized bedroom, a smaller one, a bathroom and an efficiently equipped kitchen, a living-room with a view along the valley.

'It looks smaller than your flat,' he commented.

'It's not, really. Just this poncy clutter makes it seem so.' A wave of the hand dismissed the obviously expensive furniture, the thick Chinese carpets, silk cushions, pictures and the plethora of highly decorated porcelain and glass objects with a casual wave of the hand. 'Worth pinching, though. That's why Lance Armitage is paranoiac about not leaving keys all over the place. I used to work for him, so he knows he can trust me. Have you seen all you want to see?'

'Yes, thanks. It's a very attractive proposition. I'll think about it,' Richmond said, though knowing he'd already made up his mind that, stripped of its shiny wallpaper and fancy carpets, the place would suit him to a T. The price was a bit of a facer, but he was earning a respectable salary, he'd done a lot of DIY on the small house he'd had in Bristol and sold at a profit. The housing market round here wasn't exactly booming; maybe he'd be able to do a bit of horse trading with Mr Whiteley. He reflected in passing that Steynton Fine Art must be doing well for Elvira Graham to be able to afford such prices.

'Thank you for showing me around. But before I go, I'd like to have a word with you about something else.' He produced his warrant card but she didn't look at it.

'I know who you are. Polly told me you were back.'

'Then you obviously know why I want to talk to you.'

'Not here,' she said abruptly. 'My place.'

He remarked, when they were sitting opposite each other on matching blond leather sofas, 'You're not what I expected.'

'What did you think I'd be like? Someone twee and twittery? People do, you know, once they hear that name, which I hate, by the way, and don't answer to now. They called me Elf when I was little, and that's so bloody patronising to a grown woman! Though I don't suppose they mean it, it's just habit – with Ginny and Polly, anyway. Freya meant it, though. She hated my guts.' She paused, evidently to give him the opportunity to ask why.

'Why was that?' he obliged.

173

'She couldn't do anything with me when I was little. Frankly, I was a bit of a problem. Plus, she didn't like children very much, even her own. Except Peter, of course, because he danced to her tune.' She paused. 'You know I was a poor, penniless little orphan, brought up as part of the family?'

'Tell me about it.'

'My parents died when I was a baby and I was brought to live with the Denshaws. Dot Nagle was sent for to come and help out at that time, which I gather was a condition of my being taken in. As I said, bringing up children was never Freya's scene. Just as well, seeing I was such a horror.'

She smiled mockingly, but he had a sense of something not quite right. The heavy irony was overdone, and didn't sit right on her. She was talking too much, telling him more than she needed to, an information spiel so pat he guessed it was automatic; given so many times she scarcely heard it. It was basically the same explanation Polly Winslow had given him and Elvira had obviously decided to stick to it. How much had been omitted, or embroidered upon?

'And when I was growing up,' she was continuing, watching him covertly, 'she thought I was going to take her precious Peter from her.'

'But you didn't.' He was developing an unpleasant hunch, not sure yet whether it was viable, but one he'd pursue. Time and experience had taught him that women *could* hate their own children. However unnatural or inconceivable it was to most people, it happened, especially if their birth was an embarrassment or an inconvenience. Did it apply here? It could be, of course, that he was barking up the wrong tree, but if he was right, it would explain why Freya Denshaw had been alarmed at any developing intimacy between Peter and Elf.

'No, I didn't.' She was suddenly serious, dropping the flippant manner, leaning forward, clasping her hands around her knees. The thought of Isobel, who had eventually taken him away from Freya, lay between them, unspoken. She said abruptly, 'I won't mention this again, but I just want to say I'm sorry about what happened to Beth. She was a super kid.'

'Thank you.' He wanted to believe she meant it and thought she did, sensing something deeper than a conventional expression of sympathy. He was somewhat disposed to like this stiff, aggressive, abrupt and opinionated little person. 'You were the last one to see her,' he said, taking his cue from her own directness.

'Yes. I helped her build that snowman.'

'Tell me what happened that day?' he asked gently.

'Don't you *know*?'

'Yes, of course, but I'd like to hear it in your own words, as you recall it now.'

'We-ell . . . then.'

She repeated the statement she'd made at that time, recalling it almost word for word, how she and Beth had made the snowman together, how she'd gone indoors to find the finishing touches. How, when she came out again, she saw Peter turning in at the gates and found that Beth had gone.

'It was terrible,' she said. 'We were running about like head-less chickens. I'd been gone longer than I thought because I couldn't find a hat for the snowman. I thought I knew where there was an old bowler we used to use for dressing up but I couldn't find it. I wasn't gone longer than fifteen or twenty minutes at most, though. It just wasn't *possible* she'd disappeared into thin air. For a while we thought she was hiding. We all used to do that when we were kids, Low Rigg isn't short of hidey-holes, whatever else. We searched every nook and cranny. Which took some time, as you'll imagine. Then Eddie Nagle took his car and the dogs and drove out looking for her. We thought she might have wandered off, set out to meet her mum. She'd had a watch for Christmas and it was still a novelty. She was keeping tabs on the time, looking at it every few minutes.'

Her first watch, his own present to her. An inexpensive, fun thing he hadn't expected to last five minutes, but despite fre-quent over-windings and adjustments, it had still been working by January.

'If she'd set off down the road to meet her mother, Peter Denshaw would have met her on his way up.'

'We thought maybe she'd got lost . . . or slipped and fallen into a snowdrift.'

The snow had been thick that year. A terrible winter it had been, starting with a white Christmas, snow blanketing the hills, blocking the roads over the tops, blowing into ten-foot high drifts in places, with freezing temperatures and no signs of a thaw for weeks. They had wakened that morning to a fresh, heavy fall, virgin snow under a brilliant, cloudless sky. The world had looked so innocent.

'When did you call the police?'

'After an hour or so, when we'd exhausted everything else, when Eddie came back without having found any trace of her. He'd driven right down beyond the main road but there was no sign.'

And that was when he knew how it had been done. So easy. Everyone panicking, the big old house being searched from attic to cellar, then Nagle taking her, already dead and stuffed into the boot of his car, down to East Park. Using his dogs as an excuse for being in the park, letting them loose to frolic in the snow while he put her body under the bandstand, covering his tracks. Tracks which had been covered in any case by later snow. So, had Nagle killed Beth himself or had Peter Denshaw, as Dan Brearley had at first believed, arrived earlier than he'd said? Twenty minutes Beth had been alone. Twenty minutes for some sort of quarrel to start up, in which Beth had been killed, and arrangements made with Nagle to dispose of her? It was possible, but an unlikely supposition, and it had been the point at which Brearley had stuck.

Why had the possibility of Nagle as a suspect been overlooked, his car not examined for traces? Another sloppy oversight, Brearley fixated on Peter Denshaw as the culprit? Doubtless, there had been reasons at the time. With hindsight, it was hard to see just what they'd been. Rarely could there have been a bigger cock-up.

'In the end we rang the police and went indoors and waited,' Elvira was saying. By then the snow would have been well and truly trampled over, any hope of finding traces of Beth's abductor gone. 'Philip ordered Dot to pull herself together and make some tea. She'd laced it with whisky, I remember, and it tasted horrible, but I suppose we needed it. We were all frozen, as well as shocked. Philip . . . He'd always thought such a lot about Beth – yet he was the one who took charge and got us all organised.' The admission came out reluctantly.

Philip Denshaw. An unknown quantity, as yet. An old man, even then, a kind old uncle figure for Beth. With whom any connection with Wyn Austwick, at least, seemed remote. Wait a minute, though. She'd sung in a choir, hadn't she? How many choirs in Steynton? In fact, only one came to mind, and it was the one Philip Denshaw conducted, the rather grandly named Steynton Choral Society.

Press on. Find out who killed Austwick, he reminded himself yet again, and he'd have found Beth's killer: a now familiar and somehow disturbing litany. He'd always had a sense of priorities and it had stood him in good stead: this ruthless thrusting away of anything that was going to hinder him in his ultimate aim was new, and nourished him in a way that alarmed him and told him he'd have to watch it. Truth, not revenge, was what he wanted, but he was discovering that the thought of vengeance could become addictive.

He looked at his watch and thanked Elvira for what had evidently been a difficult few minutes. 'I've already taken up more of your time than I promised, but before I go . . . I'd like to ask you something about Mrs Wyn Austwick. We found the copy of a letter she'd sent to you among her papers.'

'Yes, she did write to me. We were going to meet when she came back from holiday. She wanted to talk to me, see where I figured in the family and so on.'

'Had you met her before?'

'Briefly, once, up at Low Rigg. She struck me as a poisonous woman. I'd have had nothing to do with her if I'd been Freya. Just the sort to take advantage of the confidential material she was entrusted with, I thought.'

A snap judgement that he wouldn't have found far off the mark, had his own judgement not been tempered by what he now knew of the dead woman, what had motivated her. One side of her character didn't negate the other.

'So you know she'd been threatening Mrs Denshaw?'

'I've told you. I saw Polly yesterday. She told me what Freya had done. I couldn't believe it.'

'Yes, it's muddied the waters somewhat – which might, of course, have been the intention. Give me your opinion. Is it possible she did know who killed Beth?'

'I think she *thought* she did, which isn't quite the same, is it?'

'And what do you think, Miss Graham? You were there, you

177

must have gone over the possibilities in your mind, then and since.'

'Endlessly.' She looked suddenly bleak and pinched. 'But the only thing I am sure of is that no way would Peter have killed your little girl.'

Sonia's little Fiat had been a birthday present from her parents four years ago, and on every subsequent birthday she received a cheque to cover the costs of taxing and insuring it, plus a little something over which, her mother directed without much hope, she should spend on some luxury for herself. Her mother was right not to be sanguine – the little something extra generally went into some charity box or other. Peter's lips tightened every time the envelope came from Montignac in the Dordogne, where her parents had now retired, but he never said anything. On Monday he remarked on it no more than he ever did, giving her the bunch of flowers which was his own invariable present, with a kiss and a smile, since it was, after all, her fortieth birthday.

Her face lit up. A kiss, a smile, and flowers! And when he said, 'You're a good girl, Sonia, you deserve more than a bunch of flowers from a poor parson,' her day was made.

'That wasn't why I married you,' she ventured with a shy smile.

He might have asked her why she *had* married him, and might have received a surprising answer, but he merely smiled sadly in return. 'I have George Sedgwick to see for a few minutes at twelve, but we'll have a drink together before lunch, as a celebration.'

Sonia blushed guiltily, to think that, even momentarily, among the excitement of her birthday and preparations for the Mothers' Union Christmas carol service, she could have forgotten. George Sedgwick was the churchwarden and they were doubtless meeting to discuss Freya's funeral service, which Peter himself was to conduct. She felt even more guilty when, for some reason, he kissed her again when he left.

She watched his tall figure cross the snow-sprinkled churchyard, his shoulders bent, his long black cassock flapping around his legs, until he disappeared inside the church door, doubtless to light yet another candle for his mother. It felt like an act of treachery to wonder whether the celebration drink he'd suggested wasn't in fact a form of Dutch courage, to fortify himself for the interview later that afternoon with the police, but the thought had insinuated itself into her mind and wouldn't go away. Coupling with that other dangerous little bit of knowledge she'd been keeping to herself and was afraid she wouldn't be able to much longer: the fact that Peter had been out on the Friday night that woman had been killed, without telling her where he was. But then, he often omitted to tell her where he was going. She was being wholly disloyal and must forget it.

Freya's death had hit him so badly. He'd always been the favourite among her children, perhaps because, unlike her daughters, he could not admit to her faults, nor she to his. And because he, like her, was the artistic one, the sensitive one, and as such deserved special treatment. Perhaps, thought Sonia defeatedly, it was better not to have such sensitivities. They didn't make for happiness. Perhaps I'm too critical of him. But her innate honesty made her qualify that: he's a man of God, but that is not a state of being which automatically confers perfection.

Nor had Freya been perfect. Try as she would, Sonia couldn't find it in her heart to grieve for her. She knew it was wrong and had prayed endlessly for grace to find something good by which she could remember the old woman. But Freya hadn't shown her much kindness or tried to hide the fact that she found Sonia uninteresting and physically unattractive. Of course she would never have admitted to liking anyone Peter chose to marry. Apparently, she hadn't cared much for Isobel, either, but at least Isobel had been pretty, which went a long way with Freya. For weeks there had been a certain amount of tension between Peter and his mother when he'd announced he was going to marry Sonia, but Freya could never be angry with her son for long and she'd grudgingly accepted that Sonia was here to stay. That didn't mean, however, that she'd had to love her daughter-in-law.

Sonia had had other presents for her birthday: a beautiful knitted garment from Ginny in wines and blues and golds, a pair of swinging silver ear-rings from Polly, some personally chosen, highly scented bath crystals from Harriet, and from the twins a box of chocolates. Each child had also sent her a handmade card, full of effort, which had brought tears to her eyes, and she'd placed them on the mantelpiece in front of all the others. Even Dot had given her a pot plant, a little mock orange tree. The gift which had pleased her most, however, had come from Elvira, of all people. Sonia couldn't imagine why she'd sent it, delivered by messenger, when she often forgot to send even a card. A last-minute thought, she guessed, because someone had reminded her this was a special birthday. But how kind! A delicate, lovely piece of porcelain, a white bird, its outspread wingtips tinged with the faintest pink, an object more beautiful than anything she'd ever possessed. She looked at all her presents, eyes brimming, unbearably touched by this evidence of thoughtfulness, especially at such a time, but unable to imagine herself using any of them. Not even the chocolates, which no one ever remembered she shouldn't eat, not with her skin condition. Nor was she any good with plants, and she could all too easily envisage this one's inexorable fate. Then, remembering Peter's unaccustomed gentleness, with a sudden access of bravery and a jump of excitement, she thought, why not? Why not run herself an indulgent bath, using the bath salts, dress herself up a bit? Make an effort, Sonia! Yes, she would.

First, she went to find a vase for the flowers, forgetting her sinuses and burying her face in the bronze and yellow chrysanthemums, their bitter-sweet smell seeming to say everything about her marriage.

And as she put the stiff stems in water, she began to sneeze. Peter never remembered her allergies, either.

She had set the table with special care, bringing out the wedding present silverware and putting the solanum with its bright orange globes in the centre, displaying the chrysanths prominently on a bookshelf, though well away from her chair. There hadn't been time to prepare a special meal, but the Tesco's chicken thighs were simmering in the oven and giving out a delicious smell. There was just time to slip out to the off-licence to buy a bottle of sherry out of the 'little something over' before Peter came back.

Lifting her coat from the rail in the hall, she couldn't resist looking at herself in the mirror. What she saw made her catch her breath in surprise, while a smile spread slowly across her face. Her hair, newly washed, hadn't yet gone lank and greasy as it would later, the ear-rings danced, the stained-glass colours of the cardigan gave her a little colour. She'd even put on a dab of lipstick.

She slipped on her coat, pulled the door to and started down the path with an unaccustomed spring in her step.

It was then that she heard the noise coming from the garage.

'He must have come home when I was in the bath,' Sonia wept, sobbing into the already sodden ball of tissues crumpled in her hand. 'But why? Why?'

'Sonia.'

Polly held the other woman's thin frame in warm, loving arms and tried to control her own shock and – yes, outrage. Peter had opted out, yet again. For, although sticking a hosepipe from the car exhaust in through the car window was a fearful – and in one way, courageous – thing for him to have done, it was not unbelievable. He hadn't even left a note. To do that to poor Sonia – on her birthday, too! When it had evidently been so important to her to share it with Peter: the dining-table beautifully set for two, and Sonia, smelling strongly of Harriet's Body Shop bath salts, with her obviously newly washed hair hanging over a face now swollen with tears. Still wearing the unaccustomed ear-rings and the long jacket Ginny had sent which, even in the state she was in, did wonders for her.

'How could she, Polly?'

'She?' Sonia, hardly knowing what she was saying, obviously meant 'he'. 'Who can say what he was feeling, love?' Polly murmured, pouring more tea.

'I don't mean Peter! I mean how could *she* have been so stupid as to make that idiotic confession? If she hadn't said anything, no one would even have thought of suspecting Peter! That's what made him do it. How could he face going through all that again?'

Polly had never heard Sonia so vehement, never before heard her blame a single soul for anything.

Yet another knock on the door. Another sympathiser, no

doubt, another kind offer to help. The telephone and the door bell had never stopped ringing: neighbours, friends, parishioners – Mrs Lumb the Leveller from the Old Vicarage offering to preside over the MU carol concert, Eva Spriggs, the busybody from across the road, bringing a delicate sponge cake . . . she was answering the door now, round of body, warm of heart, not averse to being involved in the drama of the situation, but eager to help, if only by acting as doorkeeper. It was impossible not to be impressed by the warmth and sympathy coming from all corners, equally impossible not to notice the sorrow was for Sonia, rather than Peter. Not 'poor Sonia' at all, with her unassuming and compliant nature, but good, kind-hearted, hard-working Sonia, respected and evidently loved in the parish.

Viewing her in this different light, Polly acknowledged and admired the dignity with which she pulled herself together as Eva Spriggs ushered in more callers.

The police, of course, had had to be involved, and it was with little surprise but a quick leap of something she didn't quite recognise that Polly saw Tom Richmond. He was not alone. Accompanying him was a bulkier man, towering above him, though Richmond himself was over six foot: Superintendent Farr, an avuncular figure, with far from avuncular eyes. Surely a suicide didn't warrant a superintendent?

Richmond seemed well on the way to becoming a permanent fixture in their lives, and would be until . . . Until what? Until Wyn Austwick's murderer had been found? For longer than that, she knew. He would probe deeper and ever deeper . . . until he had successfully proved that Beth Richmond hadn't been killed by her mother, Isobel.

Polly had never believed that Isobel had killed Beth. She supposed no one ever wanted to admit, even in the teeth of the evidence, that someone they'd known and liked could have been capable of such a wicked thing as murder. But she felt as though she knew it in her bones as true that Isobel could never have killed Beth. Or even if, by some outlandish, freakish, chance, she *had* been the unwitting cause of Beth dying, she would never have concealed her child in that way.

She had been such a gentle soul, in danger of spoiling Beth by giving in to her rather than by chastising her. She scolded the little girl occasionally, of course she did, what mother didn't? But not so very often, for Beth hadn't been an especially difficult child – not when compared with the disturbed, violently anti-social children Polly taught. A bit rebellious, yes, disobedient from time to time, but nothing major, nothing like as much as she might have been, considering her life had been screwed up through no fault of her own, and that she hadn't yet adjusted to the changes. She'd been eight years old, for God's sake.

The fact remained that *someone* had killed her.

When it had happened, ten years ago, Polly had been spending a crazy weekend with a group of friends, after the wedding of two of them. The wedding had taken place in a village on the Cornish coast, as nearly off the end of England as you could get, so there was no chance of driving home the same night, just supposing any of them had been in any condition to drive. The group had taken a rented cottage for the weekend, meant to sleep six. Ten – or maybe more – had crammed in, occupying chairs, floors and sofas, carrying on the celebrations. One of the chaps was a stranger to Polly, a loose-limbed Adonis with floppy dark hair and laughing blue eyes and no moral conscience. Three months later, before this last was apparent, they were married.

While Polly was being swept off her feet by Tony Winslow in a Cornish village, sense and sensibility blotted out by his charm, the sombre events in Steynton were being played out. She hadn't known about it until she'd got back to college, when an urgent telephone call had brought both joy and disaster – on the one hand, news of the birth of twins to Ginny and Leon, and on the other of Beth's disappearance.

She drove home to Yorkshire the following day, ditching all her classes and commitments, battling up from London through increasingly treacherous weather, cursing her decision to drive when she found the M62 closed because of snow, and that she was being redirected miles and miles out of her way, along roads hardly less navigable. Low Rigg had still been in an uproar when she finally got there: Peter being questioned by the police, Isobel, prostrate with grief and illness. Birth, and what eventually turned out to be death, happening within a couple of days – Ginny's delight and happiness overshadowed and dimmed by the appalling tension, the endless wait for news of Beth that never came. Placid and undemonstrative though Ginny outwardly appeared towards her boisterous little boys, Polly had always sensed that the twins' birth at that particular, poignant moment had made them doubly precious in her eyes, a brush of angel wings across the darkness and misery of those long January days, the miracle of new life in some way making sense of the unutterable sadness and pain of a child's death.

For Beth had to be dead by then. Hope for her had dwindled, though the search had continued, hampered by the appalling weather. And afterwards had come the endless questioning, the suspicions . . . Sonia was right. Peter wouldn't have been capable of facing up to all that again.

She was wearing swirling layers of warm fabric, a velvet, printed waistcoat, and long boots, yet she clasped her arms across her chest, hugging herself, feeling as if she'd never be warm again.

The big superintendent hadn't stayed long after all, had been replaced by a young woman in a sheepskin jacket named Sally. She was kind and firm with Sonia and had persuaded her to take the sedative prescribed by the doctor and to lie down. She'd stayed on with Tom Richmond to manage the rest of the business, but he'd eventually sent her back to the station and was now seated in the kitchen with Polly, mugs of muddy liquid in front of them, made from a cheap, instant coffee powder, all she'd been able to find.

They sat uncomfortably wedged either side of a pine table with integral benches, reminding Richmond of those in a set-aside picnic area off a motorway. She picked up her mug and held it with her hands clasped round it, seeking its warmth, not drinking. Richmond had already manfully downed most of the repellent brew, which had at least had the one virtue of being hot.

'So that's it,' she said, her voice unsteady. 'I suppose this wraps it all up?' He looked at her without answering. She swallowed and went on, 'What Peter's done – to my untutored way of thinking, it seems tantamount to a confession . . . Perhaps you were right all along to suspect him . . . Perhaps my mother really did know the truth.'

'I wish it were as simple as that.'

Her eyes grew wide as she digested this. 'It wasn't suicide?'

'That's not what I meant, no. We'll have to wait for the pathologist's report but I don't think there's much doubt he took his own life.'

'Oh! Then . . . then, you do think he could have murdered Wyn Austwick – that it wasn't necessarily true what he told Sonia, that he spent the time walking.'

'Walking,' he repeated.

'Yes, well, that's possible, you know. Very typical, something he'd done ever since he was a boy. For miles and miles, over the moors. Alone. But . . .' She was dismayed to find her eyes filling with tears.

'I'm sorry, this is rough on you.'

'It's rough on us all.' She took a determined gulp from her mug, swallowed it down. 'Do you know what I keep thinking? I keep asking myself how he could do it when he believed in the after-life. How could he – how can anyone who believes that – be sure the agony, the punishment, will end, that it won't just go on and on?'

He was very quiet.

'Do you know what *I* keep thinking?' he answered eventually. 'That you'd be better with a nip of whisky than that coffee. And then getting off home. Or rather the other way round, if you have to drive. Mrs Denshaw won't be awake for some time, and your sister's coming later, isn't she?'

'I have to pick the children up from school, anyway. You're right, this coffee's disgusting.' She picked up both mugs, rose and poured what was left down the sink before rinsing them.

When she turned round, he saw that her face had taken on a look of determination. She leaned back, her hands on either side of her, gripping the edge of the sink. 'You asked me the other day if I knew anything about Elf's origins. I don't know why you wanted to know, and these are other people's secrets – but if it will help to clear up all this mess . . . You implied Philip was her father. Well, I think he probably is.'

'Probably?'

'I don't actually *know*, not for certain. But I've been putting

185

two and two together and yes, it explains quite a lot. I suspect Elf knows – it may seem incredible to you that the rest of us have never been told, but you see, my aunt, Philip's wife, was still alive when Elf was born. She'd been ill for a long time – but twenty-eight years ago, people weren't so accommodating about that sort of thing. Philip is rather strait-laced as well, and he's always been very sensitive to what people think about him.'

'Your mother must have been very understanding to take in his illegitimate child as one of her own family,' he said ambiguously.

'There were strings attached.' She came to sit down again, and some time passed as she gathered her thoughts. Then she explained what the family had learned from Philip a few nights ago, about their father leaving no money and Philip stepping into the breach with his offer. 'He didn't actually say so, but I think taking Elf in was a condition of the agreement. You know, it really wasn't a bad way out of a very awkward solution.'

Especially for Philip Denshaw, thought Richmond. 'Thank you for telling me that.'

'I might wish I hadn't, later.'

She smiled ruefully but the way she'd said that made him sure that there were still gaps in this story she hadn't filled in. He had a feeling she might, if he gave her time, that the results would be worth his patience. Why he should feel so convinced that this confirmation of Elvira Graham's parentage had very definite bearings on his own child's death was something he kept asking himself. So far he'd found no satisfactory answer.

He needed to talk with some person who'd been there at the time, someone unbiased and able to keep calm in the face of crisis as Philip Denshaw seemingly had. Aware that he was a man with his own secrets, and not apparently inclined to divulge them, Richmond nevertheless determined to talk to him.

Before he left, he tore a page from his notebook and scribbled his home number. 'Any time you need me,' he said.

16

Steynton never quite went to sleep. A busy main road ran through the valley town, bearing heavy traffic towards the motorway, even throughout the night. Along the road were public houses and a Chinese takeaway and a disco that stayed open late to cater for the local night life. But at half-past nine that night there was little going on. The road had been kept cleared and gritted, and snowploughs and traffic had pushed the snow into dirty heaps on the pavement edges. It was very cold. More snow was expected and, apart from carefree youth, not many people were prepared to face the prospect of getting themselves stuck in their cars or involved in a pile-up on the icy roads, preferring the comfort of their own firesides on a night such as this.

Richmond saw that the lights were still on in the Wesleyan Methodist chapel, however, and its car-park well filled. The members of the Steynton Choral Society must be a dedicated lot, or perhaps better equipped for driving in these conditions than he was, he reflected, drawing his own car up alongside a four-wheel drive vehicle and spotting several more in the vicinity.

For the first time in his life, Philip Denshaw felt glad that one of his musical evenings was nearly over.

The rehearsal for *Judas Maccabeus* had been going for nearly two hours, and the rafters rang in the old chapel where choirs had sung with zeal and gusto for generations. It had been built in the days of religious fervour to accommodate a congregation of three hundred, with an overflow in the gallery. Since then, varnished pine had given way to white paint, the walls were now claret colour, the central heating had been updated and the hard wooden pews provided with cushions. People no longer saw the need to equate religion with discomfort. But they still loved to sing.

Sheer love of music, a tradition of lusty hymn-singing that had been passed down through the generations, was inherent in this choir; they were not afraid to raise their voices in full-throated, joyful harmony, quite unlike the soft cooing of a Welsh male voice choir, say, but just as seductive in its own way.

Tonight they were not singing as well as they might: a missed note here, one voice a beat behind, a ragged finish to a phrase, perhaps infected by his own inner unease.

'Stop! That's it for tonight. Next Tuesday at eight. Thank you all very much.'

Surprise showed on all faces. Ten minutes before time, when it was usually ten minutes after, or even twenty! Especially when there was only a fortnight to go before the final performance, with all the usual last-minute hitches and complications: winter colds and coughs, a virus among the sopranos. One of the specially booked principals down with laryngitis – or temperament – and her understudy, a young woman who sang like an angel, not wishing her ill but daring to hope . . .

But Philip Denshaw, usually a rigid taskmaster, had declared the rehearsal over and, remembering the road conditions outside, most of them were willing enough to depart. Scores were shuffled together, outdoor clothes donned, farewells exchanged, and Philip, at last left alone, gathered his own things together and felt for his car keys as he walked to the back of the chapel.

A stranger sat in one of these pews at the back. How long had he been sitting there, listening? There was a familiarity about him, a face half-remembered. He stood up as Philip approached him. 'DCI Richmond,' he said, offering a police warrant card for inspection.

Beth's father. Seen as a grainy newspaper photo, ten years ago, never completely forgotten. Philip felt his pulses beating, the blood draining away from his heart, then the heat rising in his face.

'What can I do for you?' he managed, calmly enough.

'Wonderful singing,' commented the policeman, waving a hand to indicate that Philip should sit down. Philip nodded acknowledgement and took a seat at the end of the pew opposite, turning to face Richmond, the aisle between them. Richmond told him he was investigating the murder of Wyn Austwick.

'Then you've come to the wrong place. I didn't have anything to do with that book my sister-in-law was having published.'

188

'Mrs Austwick was a member of your choir here, wasn't she?'

'She was. But I don't know all the members personally. She was just one of the contraltos, pleasant voice, that's all I knew about her. Except that she wasn't very trustworthy – about turning up, I mean. Missed a lot of rehearsals.'

Richmond could see that damned her in Denshaw's eyes as not worthy of more attention, he made it clear she had impinged on him as nothing more than a voice, but Richmond pressed on with his questions. He found no further enlightenment. Philip insisted he had never met Wyn Austwick outside the choir rehearsals, had no idea where she lived. He hadn't even known about the book she was writing for Freya until after her death. *'Freya's* death,' he added.

'Distressing, two family bereavements, so close together like that, Mrs Denshaw, then her son. I'm sorry.'

'Thank you, yes, it is upsetting. You get used to it as you get older, folk dropping off one by one, but Freya was younger than me. Makes you think.'

He had to be well on in his seventies, but he looked hale and hearty enough at the moment, plump and pink-cheeked, his sparse white hair scraped horizontally across a bald pate. You could never tell how death affected people, however. And intimations of mortality must inevitably be strong after losing two close relatives in such quick succession.

'Must do. Not yet forty, your nephew, I'm told. An untimely end. It's always disturbing when something like that happens, when you can't see a reason.'

'You're asking me why he did it,' Denshaw said bluntly. 'Well, I can't tell you. Whatever made Peter do anything?' Despite his asperity, his eyes were pained. He added abruptly, 'I wasn't surprised. He was always unstable. Went off at tangents, trouble wherever he went. The last person who should have been a parish priest.' He brushed a hand across his face. 'I'm sorry, shouldn't have said that, but Peter and I never saw eye to eye.'

'Different generations . . .' Richmond offered the cliché, just to keep him going.

'It wasn't just that, I don't have any difficulty with other younger people, only Peter, and –' He stood up, picked up his music case. 'I'm talking too much. I have to get back up to Low Rigg and with the weather as it is . . . Sorry I couldn't help you.'

'Yes, of course, I'm keeping you – but I *would* like to talk to you further about your nephew. Can we arrange another time?'

'Another time? Why?'

'Peter's death is still unexplained.'

Denshaw heavily resumed his seat. 'You'd better carry on and get it over with now then. Just tell me what you mean by that.'

'All right. As you wish. He didn't leave a note and there'd been no indications that he'd ever had suicidal tendencies. We have to be satisfied that there were reasonable causes for him to have taken his own life.'

'What are you suggesting, Mr Richmond? Peter was a very unhappy young man. Apart from his mother's death, which affected him deeply, he'd suffered two previous bereavements, both of them tragic, and he'd been under suspicion for one of them . . . I hardly need to remind you of that. He never got over it.'

'He had a certain difficulty with personal relationships, or so I understand.'

'With me, you mean. I can see somebody's been talking.'

'Not only with you, with Elvira Graham, too, I'm told.'

If he'd hoped to shock Philip, he'd succeeded. The old man suddenly looked his age. A kindly old man, on the surface, yet there was something that jarred, made Richmond wonder if he might not be a bit of an old humbug . . .

'Let me help you,' he said. 'There was some trouble, I believe, when Elvira was a young teenager, between her and Peter and yourself. It must have been serious to warrant an enmity that's lasted over – what, fifteen years?'

Philip was silent for so long, Richmond thought he wasn't going to answer. Finally, he said, 'Don't make a big mystery out of this, there's no need. I'll tell you exactly what happened and you can draw your own conclusions. I came across Peter painting Elvira. In the nude. She was eleven years old, and he was twenty-one. Elvira meant a great deal to me, and I can tell you I was very shocked. Protestations of innocence from Peter –

190

simply *art*, he said – cut no ice with me, he knew what he was doing. I was very angry with him, told him it must never happen again and that was that, as far as I was concerned. I was prepared to forget it. But Peter's resentments always went deep. He never spoke to me after that if he could help it, was barely civil when he did. He tried to poison Elvira against me too, and for a long time succeeded. Children in their teens can be very unforgiving. I persisted, though, and we were just about getting somewhere when . . .' He looked thoughtfully at Richmond. 'May I speak frankly about your daughter? It won't upset you?'

Richmond waved a hand.

'It seemed to me that Beth needed a lot of love. She'd been very troubled about the divorce and I didn't think Peter was the best person to act as a stepfather. So I paid her a lot of attention and she responded. I was very fond of her – and she was fond of me, I think. Well, when that terrible thing happened to her, I found that Elvira and I were back where we started. I have to say I think she was just a bit jealous, even at eighteen. She's a determined little madam, and she'd got it into her head that none of it would have happened if I hadn't kicked up such a fuss about that painting . . . Peter wouldn't have felt so guilty, wouldn't have got religion, wouldn't have met Isobel, all that psychological rubbish everyone talks now, nobody responsible for their own actions. Go back far enough and you can find a reason for anything, I say, but Elvira . . .' The old man looked at him wearily and stood up. 'The situation has upset me very much over the years.'

'I can understand that. Thank you for being so frank,' Richmond said, but waited in vain for more confidences.

'And now I must go.'

It wasn't the right moment, when the old man had been so forthcoming, to probe further. Philip followed him to the door and waited outside with him while he locked it. When they reached the car-park, Philip held out his hand. 'We've talked about death – but the death of a child is the worst thing of all. It may comfort you to know that none of us at Low Rigg wished Beth harm.'

The words had the ring of sincerity, and Richmond wanted to believe them. But again, that feeling of something out of synch.

And, unfair though it was, he'd always had a personal antipathy to damp handshakes.

He watched Philip Denshaw drive out of the car-park and sat on in his own car, weighing the implications of what he'd just heard, wondering whether the conclusions he was coming to could possibly be the right ones, or if his theories weren't going a little on the wild side.

He'd learned nothing new tonight, nothing that he hadn't picked up or been told by Polly, apart from gaining an insight into Philip Denshaw's character. He thought about that, long and hard, sitting alone in his car in the now deserted car-park, then drove home, pausing only to buy a parcel of what Charlie vowed were the best fish and chips anywhere in the northern union. Whatever or wherever that might be, Charlie was right about the fish and chips, as he usually was.

Feeling better after his first square meal that day, Richmond settled down in front of the fire with a scotch and allowed himself to think about this compulsion he had – this need to dig into this case. Deep down, right to the very bottom of the affair. To where it had all started. Long before Beth had been killed, he was sure. He had developed a conviction that her death was only incidental to some other purpose, which was not a comfortable conclusion to come to at one o'clock in the morning.

Perhaps he was wrong.

But . . . bits and pieces, the bits and pieces he'd talked about to Polly Winslow, were beginning to attach themselves to one another, like floating amoeba. A small fragment picked up, a sense of something not quite right, his antennae tuned to nuances and echoes from the past.

Everything in this case turned on the advent of Elvira Graham into the Denshaw family, of that he was sure. And on Philip Graham Denshaw: he thought to himself, here we have the picture of a man with an ailing wife and a beautiful, possibly available, sister-in-law, already with a family of her own. Into this situation comes a new baby, parents having been conveniently killed. The fiction is kept up about Elvira's parentage so that his wife (and everyone else) would never know the truth. Dot Nagle apart, perhaps. Someone must have helped with the cover-up and he could think of no one more likely to keep her mouth shut. Cynical it might be, but the explanation for all this seemed self-evident to Richmond. Especially since, when his wife had died, Philip had moved in permanently with Freya at Low Rigg. A convenient arrangement that had suited everyone – until Beth's arrival into the family, when Philip's attention had turned to her from his own daughter, with whom he was having problems. Philip himself had admitted Elf was a little jealous . . . perhaps there had been rather more to it than that. Richmond closed his eyes. Supposing Philip had been a little *over*fond of Beth . . . and his natural predilection for children masked something more sinister. Beth, thank God, had not been sexually molested, but supposing events had somehow taken a wrong turning before that could have happened? So that, with Eddie Nagle's paid connivance, her body had to be got rid of. Were it not so tragic, it would be ironic if Nagle had been paid by Philip *and* by Freya, who had imagined her son to be the culprit.

And if Elf had known, or guessed, what was happening . . . that might explain how, despite her differences with her father, she had been able to buy that expensive flat, that art gallery.

He sat there until three, back-tracking, rehashing, running it all through his mental computer. Then he went to bed and slept for four hours. Three cups of coffee and a bacon sandwich later, he felt nearly ready for anything the day might bring.

But it wasn't to be solved as easily as all that.

The day was Saturday, Saturday morning, the day of Freya Denshaw's funeral. It had been scheduled for Wednesday, but had been postponed in view of Peter's death. The double funeral her daughters would have preferred, not wishing to prolong the trauma of grief any longer than necessary, wasn't possible, since the coroner had not yet released Peter's body. Freya Denshaw was going to her grave alone.

Richmond went to the funeral. The town was busy as he drove through. Regardless of the fresh snow that had fallen overnight, the Saturday morning, pre-Christmas crowds, loving the razzmatazz which everyone professed to hate, were thick as he drove

193

through the town, the market, with its striped awnings over the stalls, doing a brisk trade in cheap wrapping paper and baubles. The Rotary Club's decorated float carried Father Christmas round the streets to the accompaniment of piped carols. It would be the turn of the Salvation Army next week, but meanwhile Rotarians rattled collecting tins at shoppers and the lunch-time pub trade alike while shepherds watched their flocks . . . A tall Christmas tree, set up in front of the town hall, sparkled with fairy lights and real snow.

The interment was to be in the cemetery where, at Charlie's request, Isobel and later Beth, had been buried, near to Connie, and knowing how testing the occasion would be for him, Richmond might well have cried off. Remembering the last times he'd been there, he knew the occasion was bound to be painful, and he had no idea if he was likely to gain anything from putting himself through the mincer by being there.

There was no need for him to have gone, but something drove him to be there, perhaps the traditional belief of police officers that a murderer might have a compulsion to attend the funeral of his victim and thereby reveal his guilt in some way. Freya Denshaw's death had not been suspicious, but all the people who were involved in his investigation would be present, and the more he could observe them, the better.

The name Denshaw still meant a lot in Steynton, and there was a fair crowd, which meant that Richmond was able to keep to the back and remain unnoticed by the mourners as they stood round the graveside. Leon Katz, exuding gravitas, holding Ginny's elbow. Polly, straight-backed and looking at no one. Sonia, hands clasped, head bowed. Eddie Nagle and Philip Denshaw, with Elvira Graham and Dot Nagle, two small women standing close together between them. Philip put out a hand and placed it on Elvira's sleeve. It wasn't repulsed.

A strange thing happened as Richmond looked at this quartet, at Nagle – his split lip scabbing over and obscenely swelling even further his wide, fleshy mouth, at Philip Denshaw, plump and secretive, at Dot Nagle, and Elf. For the first time, he seemed able to see them objectively. Several thoughts which had been separately nagging at his conscience ever since the night he'd spoken to Philip Denshaw came together as he looked at them all, and a subtle reversal of ideas took place. The players began to move around, grouping and regrouping and, standing there watching them, he began to see the emerging pattern. Bizarre. Looking at them all, at Elvira Graham, however, he really didn't think it was so *very* bizarre.

17

It was after the funeral, late in the afternoon, and the sun was a little, angry red ball going down behind the moor, the branches of the elms were soot-black against the cold, pale green sky, the crows noisily flying home to their ragged nests in the forks of the trees. Elvira Graham pedalled her mountain bike up the familiar road, past the Moorcock and up towards Low Rigg Hall.

The cold had brought fresh colour into her normally pale cheeks. She was blown and breathless with the exercise, but the blood pumping oxygen and endorphins strongly through her veins was making her feel alive, clearing her brain, letting her ignore her trembling muscles. Riding to and from school had never been like this. She'd thought more than twice about taking up cycling again for pleasure (or rather from guilt that in her present existence she didn't take nearly enough exercise) when she remembered the daily grind they'd all had to endure as children, in all weathers. But that had been on heavy old bikes with not enough gears, which had to be pushed up hills too steep to ride. Blood, sweat and very nearly real tears *that* might have induced, had she been the crying type. Sadistic it was, at the end of a school day. Wonderful, though, when you got your first sight of the Moorcock, signalling the last stage to home. Only when the weather was too bad had Eddie Nagle driven them in the car, and then merely three miles, just to where they could catch the nearest bus to take them to and from school.

Nobody had ever guessed, when the others had left school and Elf had to make the daily journey alone, that she'd made her own arrangements. Thereafter, she'd cycled those three miles to the bus stop, jettisoned her bike in a friend's garden, and ridden to and from school in comfort on the bus, paying the fares out of her lunch money and making do with a bag of crisps. She'd always been devious. Nobody had ever seemed to notice that she was home so much earlier. Nobody had cared, she'd thought then, pretending she didn't care, either.

For years she'd smarted under a sense of injustice. Feeling sorry for herself. Deliberately ignoring what was right under her nose, because she didn't want to see and acknowledge it. It had taken Peter's death to show her that. She drew in a breath of the sharp air, like knives into her dry throat, stinging her eyes. It was the cold that was bringing the tears – she wouldn't cry. She would *not*. It was inappropriate – feeble – to cry when you weren't sad, just bloody angry at what he'd done, the fool.

She hadn't meant to come here when she set out, but half-way through her designated route, she'd at last given in to the compulsion that had been driving her towards this ever since Freya had died, the sense that matters were coming to a head. In one way she was glad, but as she turned off towards the moors, she was primarily very afraid of facing what she'd been trying for most of her adult life to avoid. All the same, she wouldn't have ridden up here had she thought it through, remembered that it would be dark when she cycled home, that it might well snow again. She didn't relish the thought. There was always her old room at Low Rigg, only needing the bed to be made up, but that wasn't a solution she cared to contemplate, either.

Seeing that funny little red car of Polly's pulled up in front of the house, and light pouring from Freya's old bedroom, she dismounted and wheeled her machine through the gates and round to the back.

A dark glow from the kitchen flooded out into the yard as she came round the corner, and she paused to peer in through the window as she passed. Dot had left open the door of the stove, as she often did for warmth, and the ruddy heat from the glowing anthracite filled the huge, unlit cavern of the kitchen, making the sky outside suddenly dark by contrast. Her white face was stained with colour from the incandescent heart of the boiler, and wreathed in smoke from her cigarette; the whole thing looked like a picture from Dante's *Inferno*.

What was she doing, still there, staring at nothing, smoking, drinking tea? Why hadn't she gone straight home after the funeral? But let's face it, she'd always spent more time here than in the cottage, with Eddie – and who could blame her? Not me, thought Elf, who had wasted years blaming Dot for many things.

But her responsibilities filled her with dread and foreboding, her inadequacies overwhelmed her.

It was clear she would have to do something about Dot. She was going to pieces now that Freya was gone, empty days to fill and nothing to fill them with – no gossip, no pleasurable bickering. She was in limbo, left alone with Eddie. Elf shuddered and suddenly decided she would rather face Polly's clear-eyed questioning than Dot at the moment, though that wasn't going to be easy, either, what she had to say to *her*. She bypassed the kitchen and made her way upstairs. The door to Freya's old room was open, and she could hear Polly moving around inside.

Polly looked up and saw Elf standing in the doorway. 'Dot's going to need a removal van for all this lot,' she remarked, indicating the cardboard boxes and packing cases containing Freya's clothes, occupying much of the floor space.

'Crikey! What's she going to do with them?'

Polly shrugged. 'Auction them, maybe. Private buyers, or some museum will want them as a collection. God knows what they're worth.' The boxes represented three days' careful work on Dot's part, folding and swathing the gowns and coats and suits in the same sort of acid-free tissue paper that had kept them in a perfect state of preservation all these years. 'Better that than leaving them hanging useless in the cupboards.' She seemed to notice the way Elf was dressed for the first time. 'You haven't *cycled* up here?'

'I suddenly decided. Wish I hadn't, now.'

'I'll give you a lift back. I can't get your bike in my car, but you can pick it up in your own, later.'

'Thanks.' Elf stood awkwardly, on the verge of saying something more. Polly, who had only come back to pick up some clean clothes for herself and Harriet, and was impatient to get back to Garth House, and wondering what on earth Elf was doing here, waited for an explanation, but Elf stayed silent, biting her lip, looking uncertain.

After light refreshments at the Woolpack, Ginny had invited back to Garth House for a cup of tea anyone who wished, but Dot had looked at her as though she was being invited to some Bacchanalian orgy and said she and Eddie would be getting back to Low Rigg, thank you.

Polly had followed them, and been trailed all the way by a

battered Volkswagen. She guessed it would be the Press again and, sure enough, the VW had followed her right in through the gates and up to the front door. Freya was still news, in certain quarters. Let them speculate, she'd thought, refusing to comment to the young woman who'd jumped out of the car's passenger seat, notebook at the ready, manoeuvring to stop Polly entering the house. Polly had been adroit enough to unlock the door, slip inside and close it firmly behind her, without answering any questions. Probably not wise, she reflected afterwards, better to have fed them platitudes, but she hadn't felt up to answering questions about Freya Cass's life since she'd retired to this back of beyond, nor about the circumstances of Peter's suicide, which was bound to have leaked out . . . and it was more than possible that Freya's connection with Wyn Austwick would have been sussed out . . . even Beth's murder could have been resurrected . . .

Passing the open door of Freya's room, she had stepped inside for a moment, which had been another mistake. The pathos of the stripped bed, the absence of all the inconsequential clutter with which Freya had liked to surround herself hit her harder than the funeral itself had done. Sooner or later, they would have to sort through her personal effects, what jewellery she had left . . .

'I want you to have this back,' Elf said at last, uncannily picking up her thoughts. 'I've worn it ever since we spoke, in case I saw you.' She unfastened the gold chain around her neck and slipped off the black opal ring suspended from it. 'It's yours by rights.'

Polly refused to take it. 'Freya never cared for jewellery, never wore much, did she, except a few favourite pieces? If she gave this ring to Dot, she wanted her to have it, and Dot had a perfect right to give it to you, like you said.'

Elf sat down suddenly on the edge of the stripped bed that looked so strange and hard and uncomfortable without its sumptuous lilac spread. She looked down at her right hand, clenched into a fist around the ring, without saying anything for a while. 'Oh, Lord, Polly, didn't you know . . . didn't *any* of you suspect? Freya didn't ever *give* Dot anything. Her jewellery was always in such a muddle, costume jewellery mixed up with what was left of the real stuff, you know what she was like. Always misplacing things, no idea what she really had. It was easy for

Dot to pinch things, this ring, plus a whole load of other bits and pieces as well, I have to say.'

Polly was stunned. 'Did you know that when she gave it you?'

'No. I thought she was telling the truth. She gave it me, trying to win me over, but it was twenty-eight years too late. When . . .' Her voice shook. She took a deep breath. 'OK. When she finally admitted she was my mother.'

The room went very quiet. It was full of dim shadows, only one small lamp switched on. Outside, it had become very dark. Elf's face had taken on that tight, pinched look again that might very well become permanent as she grew older, that made it possible to see the resemblance to Dot.

'How long have you known?' Polly said at last.

'Officially, about six months, but long before that, really. Nobody would ever tell me anything about my origins, even when I was growing up and beginning to ask questions, as you do. Which of course made me even more curious. Then gradually, I knew. Just feelings I had, absorbing hints and facts and putting two and two together . . . but long before I suspected Dot might be my mother, I knew .Philip was my father. You'd guessed that, hadn't you? I asked him outright one day and he told me the truth, but even then he wouldn't say who my mother was. I decided there must be some awful, compelling reason why I wasn't to know. And then I came across an old family snapshot . . . and you know what they say about curiosity.'

Came across. More likely looking for, searching, needing to know. Polly wanted to hug her, to banish the cold tightness and the bitterness from her shut face, but she feared Elf was in no mood to respond to that kind of sympathy.

'It was the only photo I've ever seen of Dot,' she went on, 'and I just knew. It was like looking at a slightly distorted view of myself.'

'The snap taken on the beach at Filey? I saw it for the first time the other day. Soon as I saw it, I knew, as well.'

'Did you? You've been sharper than I gave you credit for.' A crooked smile robbed the words of malice. 'Well, it explained a lot, didn't it? Why she'd come to live here permanently, supposedly to look after the little orphan babe – God, can you imagine a more unsuitable child-minder? Why she always seemed to like me that little bit better than the rest of you – though that's not saying much, is it?' Her defences were down, all the hurt and confusion was surfacing. She added bitterly, 'It would have made a difference to me to have known all this. I – I used to think Freya was my mother.'

'What?'

'Yes I did, for years. And I despised both her and Philip for not admitting it. When he eventually brought himself to tell me he was my father, ages after that fuss about Peter, we became better friends for a bit . . . I think he was actually on the verge of openly acknowledging me, and then, Beth died, and we were back where we started.'

Polly, who had sat down on the dressing stool, feeling in need of its support, turned an arrested face to her. She had a sudden premonition, as if some terrible revelation were about to take place. With an effort, she reorientated herself. 'Beth? What did she have to do with it?'

'That day she disappeared, when we were all frantically look-ing for her, I found – well, what I found was her red woolly glove, all wet with snow, half-way up the middle staircase.'

Polly's mind whirled. 'But that means she wasn't playing outside all the time. She must have come back into the house.'

'That's what I'm telling you! Didn't you hear what I said? *I found the glove on the middle staircase! On the way up to Philip's rooms!*'

The shadows seemed to move in, enveloping them in an endless silence, until Polly said, 'Why? Why didn't you ever *say*?' Though even as she spoke, she knew why. And for the first time understood something of that compulsion people had to shield those whom they loved, the dilemma they faced, to speak or not to speak, the impossible choice. Because how could you live with yourself either way?

'Didn't you even tell *him* you'd found it?'

'Not in so many words. But he knows what I suspect, must do. Why else do you think he bought the shop, the flat? Unless it was to keep my mouth shut?'

'Perhaps he gave them to you just because he loved you.'

Elf began to laugh, a choking, hard little laugh that was only a breath away from tears. 'You think he's *given* them? To *me*? Oh, that's rich! He might just have wanted to make amends, but not that much. The only name on both sets of deeds is Philip Graham Denshaw. I'm merely the tenant.'

Polly stood up and switched on the central light. It was a low wattage bulb, its output not sufficient for the big room, and the light it cast was dingy and miserable. The colour whipped up in Elf's cheeks by her ride here had faded to the extent where Polly was alarmed by her extreme pallor.

'A fine heritage I have, between the two of them!' Elf said bitterly. 'Philip, so pathetic, and Dot . . .' Her voice broke. 'Polly, I know it's wrong, but all those years without one iota of affection – I can't – I just don't even want to *begin* thinking of her as my mother!' Unstoppable tears began to pour down her cheeks. She looked utterly lost. Then angrily she scrubbed at her face. 'So what makes me feel I have to act so bloody protectively towards them?'

A bond, a blood-tie, however hateful, was the only possible answer, and yet . . .

'I don't know, love,' Polly said helplessly. She only knew that she, too, would have felt the same, shamingly, had it been her misfortune to have Dot as a mother.

After the funeral, Richmond had gone straight back to the station to have another look at the forensic reports. He studied them carefully for a while, then rang the lab and asked to speak to Marianne Turner, the woman who had dealt with Wyn Austwick's clothing. He knew her fairly well, a pretty young woman with owlish spectacles, wheelchair-bound, who took her job seriously enough for it to be quite on the cards that she might be doing some overtime at the lab. She wasn't, however, so he had to spend time finding out her home number. She answered on the third ring and he apologised for disturbing her weekend.

'I take it it's important, or you wouldn't have interrupted United v. Spurs.' The swelling roar of television football sounded in the background.

'Sorry about that, I'll be as quick as I can. It's about that smear of face powder found on Austwick's jacket . . .'

'Pressed powder. It's lanolin-based, which means it contains a certain amount of grease, so it's difficult to remove, as any woman who gets it on the collar of a jacket will tell you.'

'What I'm wondering is, would she have been wearing make-up when she was on her way into hospital?'

'Depends on how vain she was, I suppose. Or possibly, I suppose, how much wedded to routine she was, so that she used it automatically. If she did wear it, she'd have been ordered to remove it immediately, or I'm no judge of nurses. Doctors aren't keen on trying to assess their patients' pallor or otherwise when they're daubed up with make-up.'

'That's what I thought.'

'The mark might have been made previously, of course, but I doubt it. She'd have been blind not to notice it, being it was right across the front of her jacket lapel. She was naturally very pale-skinned? I'm assuming that, not having dealt with the corpse myself, only the clothing.'

He held his breath. 'No. She was sallow. Yellowish, really.'

'Ah. Then we're possibly talking transfer traces,' Marianne said briskly. 'If she'd that kind of complexion, I doubt she'd have worn that shade of powder. She'd have looked a bit clownish. It's just about the lightest one you'd ever find – made for someone with a very pale complexion.'

Which was the answer he'd expected. He released his breath and thanked Marianne, apologising again for interrupting her match viewing, went home and made himself a substantial sandwich. He didn't see there was anything further he could do, over the weekend, except collect his thoughts and ideas together, test his theories and see whether they hung together as well as he had begun to dare hope that they would.

Half-way through his sandwich, the telephone rang. It was Polly Winslow. 'I'm at Low Rigg. I think you'd better come up here,' she said. 'Quickly.' Her voice sounded urgent, slightly breathless.

'All right, hang on. I'll be there.'

He raced for his car, tried to contact Manning, without success, and had to be content with leaving a message for him. The weather had worsened, his wipers were scarcely coping with the snow driving across the windscreen, his tyres were skidding on the new layer of snow. He was half-way there, headlights making a narrow tunnel of the twisting road, already narrowed by banked snowdrifts either side, before he realised he hadn't even asked Polly what it was all about.

*   *   *

It was fully dark by the time he reached Low Rigg hamlet. Lamps glowed behind curtains in the windows of the cottages. The Moorcock was brightly lit and its cramped car-parking space, despite the bad road conditions, already occupied by several cars, the drivers either fools or optimists. His car's ventilation system pulled in the smell of frying chips as he passed, reminding him of his abandoned sandwich.

He thought he wasn't going to make the last steep pull up to the big house, but the heavy Volvo proved itself up to it. Lights were on all over the house, casting blue shadows against the snow when he turned in through the gates. She must have been waiting for him, the door was opened immediately to his ring. She took his hand in both of hers, in a warm, spontaneous gesture, and drew him inside, showing him again into the yellow room after he'd stamped the snow from his boots. This time there was no fire, and the barely adequate heating made him realise the necessity for it. The house already had a dusty feeling of abandonment and when he saw Polly herself properly, he knew something was gravely wrong.

'Sit down, you're trembling,' he said, putting hands which were strong and steadying on her shoulders. She raised her eyes to his face, and in that brief moment of contact they both, at last, allowed the knowledge of mutual attraction to vibrate between them, a promise that there might be something beyond this black moment.

It lasted no more than a few seconds then, driven by some inner compulsion, she turned away, waved him to a seat and began her story.

'I'll have to ask you to be patient with me, and hear me out, but I promise you won't think it's a waste of time when you have.' Courage was a tenuous thing, and she seemed to think if she paused she might lose it. The words came tumbling out as she related what had passed between her and Elf. He listened quietly, unsurprised. From that moment at Freya Denshaw's graveside, when he had seen Dot Nagle and Elvira Graham standing close together, there had been no doubt in his mind about the relationship between the two women. Not because of any strong facial resemblance, feature by feature – there was some, perhaps, but not to any remarkable extent. Yet, imagining Dot as she might have been thirty years ago, her tightly permed grey hair as dark and sleek as Elvira's, without the heavy, ageing make-up, he had had no doubt that these two small, slightly built women were closely related.

And Philip Denshaw was certainly, as he'd suspected, Elvira Graham's father. Stranger liaisons occurred, but surely, Richmond thought, some better way of coping with the situation which had arisen when Dot found herself pregnant could have been arranged, other than bringing his illegitimate child and her mother here to Low Rigg Hall. A partial explanation occurred to him, one he knew some women found difficult to accept, revolving around the concept of fathers loving and desperately needing their children every bit as much as their mothers did. Philip Denshaw, for all his faults, loved children . . . one could, perhaps, sympathise with his need . . .

And then Polly, swallowing, told him about Elf finding Beth's glove.

For a long time, he said nothing. Then he nodded. 'Where is he?'

'In his own rooms, playing music. Not answering the door. But wait,' she said, as he began to lever himself up. 'I'm afraid I haven't finished, yet.'

This was extraordinarily difficult. Impossible. She couldn't hide it from him, nor spare him pain. And this time, she felt unable to touch him, either, unable to communicate her sympathy, not even by a hand laid on his, as she had before. Now, it would seem an intrusion. This was a private grief, in which she had no place. But to let him go in, unprepared – no. In the end, she told it in bald phrases, like inadequate subtitles on an emotional foreign film drama, words which could in no way convey the impact of the unbelievable pictures still scrolling themselves in her mind.

Dot had still been sitting in the luridly lit dark when she and Elf had gone into the kitchen, unable to reach Philip, hoping he might respond to a plea – or a command – from Dot to open the door. The old joke about Dot being able to make Philip do anything, if she so wished, had taken on rather different overtones now that the truth about their one-time relationship was out in the open.

Polly had switched on the centre kitchen light, like most of the lighting in the house, mean and not equal to the job. Dot blinked, her face losing its rosy glow as Elf shut the door on the glowing coke interior. There was a strong smell of bleach, a sure sign that Dot was upset. At no other time did Dot willingly apply herself to cleaning, but in all crises of her life, she went for the bleach bottle, swabbing the sink, scrubbing the big deal table, even the floor, so that her hands stank permanently of it. The kitchen had reeked of it for weeks after Beth disappeared.

'Oh yes, I knew she'd come back inside,' she said casually, when told about the glove. 'She came into the kitchen. I was making an apple pie for the supper.'

Oh, those apple pies! Dot's specials, to be avoided at all costs – pallid pastry, burnt round the edges, apples only half-cooked, too much or too little sugar, depending on how she felt at the time. Polly wondered what had happened to that particular one, had anyone forced themselves to eat it? She said slowly, 'You never mentioned she'd been indoors.'

'Nobody asked me.' She began to hum, tunelessly, under her breath. Another bad sign, like the bleach.

'Leave this to me,' Polly said to Elf, but Elf showed no signs of wanting to be involved. She had backed away and was standing with her back to the dresser, hands clenched round the knobs of the top two drawers, as if for support. 'Go on,' Polly said to Dot.

'She kept snitching bits off the edges as I was rolling out. I told her to give over, she'd make herself poorly eating raw pastry but she took no notice, so I slapped her wrist.'

'*Slapped her wrist!*' Any child brought up at Low Rigg knew Dot's slaps on the wrist, or anywhere else. 'Some slap, it must have been!'

'I didn't *mean* to hurt her!' Dot said sharply, offended and unremorseful. 'A clip round the ear when they're misbehaving never did any child any harm that I've ever heard of.' She was talking about it as if she were discussing the weather, and as if it had about as much importance to her. She sounded indifferent, but she couldn't meet their eyes.

It was at this point that Polly began to wonder if Dot was quite sane, if she hadn't been more than a little mad for a long time. At this point too, she and Elf had exchanged looks, and the truth flashed between them, both of them knowing that it wasn't Philip Beth had had to fear, while Dot unconcernedly lit another cigarette, as if all this had nothing to do with her. The stink of cigarette smoke, mixed with the pervading odour of bleach, was sickening.

'But it was more than that – you must have really hit her! Hard. Several times!' Polly looked at her with growing horror. 'What did you hit her with?'

She closed her eyes on nightmare, a familiar scene made surreal. A snowy day, just like today, freezing cold outside, warm in the kitchen . . . 'You were rolling out *pastry*!' she said.

The rolling pin, the same one which had been in use in this kitchen as far back as she could remember, for generations, maybe. Her grandmother, rolling sheets of oatcake and leaving them to dry over the creel. Herself as a child, the rolling pin too cumbersome in her small hands, nearly as big as she was, but determinedly using it to flatten leftover dough and stamp it out with a thimble into hard, grey little dolls' biscuits. And Dot, regularly employing the same stout rolling pin for bashing steaks into tenderness before cooking. Her stomach churned. She gagged. Elf, too, traumatised into silence, had her hand to her mouth, her eyes were huge above it.

Dot went to the sink and began washing her mug, furiously rubbing it dry with the tea towel. Filled the kettle and put it on again, uncaring. Polly, herself a compulsive mover, watched, appalled, but knowing how it was. You couldn't go on talking, talking, without doing something to occupy yourself until the words came. But when Dot at last turned round, her face had grown ugly, her eyes were sparking malice, her mouth thinned so that it almost disappeared into the powdery whiteness. 'She wouldn't be told – spoiled little madam! She started whinge-ing for Philip. I gave her a little tap, and she fell, and went quiet, and . . .'

'And you hit her again? With another little tap, I suppose, and another?'

Sarcasm, anger, did nothing to make the nightmare better. Which was, after all, such an easy thing to believe. Always free with her hands, Dot, with anything that happened to be in them. If you were a child, you learned to dodge if you could, to run away and nurse your ringing ears, your hurting arms and legs in silence, until her rage had cooled. Which it soon did, give her her due, and then you'd be given sweeties and allowed to watch rubbishy television programmes. On the tacit understanding that you didn't tell your mother about something she never guessed at. Never seeing the marked bodies, because Freya never bathed or undressed her children herself.

Polly remembered Eddie, too, tough and frightening, yet with eyes filling with sentimental tears when he'd witnessed the blows and slaps and pinches. But too afraid of Dot himself to do anything about it. So that they'd laughed when it was Eddie's turn, too, for bruises and black eyes, when they'd realised where his injuries came from – not from fighting outside the pub after getting drunk, as the fiction went, but from his skinny little wife. Giggling then, and Ginny singing in a Cockney voice that old music hall song, a favourite of their grandfather's: '. . . 'itting of a feller wot is six foot three, and 'er only four foot two!'

They'd laughed, cheeky, not understanding.

'If she belonged to me, I'd let 'er know oo's oo,' went another bit. But Eddie never did let Dot know who was who. Or at any rate, he went on letting her hit him. Eddie and Dot, that was a different ball game to Dot hitting children, smaller and more defenceless, Polly realised as she grew older. Something secret, darker, there. Some kind of tacit agreement between them. Collusion. A kind of love, maybe. Who understood the inner workings of a marriage?

Or the compulsion to hit a child? To kill?

What had made the rage so unstoppable, that time? With *Beth*? A delightful child, with a mind of her own. A bit mischievous at times, but laughter easily overcoming tears and tantrums. Enchanting. A surprise and a delight, a treasured gift to a grown-up family, through Peter, of all people! Quickly becoming a favourite with them all, with Philip especially, who was patient with her over her piano lessons, not averse to spoiling her a little, talking of making money over to her in his will . . .

Polly's heart gave a lurch. Why hadn't she ever thought of that before?

'Well, aren't you going to send for the police?' Dot demanded.

The police, yes. Tom Richmond. She began to move, mechanically, and Elf sprang away from the position in front of the dresser, where she'd seemed to have taken root, at the thought of being left alone with Dot. 'I'll get Philip – even if I've to break his door down!'

'No!' Dot commanded her sharply. 'What good has Philip ever been to me? Go down to the cottage and bring Eddie back. I'll wait here until he comes. You don't have to worry,' she added wryly, 'I won't run away. It's far too late for that, now.'

18

It was money, of course, that had made her hit that child, though it wasn't the thought of money that was running through Dot's mind at the time. Then, she'd been curiously detached. Like now, as she waited for the police.

But before then, for weeks, ever since he'd so casually mentioned it, the words had festered. All that money of Philip's going to a stranger, a child he barely knew . . . Oh, what fools girls were! Wilful, she was, Elf, not to make it up with Philip, blind not to see which side her bread was buttered, that it would cost her nothing but smiles and a bit of flattery to put him back in the right humour. So that she'd end up with what was only hers by rights, anyway.

These were not maternal feelings stirring in Dot's breast, she told herself. She'd never had any, not even when the baby was born. Love? No, not she. She'd been born lacking that capacity, hadn't she? But the instinct to look out for her own was deeply ingrained in her sharp Cockney nature – a creed instilled into her since birth. An inborn sense of survival.

She felt drowsy in the heat of the kitchen, the last fifteen minutes had passed like a dream since Elf went to find Eddie, and Polly . . . well, Polly, of course, would have sent for the police. Dot was calm, she'd known it was all over since she'd raised her eyes from Freya's coffin and seen Richmond's gaze on her. She told herself she was glad. Ten years of keeping it held inside herself had wearied her. No one knowing except her, and Eddie.

She made herself yet another pot of tea, waited for it to brew, to become strong and dark with tannin. Whatever anyone else thought of Eddie, he'd been like a rock. Getting rid of the bodies for her, first the child, then the woman. Never mind that he had as much to lose as she had. She told herself that neither act had been premeditated, and perhaps that was true of Beth, it was something she couldn't help, a product of this rage inside her.

She'd always known she was worth more than the raw deal

she was destined to get from life. It hadn't been much of a life, all told, and sometimes the anger at it came boiling out, unstoppably, vented on those who wouldn't tell.

The Austwick woman would have told, if she'd lived. She had a mouth on her, that one. But she needn't have died, if she hadn't tried to be too clever. If she hadn't threatened to tell what she knew, or had guessed. Not as a means of getting money, that Dot might've understood, but merely as revenge because Eddie had ditched her.

Eddie and his women. They'd been no surprise to Dot. She'd known before she married him that she wouldn't be the only one in his life, especially as she grew older, as what looks she'd had faded. Twenty years ago she hadn't been so bad, still had her sharp, piquant looks, which other men besides him had found attractive. Thin as a whippet, but Eddie liked his dogs and his women thin. And he'd said he loved her, though she knew it was the cushy number here, her expectations that he'd loved more. But what the dickens do they see in him? she'd thought, God knows, he's no oil painting. Hasn't much at all to recommend him, except his virility . . . She hadn't really minded these other women, though – the other *girls*, always pretty, always young . . . At any rate, until he'd taken up with that old crow. And *that* Dot had minded.

Dot didn't drive, had never learned. That night, after Eddie had gone to his darts match, she'd walked down from Low Rigg to the main road and then taken the bus that stopped at the Clough Head Estate. She hadn't meant to kill the woman, only give her a piece of her mind, but the big torch she'd needed to see her way on the unlit moorland road was still in her hand when she knocked on the woman's door . . .

She shouldn't have laughed. She shouldn't have pleaded, either, when she saw Dot raising the torch. 'I'm ill!' she'd lied. 'I'm on my way to hospital!' Maybe she hadn't lied after all, though. Illness of any kind had always disgusted Eddie, and maybe that was partly why he'd been as glad to see the end of her as Dot was. Putting her into a dustbin liner wasn't difficult. Dragging her into the tiny kitchen had been less easy, and she'd had to lie her diagonally across the floor, but she'd had to do it, to get her out of the way to clean up the hall. The woman had no bleach under the sink, to get everything clean, but she'd made do with what there was. Then left her there until she could come back with Eddie to dispose of her.

Eddie, as usual, had known what to do. No blame, no questions. Picked her up as though she was nothing, put her in the car boot, driven her to the quarry. Dot thought it was as well she'd been there, he'd have thrown the woman in just as she was. Dot was the one who'd had the idea of weighting her with her own suitcase, only it hadn't kept her down. They hadn't said, the police, but her belt must have come undone or something.

She poured some tea into the clean mug, eager for the revivifying taste, then stared in disgust at the pale liquid which emerged from the pot. Tea begrudged and water bewitched. What had she done? Forgotten to empty the pot, poured boiling water on to already used leaves, that's what. She filled the kettle to start again.

It was the look Elf had given her before she fled the kitchen that she couldn't bear to think of. It came as a revelation to her that she cared, after all, about the child she had borne twenty-eight years ago, the result of what had happened when she'd gone with Philip Denshaw, met when she'd visited Freya, his wife already an invalid – flattered, but never expecting he'd marry her – oh no, his kind didn't marry the likes of her – but wanting more than she'd ever got from him.

He'd wanted her to have an abortion, terrified of the scandal. But legal abortions weren't yet ten a penny in those days, and she'd seen too many disastrous results of back-street operations to risk one herself. The solution he'd put forward, in return for her silence, and with Freya's compliance, had a lot of drawbacks, but on the whole, it had worked well enough. He'd seen her all right for money – she, like Eddie, wasn't greedy, she only wanted enough to feel secure and comfortable. And to be sure that her daughter would be, too.

It was only when she'd seen all the years of keeping herself held in, never able to show any feelings or emotions she might have, all she'd hoped for slipping away because of Elf's stubbornness and Philip's attraction to the child, Beth, that she'd balked.

All, all for nothing.

In a sudden excess of frustration, she swiped her strong, wiry arm along the dresser top, sweeping it clean of all its accumulated clutter, something she'd wanted to do for years. Chipped plates, mugs, the pewter tankard with the milkman's money in it, an old date box containing pencils, rubber bands and pins, an ugly, orange-coloured 1950s moulded glass vase crashed satisfyingly to the floor. A storm of old letters, forgotten shopping lists and abandoned junk mail whirled like the snow blowing outside the window. The 1937 Jubilee painted tin tea caddy with the King and Queen on it, now black with age, the edges of the lid and a half moon just underneath it rubbed shiny like silver with wear, spilt its contents over the floor. She'd forgotten the teapot, still full of weak, boiling tea, and that went, too, its lid falling off and its contents scalding her leg and foot. She screamed with pain and didn't see the bit of paper, that month's paper-bill, as it happened, which wafted, light as a leaf, on to the kitchen table, right on to the ashtray where her cigarette was still burning. The paper browned and crisped and finally caught fire, setting light to the morning paper, which became kindling for the tablecloth. Flames spread. Charred fragments of paper and burning cloth floated around, a foam-filled cushion began to smoulder evilly, flames licked round the table edge. The square of coco matting under the table started to burn with a brisk crackle as a flaming piece of tablecloth dropped on to it and ignited it.

Dot was too busy dashing cold water over her leg and foot to notice what was happening behind her until, whimpering with pain, she looked around for a tea towel to mop up the excess water. She couldn't believe what she saw, and now smelled, how quickly so much of the kitchen was fully alight. She screamed louder and tried to pick up the heavy old tab rug which lay in front of the stove to smother the conflagration but it was one that took two to lift and was too big for her to manoeuvre. Trying to lift it, to drag it over and beat out the flames, she inadvertently stood on the end, tripped herself up and fell to the floor with it. Her black mourning clothes caught fire, then her hair. The rug, impregnated with years of grease, caught fire, too.

Eddie, opening the door a few minutes later, sent in a freezing draught which fanned the now roaring flames further, through the doorway and into the long corridor alongside the back stairs. He saw his wife stagger to her feet, and then collapse back into the incandescent heart of the fire. He yelled, ran forward, but was beaten back, his face blistered by the tremendous heat.

It was Eddie's turn now, to begin screaming.

Epilogue

On another dry, sunny day of piercing cold, this time in March, Richmond again parked the Volvo by the reservoir and climbed to the top of Clough Edge.

The force of the wind flattened the stiff, moorland grass and bent the whin bushes in its path, hitting him like a blow in the chest as he breasted the ridge and stopped, focusing his gaze on Steynton spread below. He turned his head slowly towards the hamlet of Low Rigg and what was left of its ruined Hall, crouched like a black widow spider against the unsullied purity of a thousand daffodils.

Not that either the Hall or its garden could be discerned properly from here. The house was but a dark, distant huddle and the flowers were simply the dancing, golden haze he remembered from the previous day, though the vision of both was one which would be permanently, indelibly imprinted on his memory. He'd gone there yesterday to say his farewells, intending finally to lay the last of the ghosts. He'd left his car outside the Moorcock and walked up the last yards of the steep road and through the stone gateposts, stepping across the flagged garden, feeling as though he were almost wading through daffodils. Coming suddenly upon desolation.

Time no longer existed there. Left to its own silence, Low Rigg Hall was a heap of stone slowly returning to the earth from which it had once been gouged; jackdaws and crows had already begun colonising its treacherous chimney stacks and the parts of the roofs which hadn't caved in. He was appalled to find how soon disintegration had taken over after the fire, aided by a severe winter. Now the winds were blowing through the eyeless windows, chimneys were crumbling, wind and weather had caused an avalanche of stone slates to relinquish their hold and slide to the ground. Only its thick, stout walls remained to show where rooms had once been.

The old building, once the fire had caught hold, had never really stood a chance. Its dry, ancient timbers fed the flames, and by the time the fire engines had arrived, hampered by the appalling road conditions, the place was an inferno. Now it was nothing but a shell, save for one wing which had partially escaped, though most of its contents had been consumed, gone the way of all the other furniture in the house. It was a miracle that the only life lost in that conflagration had been Dot Nagle's.

After three and a half centuries, Low Rigg Hall, as such, had ceased to be, and common sense dictated it was better left so, at least until its departed spirits were at rest. In time, someone with money or pretensions might see possibilities in it, might buy it and remake another home where the old one had stood. Put in a modern central heating system and hang coach lamps by the front door. Install state-of-the-art bathrooms and a country pine kitchen, complete with Aga. Tame the garden and lay patios. Come summer, they might discover a rampant, defiant rose spilling itself unchecked on the back wall, in spring look out on the ocean of daffodils which had lain dormant and unsuspected beneath the cold winter earth. Maybe that's how it would happen. Meanwhile, the house waited, a ruined, brooding presence in an inimical landscape.

Richmond had spent the last three months preparing the evidence. Eddie Nagle would face prosecution when he was fit. The severe burns he had suffered had not added appreciably to his good looks, but he would live to take the blame for his part in the two murders. He was freely admitting that part in the hopes of a mitigation of his sentence: he had made a full and detailed statement of what had taken place on both occasions. He'd survive. People like Eddie Nagle were natural survivors.

As was Philip Denshaw who, without any effort or demur on his part, was now installed with Elvira in her flat, with a new piano and the task of tracking down and replenishing as many of his lost music scores and books as was possible, a fact he appeared to mourn more than the tragic events which had caused their loss, and which seemed scarcely to have made a dent in his conscience.

Richmond thought fleetingly of the spare, elegant, self-sufficient lifestyle Elvira had created for herself in the flat high above the town, and asked himself if we didn't all have a streak of masochism in our natures.

What had made her offer to share a home with her father? The same sort of instinct which had caused her to make one last determined effort to make up the differences between herself and Peter, that had got him to agree to come to her flat on the night Wyn Austwick was killed? A genuine desire for reconciliation? That was what she said had been her motive.

Sonia at least believed her. But then, scepticism wasn't in Sonia's nature. She'd been destined from birth to do what she was now doing: training for ordination, intending eventually to become a parish priest. Perhaps she'd help to redress the balance by becoming almost certainly a better one than ever her husband had tried to be, Richmond suspected.

He stood thinking about them all, hands thrust deep into his jacket pockets, collar turned up, almost blown off his feet, his eyes watering, ears aching with the penetrating wind, every breath a knife-thrust into the lungs. The sad-green hills, from here descending to the grey valley, were blue on the other side, three-dimensional in the translucency of the air; except for a few white, puffy, racing clouds the sky was blue as a dunnock's egg. The scene had its own harsh, unique and, for him, unforgettable beauty. He doubted whether he'd ever see it again.

He had, for a time, entertained the notion that he might find a life to live here in Steynton, one of some meaning, only to discover that he had succeeded in exorcising his own personal ghosts, but not the memories. At first, it had been tempting to believe he could have re-made his world here. With a woman possessed of a wide, warm smile and a loving and impetuous nature. There had been a moment when the words which would have sealed their fates might have been said: but he had paused too long, she had read too much in his face, and the moment was lost, perhaps for ever. Chiefly, he thought, because he'd had no choice but to pursue the truth to its bitter end, and its consequences had left too much emotional baggage between them. Richmond, who had seen the disintegration of relationships for much less than this, knew that to be true. Some day, perhaps, he would find a sort of peace, but not here. He didn't belong here, he never had.

He turned abruptly away from the prospect of Steynton, the wind at his back, scattering a slither of small stones on the thin

217

soil under his feet in his haste to reach the Volvo. He threw his jacket on to the back seat and slid into the car's enveloping warmth.

He sat for a moment, getting his breath back. Then he turned the key in the ignition and headed south.